The Daughter of the Puppet King

VERONICA BROWN DUBROC

The Daughter of the Puppet King

ISBN
978-1-959365-16-7 (Paperback)
978-1-959365-17-4 (eBook)
978-1-959365-15-0 (Hardcover)

DEDICATION

I dedicate this book to my mom, Diana, my tenth and eleventh-grade English teachers, Ms. Grace and Mrs. Abraham, and to the late Mr. John Sutcliffe, my very first English professor in college, for telling me to pursue writing even though I am dyslexic. They wouldn't let me listen to those who told me to give up! Thank you. This book is also dedicated to those people like me who learn in a different way—this book is proof that you can succeed at your dreams too!

PROLOGUE

Hello, I am Cadmus. I am the keeper of the history and stories of this land. This land is the kingdom of Ashenland. The kingdom is a valley; we have tall mountains on three sides and a sea to the east. Our ancestors came over the mountains from the west or the south. That history is lost to the world now. We know only that the journey was difficult and took several weeks. When they finally emerged from the mountains, they discovered a large amount of fertile land that led to a vast sea.

The founders of Ashenland came across those mountains as refugees from a terrible civil war. The place they came from has been lost to the years we have been here, as Ashenland grew into a great and prosperous kingdom. We are left alone by other kingdoms because crossing those mountains in large numbers is vastly difficult, so we are not at risk of being attacked by an army.

Most of the people of the kingdom stay away from the sea. There are fishermen and trappers who live near the waters of course, but they keep to themselves. There are stories of dangerous sea monsters and pirates from lands south of us on the other side of the mountains.

We have no trouble with the pirates ourselves; our land has few minerals that are naturally occurring here. The fishermen and the farmers closest to the water do trade with the pirates when they need supplies. I suspect that is how much of the capital city and the palace of the king acquired the gold that is used there. We acquired a few of their words into our language as well. The most common word you will hear us say is *aye*. That is the last you will hear of the pirates. They do not play a role in our current situation.

When our ancestors crossed the mountains, they had two or three in their number with special magical powers. These were powers they were born with but could not gain full use of them until they were near or past adulthood. These people became known as sorcerers.

The sorcerers grew into protectors of this land. Their offspring are still here and are still protecting this kingdom. Some of the sorcerers have crossed the mountains and know what is on the other side. They are also the guardians of the town and cities. They use their wisdom to solve disputes and keep the laws. In this way they keep us safe.

However, one of these sorcerers was enticed by evil to turn on his people. His name is Kybon. Kybon holds the position of high advisor to the king. This job is considered the highest honor. Who better to advice the king than someone who possesses magic in his bloodstream? But Kybon is no longer advising the king. He is ruling the kingdom while holding the king captive in the king's own weak and sick body.

So this is where the kingdom stands now—on the brink of a civil war sparked by Kybon's desire to wipe out any threat of a stronger king that could replace his puppet on the throne.

But you will see as the story unfolds that there are those who can still save Ashenland and restore the peace that we had enjoyed since our ancestors came here so many years ago.

There is a great and ancient magic that was set forth to protect us from corrupt sorcerers like Kybon. It has weakened and eroded over the years, but not even Kybon can end its power of protection over us.

I will say no more. I bid you farewell until we meet again on a cold winter's night at the solstice festival in the forest near the town of Bale.

CHAPTER 1

Secrets Revealed

Rupert shivered in the cold. He had not meant to fall asleep in the stable. Now stretching his legs outside in the snow, he looked toward the familiar house in the moonlight. There was a fire burning inside. Rupert could almost hear the fire crackling as the flames licked the wet wood while it burned white.

He knew the rooms in the small house were warm. It was always warm in "Uncle" Thomas's house. Rupert had no uncles by blood, nor did he have a father. Thomas was the only man around to look after him, and Rupert called him uncle to show respect. Because of the fire, Rupert could see into the small window.

Thomas was awake and sitting in a chair close to the fireplace. His niece, Victoria, was asleep in a cot nearby. Rupert could not see her, but he knew she was there. She always slept in the common room close to the fire when she was fighting an illness in winter.

In the dim mixture of moonlight and firelight, Rupert could see as Thomas's tall, broad-shouldered frame got up and walked to the door, opening it just enough to slip out so he would not wake Victoria. Quickly Rupert slipped back into the stable. He didn't want to tell his surrogate uncle he had been so irresponsible that he hadn't gone home. It had been many years since he had fallen asleep in the stable, but with so many things happening now, he stayed too long in the barn because it was the place he was most comfortable. He had always stabled his horse Thunderstorm in Thomas's barn. There was no adequate barn on his mother's property.

There was a special bond between Rupert and his horse. Thunderstorm was from a special breed of horse that carried with them some of the magical properties and longevity that their sorcerer counterparts had. Rupert was seventeen now, and the horse had been his companion since his birth. The horse was still young for his breed so he would be with Rupert for another many years. Being near his horse made Rupert feel safest. Thomas understood that, but he still would not have been happy that Rupert had not gone home to his mother the night before.

Rupert peeked through the door as Thomas trudged in the dark, through the shin-deep snow that covered the path he had helped shovel clear at nightfall, to the stable. Rupert ran to the farthest stall where Thunderstorm was housed.

Thomas walked in, sighed, and shook off the snow. He lit the small lantern hanging by the door. It gave off very little light, but Thomas had done this many times before. Then he went to the firewood and stacked several pieces onto a small litter so he could pull the wood back to the house in only one trip. Rupert rubbed his horse and whispered to him to keep quiet. It was not easy to hide the oversized horse and himself in the stall. If Thomas found out that he was there, Rupert would have to endure another lecture on being careless. He would hear it from his own mother soon enough. Thunderstorm woke the other three horses in the stable somehow. They made a little bit of noise in their stirring, enough at least to mask the fact that there was an extra person in the stable.

Rupert hoped the darkness would conceal their presence also. He was afraid that Thomas would figure it out anyway. He didn't want to startle Thomas while he was stacking logs, so Rupert remained hidden and quiet.

As Thomas stacked, a woman appeared next to him. Rupert had nearly jumped out of his skin but was able to stifle a scream as he hid. Thunderstorm shifted in his stall to hide the sound Rupert made from being startled. Rupert was thankful again for his extraordinary horse.

Thomas was not startled when the woman appeared. He didn't even look up to speak to her.

"Hello, Ashel," Thomas said in a dry tone.

"It is time, Thomas."

"I know! But she is all I have left. Your magic has taken everyone else." He was just short of scathing.

"Our magic, Thomas."

He took a deep breath and looked up. Rupert couldn't see his expression in the darkness, but he could feel the wave of sadness that filled the small room.

Ashel stood only a foot from Thomas, but she had appeared just in front of the lantern. Rupert could see her clearly from the side. She matched Thomas's height of six feet; a long auburn braid fell down her back. Her clothes were black and very plain, but in contrast, she wore a vibrant red cloak. Rupert was taken by this woman's beauty and agelessness. He had seen her once in a painting when he was a boy. He had been told then that she had been born long before his father. He nearly gasped again when he remembered who she was. Despite her youthful appearance, she was the leader of the council that governed the sorcerers and wizards in the kingdom. Her decisions on any matter that had to do with magic were final. Rupert wondered what business she had with Thomas. His mother said Ashel did not often leave the council.

Thomas's voice broke the silence; his internal sadness had been brief. "Yes, you are right. It is everyone's magic, especially now. Are you staying for breakfast?" His tone had softened as he finished speaking.

"No, I only have a few minutes. Kybon has found our hiding place again. I have come to tell you that I have sent Colin here. And remind you firmly that his mistakes will catch up to him."

Thomas said nothing. This time, Rupert felt anger fill the room, but it wasn't just from Thomas. He felt it welling up inside of himself. He wondered why the name Colin had made them both so angry.

"Whether you like it or not, Thomas, most of this is out of your control. The council and I are very busy protecting the rest of the sorcerers from Kybon's tyranny. But I will be keeping an eye on Victoria and her friends."

"Can you keep a spell of protection on them?"

"They will not need it. There is enough magic on our side until Rupert gets his full powers."

"I wish I had your faith."

"Your lack of faith is what is keeping you miserable! I am sorry about the tragedies in the past, but our lives go on. I did not come here to argue with you again. I know where you stand. Colin will be here any minute. While he is here, we will move to a new location. He must think he is on a mission from us. And he must stay a full day."

Thomas still did not respond.

"I must leave. I cannot be here when Colin arrives. Do not worry about things you cannot control."

Rupert thought he saw her glance in his direction, but it had been so quick, he wasn't sure if he was just nervous about being caught hearing something that was not his business.

Ashel reached out and put her hand on Thomas's shoulder. He was not an affectionate man, but they appeared to have had a long history. Rupert was only mildly surprised when Thomas leaned in reluctantly and accepted a hug. Before Thomas released his arms, she was gone. He finished stacking the wood and dragged the litter out of the door.

About a minute later, Rupert left the stable with his horse. Thunderstorm, despite being larger than a normal horse, had a knack for walking lightly when he felt it necessary. He looked back as he walked slowly next to his horse, watching Thomas in the dim moonlight.

It took Thomas only about five minutes to unstack and restack the wood on a small platform under the overhang Rupert had helped him build several years earlier to keep the wood out of the wet snow or rain. When Thomas was finished, he slipped back in quietly with three logs to set on the stone hearth. Rupert watched as Thomas came back into view from the window and settled into his chair to presumably wait for Colin.

When Rupert reached the gate, he mounted his horse and headed for his mother's house, which he could barely see just down the road in the first beams of sunlight.

CHAPTER 2

The Dream

The room was large but dark. She was a very small child being taken away from a man sitting in a large chair. He tried to stand but fell to his knees. His blue-gray eyes were now on her level. The eyes looked into her face.

"I am sorry it has to be this way. I will never stop loving you!" Then the man raised his eyes to the person behind her that she could not see but knew was there. "Tell Thomas to take good care of her!" He looked back at her. There were tears in his eyes. "I will always love you, Victoria." The man reached out and stroked her face.

She began to cry. "I don't wanna go" came from her own throat.

The sound of footsteps outside the room could be heard faintly in the hallway. The man retracted his hand. "Go!" he said, looking to the wall in great fear. Then two arms grabbed her and hastily took her from the room.

The man holding her was running, but he was going the wrong way. They could not get out this way. But then they went through a door in the wall. There were disembodied sobs. But somehow her two-year- old form knew that they were her own sobs. Someone was carrying her through a dark corridor. She didn't want to go. The man tried to console her and told her things would be all right. But she didn't believe him.

Victoria awoke with a start. The pain in the pit of her stomach was there again. She was cold and shivering even though she shouldn't be cold in the house. She sat up to grab the extra blanket Thomas had left for her.

Her long brown hair was still braided. She did not want to be sick today. It was too important of a day. But this dream always made her feel sick. It was happening more and more. She had hoped the years would make it stop, but she now knew for sure that she was wrong. She sighed as she rolled over and tried to will herself back to sleep by thinking about the fact that it was her sixteenth birthday at last. After a few minutes, she grabbed her journal and flipped to her favorite page. She rubbed her green eyes and began reading the familiar words she had written years ago.

> *I met a strange but interesting boy today. He is a friend of Rupert's. I remember seeing him a few years ago at school, but he stopped attending soon after. I am looking forward to getting to know him. He is thirteen.*
>
> *I was in a carriage on my way to school with Rupert. I would rather walk, but Uncle Thomas will not allow it in the rain. Something very strange happened today! We were attacked!*
>
> *There was a scream from the carriage driver, then a very sudden lurch. The carriage skidded to a stop. I could hear shouts outside. Rupert looked out the small window and pulled his head back in.*
>
> *"Highwaymen!" he said in a hushed, confused voice. The carriage driver was being robbed. His angry shouts were not decipherable over the rain on the carriage top. Then there was the sound of something hitting the side of the carriage and another voice shouting.*
>
> *Suddenly, a boy who knew Rupert's name burst in through the cab door and announced that the Highwaymen were gone and that he was going to accompany us to school but that we would have to walk the rest of the way because one of the carriage wheels were broken. He introduced himself as Cornelius. He reached out and shook my hand. "Nice to meet you finally! I have heard so much about you." I shook the boy's hand, and a chill ran through my spine at the contact. It was a strange feeling. I have never felt that before. I stepped out of the cab into the rain still holding his hand. He took off his cloak and put it around me…*

She awoke again, feeling nauseous and cold. She was very nervous about her birthday. Something important was going to happen today. She hoped for a betrothal agreement, but she could only tell that Thomas had something planned. He had been quieter than usual for the last few days and had reminded her again and again, "Do not get your heart set on a quiet life! The world has other plans for you!"

She had been hearing this from him as far back as she could remember. The words went through her head again. At least she would know soon what he meant by those words.

She closed her eyes and tried to regain the picture of Cornelius at thirteen. She couldn't quite remember the details when she was awake. All she could remember was his smile and only because it had not changed in the five years she had known him. The window was visible from her position on the cot. She could see that the sky was graying. She closed her eyes once more to get a few more minutes of troubled sleep.

CHAPTER 3
The Awakening

Victoria awoke for good to the sound of Thomas's voice, deep and heavy and low across the room. There was another voice too, much higher but definitely male. She could sense fear in the second unfamiliar voice. She listened intently for a moment as her senses returned to normal. It became clear that the two men were speaking about her and Rupert, her best friend.

The stranger's voice was louder than her uncle's, and she heard his last sentence clearly.

"The war is finally upon us. It will be the girl and Oberon's son. What's his name? Rupert, I think, that will decide the outcome."

She knew that a civil war was coming, and the tough times were going to get tougher, but she couldn't figure how she and "Oberon's son" would figure into the outcome of anything. It was widely accepted that war would be useless and the outcome predetermined by the evil power contriving it. Rupert might be important to a war since Oberon had been a powerful sorcerer, and Rupert stood to inherit his power, but not her, she thought to herself. She was not special at all.

She opened her eyes slightly. Sunlight was starting to fill the room. Thomas rarely let her sleep past dawn. She took a deep breath. There was no pain in her chest, and the air filled her lungs completely. She was well again. It was time to get up and find out what brought a stranger to see them so early on her birthday.

"Uncle Thomas, can you and your visitor leave the room for a moment so I can change out of my night clothes?"

The stranger gave a start at the sound of her voice. Thomas let out a chuckle. Victoria could tell that he had already known she was awake.

"Yes, Victoria, and then we must talk. Are you feeling better today?"

"I feel much better, I think. With a good breakfast, I'll be completely myself again."

Thomas stood up and motioned the visitor to do the same. It was still to dim in the room for Victoria to see the features of the man, but she did not know him.

Thomas shoved the stranger to the door and then led him outside. "We must go to the stable and check on the horses anyway. There was more snow last night. I must make sure they are warm and dry." His voice tapered off as the door closed behind them.

Victoria got up and looked out the window. The stranger was a gangly middle-aged man, with short graying hair; he had sharp features that reminded her of a portrait of the king she had seen in school. The stranger looked familiar, but she was sure she had never met him before. Her stomach growled loudly, so she left the window and quickly dressed so she could begin breakfast. She could hear the muffled voices of the two men outside. She went back to the window and opened it slightly so she could hear what they were saying.

"Colin, there is an open stall for your horse. I am sure he is tired from steady riding in the snow." Thomas's voice was carried back to the house. Victoria saw an unkempt brown horse already covered in a thin layer of bright white powder tied to the lone tree next to the house.

"Get your horse to the stable. I see you have the same disregard for horses as you do for humans," Thomas said with discontent.

"He's an animal, Thomas!"

"Yes, and for many days, he is your only companion, and to repay him for his labors, you leave him to freeze the first chance you get. That horse may be the only friend you have left in this life. I hope he teaches you a lesson you so richly deserve."

Colin scoffed. "Dumb creatures cannot hurt the likes of me. Sorcerers need not worry about the lesser four-legged." He untied the horse and pulled roughly on the reins. The horse did not move. "Come on, stupid!" he screamed and kicked the horse in the leg.

The horse whinnied and reared up wildly. Colin jerked harder on the reins causing more pain and discomfort for the horse's mouth. The horse pulled away from him because of the pain, causing his master to lose his grip on the reins. Colin raised his hands and began to mumble words of a spell.

Thomas shoved Colin roughly to the ground in front of the spooked horse. "Never treat an animal that way!" he yelled. "And never use magic on a defenseless animal!"

Victoria gasped from the house. She had only heard stories of her uncle's temper, but she had never seen it.

Colin fell under the rearing horse. Thomas grabbed the horse's reins carefully with one hand and rubbed the animal's nose with the other. The horse clearly calmed just at Thomas's touch but not enough to keep him from stomping the ground. Victoria smiled at her uncle's special talent for soothing animals.

As he calmed the horse, he kicked Colin hard in the ribs, getting him out of the way of the horse's powerful kicking legs. The horse stomped the ground with enough power to rattle the door of the house. Colin sputtered and rolled over, wincing in pain from Thomas's foot.

"That hurt!" he yelled, finally wheezing and wincing as he got to his feet. Clutching his ribs, he hobbled forward and took the reins from Thomas weakly.

"I am sure it did hurt. I should've let him stomp on you! It would have been an accident. Your own neglected nameless horse would have killed you. Ashel would have to accept that! Now get a move on! No horses will be neglected or abused on my property." Thomas pushed Colin roughly again with one hand while he kept his other hand on the horse to keep him calm. They both started toward the stables twenty yards away.

Victoria continued to watch as they entered the stable. She pulled the window closed. She thought for a moment about what Colin must have done to Thomas. But her uncle had taught her to concentrate on the task at hand. She looked out the window one last time, took a deep breath, and turned back to start breakfast.

She noticed that five chairs had already been placed around the cluttered table, and a smile crept into her face. Cornelius would be back today. He told her he made sure to leave with enough time to be back for her birthday. Whatever today would bring, she was happy to know that Cornelius would be with her.

CHAPTER 4

Rupert Overhears Again

As Thomas pushed Colin inside the stable quickly, he again did not notice that there was a teenaged boy sitting very still in the farthest stall. Rupert had returned in clean, warmer clothes only a few moments before the door of the house opened. He always went directly to the stable to stow Thunderstorm before going to the door of the house. Thomas and taught him to take care of his very special horse. Thunderstorm always went to the last of the eight stalls in the stable, though Thomas had never stabled more than three horses of his own since Rupert could remember.

When the men entered, Thunderstorm went to the very back of the stall, trying to hide his large frame from Thomas's sight, but he tried to keep an eye over the stall. Rupert smiled. His horse was as curious as he was to see how Thomas would react to this stranger.

Colin and his horse were in front of Thomas. The horse went into the fourth stall. Thomas did not take his eyes off the man in front of him. Rupert sat perfectly still out of fear and guilt of being caught eavesdropping for the second time that morning.

Thomas's voice cut through the silence that followed the stable door closing.

"I will tell Victoria what I feel she needs to know. You keep your mouth shut. It is my place to tell her. I know the high sorceress sent you here to make sure I send Victoria and Rupert to help lead in the war. But I will do it as I see fit."

"Thomas, I know that you dislike my being here, but we are old men now. For the sake of the whole kingdom, we must be civil to one another." Colin sighed and continued. "I will stay quiet, but I've got to tell the Sorcerers Council everything that you tell Victoria and Rupert. You know Oberon was a dear friend of mine. I was as sorry as you when he was killed, leaving his infant son as the best chance we have to stop Kybon. Oberon was the only sorcerer that rivaled his powers. If his son is as powerful, there may still be hope for us all."

Rupert had to make a conscious effort not to jump at the sound of his father's name. His mother had told him many stories about his father, but he knew little about how or why his father died just weeks after his own birth. He knew only that Kybon, who was now ruling the kingdom in the ailing king's name by means of dark and evil magic, had been in some way responsible for Oberon's death.

"Do you think, Colin, that I haven't thought of that? I want more than anyone for the sorcerers to be out of hiding. But there is still nearly a year until Rupert is eighteen. He is vulnerable. If he dies before he gets his full powers, all will be lost," Thomas said in a matter-of-fact tone.

"There is another way to end Kybon's reign," said Colin scathingly.

"No! That is not an option!" Thomas said this with such force that his voice reverberated off the wooden walls. Again Rupert could feel overwhelming anger. He saw Thomas take a very deep breath.

Then Thomas spoke again. "Give your horse more hay than that! Now it's time for *me* to tell Victoria the story of her birth. If you speak one word, I will give you the punishment I owe you!" There was malice in Thomas's voice. Rupert shuddered at the thought of the tortures Thomas could inflict if he chose to. Colin rubbed the bruise on his ribs and winced again.

Thomas laughed. "Imagine a powerful sorcerer getting kicked in the ribs by a mortal to save him from being killed by a mere animal! I can imagine your brother's reaction!" Thomas's voice held no emotion at all.

Colin mumbled, "Which one?"

Rupert closed his eyes and bit his lip to keep from rushing out of his hiding place and asking one hundred questions. He knew that Thomas would not be happy that there was an eavesdropper in his stable nor would he have wanted Rupert to see him this angry.

Thomas grabbed Colin by the wrist and pulled him roughly out the door. Rupert hurried to the door, being careful not to make any loud noise that might give away that he was there. He peeked through the stable door as they trudged again through the deepening snow back to the house. Thomas glared at Colin as he opened the door to the house. Rupert's mind was racing at the information he had just heard.

CHAPTER 5

Birthday Gift

Victoria was dressed. She was leaning over the fire, preparing breakfast. She looked up when Thomas and Colin walked in.

"I'm cooking enough for us and your guest and Cornelius! He should be back today, and I expect him to stop here before he goes home. Rupert will eat before he gets here, I bet." She paused, looking intently at her uncle. The anger in his face had not yet completely subsided.

"Yes, I suspect Cornelius will be wanting hot food when he arrives." He paused, pushed Colin back to the chair by the fire, then continued speaking. "This is Colin. He is a spy from the sorcerer's council. He is here as a witness to make sure I tell you your history. I will wait for the others so I will not have to say this twice!"

Victoria hoped the harshness in his voice was meant for Colin. Just as the eggs she was cooking in the pan on the fireplace grate began to sizzle, there was a knock on the door. Victoria ran to the door. She already knew who was knocking before she opened the door. She quickly pushed her hair out of her face, smoothed it down a bit, and opened the door.

There stood a young man of eighteen years wrapped in a wool traveling cloak that fell below his knees so the tops of his boots were not showing. His eyes were bright blue, and there was a smile on his lips. The light-brown hair that was exposed from under his hat was windblown and wild.

He had not shaved in nearly three days. Victoria smiled brightly. She hoped her visitor would put her uncle in a better mood. Cornelius always made the days brighter.

Just behind Cornelius stood Rupert. Though he was a year younger than his friend, he was taller and looked older. He had deep-green eyes and dark hair. He was wearing a cloak as well, but one of a nobleman's, made of much tighter weave. His hair was shorter and well kept. His clean-shaven face held a look of tension or uneasiness. Victoria began to feel that her birthday breakfast was not going to be a joyous one. Rupert knew something she didn't—something big. She was not sure she was ready for it.

"Come in, you two. Victoria has breakfast nearly ready," Thomas said from behind Victoria.

Cornelius rushed in, half-hugging Thomas as he came through the door. Rupert walked in slowly and carefully closed the door after he wiped the ice from his boots. He removed his gloves and blew into his hands. When he looked up, Cornelius and Victoria were embracing and chattering quickly about Cornelius's travels.

"I am glad to see you are feeling better. I have a present for your birthday." Rupert heard Cornelius say. Victoria giggled and took his hand in hers.

"Uncle Thomas," Rupert said from the doorway, "I am here to listen to what you need to tell us. Mother said she would leave it to you to tell me what I need to know. Is the council messenger here?

"Yes, he is sitting by the fire. He is forbidden to speak. Have you eaten?"

"Yes, I have eaten. But Corn hasn't. I will tend to our horses while the rest of you have breakfast."

"Yes, they will freeze out there tied up."

Rupert smiled for the first time. He knew well that Thomas had a soft spot for animals. Without responding, he went outside and led Cornelius's horse, Kob, through steadily falling snow to the stable. He unbridled the chestnut-brown horse and brushed him down. Cornelius took great care to make sure his horse was cared for. The horse's black mane and tail were always brushed. Rupert thought of how scruffy Cornelius looked compared to his pristine horse. He smiled at the thought. Thunderstorm walked out of his stall and nudged his keeper's shoulder. Rupert reached back and rubbed his horse's nose.

"Come on, boy, back to your stall. I won't latch the door, but you can't leave this time, understand?"

The horse gave no indication that he understood or cared, but Rupert knew his horse could understand him. Thunderstorm came from a breed of magical horses. Sometimes Rupert felt his horse understood the world around them more than he did. Rupert carefully put hay in both of the stalls. Kob got considerably more because Cornelius had just returned from a much longer distance. Rupert's own horse was content to let his counterpart eat, so Rupert checked the other horses that belonged to Thomas, and he looked in on Colin's horse. Then he grabbed two more logs for the fire and walked back to the house, careful not to trip on the snow-covered path. Thoughts of what he overheard less than an hour earlier began to haunt him as he walked. He went inside the house just as the four others were finishing their meal.

Colin glanced at Rupert but looked away very quickly. Then he looked at Thomas and said quietly, "He looks just like his father."

"Yes, if you didn't know any better, you would think you were seeing a ghost," Thomas said tauntingly.

"No, I don't look exactly like him," said Rupert. "Mother says I have her eyes. My father's eyes were gray." He set the wood on the hearth, and then he sat down in the empty chair.

"Corn, will you help Victoria clear the dishes," Thomas said. "Rupert and I must clean off the chest over there. It is time to give Victoria her inheritance."

Thomas pointed to the corner opposite Victoria's cot. Next to the door that led to another room in the house sat a large wooden box. If you looked closely enough, you could see the hinges that proved it was a chest and not just a block of wood.

For the past thirteen and a half years, Thomas had been using the chest as a shelf. There were a few books stacked on one side and a collection of very small figurines made of silver on the other. The statues depicted warriors with long swords poised for battle and sorcerers with long staffs. Some looked evil; others looked wise. The tallest was a female in an intricately carved flowing dress with her arms high in the air and a look of concentration on her beautiful face. Rupert knew that this was a representation of Ashel. For the first time, he wondered where the figures came from.

Cornelius stood up and took Victoria's hand. She calmly began clearing off the table even though she was excited and nervous at receiving an inheritance. Suddenly she realized why Thomas had kept the chest all these years and what he meant when he said the contents were not his.

CHAPTER 6

Secrets Unveiled

Thomas swept the books off with one motion. They slid to the floor with the sounds of fluttering paper. Then he carefully removed the figurines and placed each one carefully on the mantle in nearly the same placement they had been in on the chest. When he had placed the last one, the one of Ashel, he turned quickly back to the task at hand.

Rupert started to pull one side while Thomas pulled on the other. Colin quietly tried to help. Thomas didn't stop him, mainly because he knew that it would take more strength than he and Rupert had to move it fully.

As they tugged it away from the wall, Rupert asked in an exhausted voice, "What is in this thing? Boulders?" As he finished speaking, he lost his grip and fell to the floor.

"The chest is made of iron and covered with wood on the outside. It was important that the contents be protected," Thomas answered. He looked at Colin, who had a very confused look at his outstretched hand as if it did not work correctly. "It's also protected against sorcery. Kybon can't get into this chest much less the likes of you! So stop trying to use magic."

Colin sheepishly smiled and began to actually pull on the handle of the iron trunk. After nearly ten minutes of heaving and pulling, the three of them were still unable to pull it completely away from the wall. Cornelius left Victoria to finish the dishes and came over to help. Thanks to Cornelius's added strength, they finally got the trunk turned around and in a position where they could fully open it.

Thomas unclasped a chain from around his neck that had been hidden by his shirt. From the chain, he removed an iron key. Victoria noticed a thin ring was also on the chain. He put the key in the small built-in lock and turned it slowly until the lock clicked. He withdrew the key and quickly replaced it on the chain. Then he lifted the lid. He reached inside and pulled out a thick folded piece of cloth and a sword wrapped haphazardly in another piece of cloth.

He turned and walked back to the table followed by the rest of them. Victoria had sat back down when the dishes were finished, waiting for her uncle to begin. Rupert did not sit as the others did; he walked to the fireplace, put another log in, and began to pace.

As Thomas stepped up to the table, he began speaking in his deep voice while the others settled down at the table.

"Twenty years ago, our King Marcus was coronated. He was still mourning the death of his father, Victor, not to mention gravely ill himself, but he was bound by duty as the only child of the king to take the throne, though he really didn't want it." Thomas stopped. Victoria could tell this was not a story her uncle wanted to tell.

"He wanted his half-brother, Kybon, to take the throne, but everyone knew that the late king was not Kybon's father. So Marcus reluctantly took the throne."

Rupert gasped at the realization that Kybon was the king's half-brother.

"Because of his poor health, he was easy to manipulate, making him easy prey for a much stronger and evil man to control him." Thomas turned and looked at Rupert. Thomas paused again to make sure this information was clear to his listeners. "Yes, the queen was in love with Korgan, who was Victor's highest advisor.

Victoria thought for a second she had learned some of this in school. "Korgan was a sorcerer, right? He had to be to be the high advisor!" Victoria said before she realized she was interrupting.

Thomas smiled at Victoria and nodded. "Victor and Queen Constance were betrothed at birth. Kybon was born before she married the king. Victor was a generous man and allowed Kybon to live in the castle with his father. It seems that was a mistake now as Kybon has become a tyrant as he rules in Marcus's stead."

Cornelius spoke too. "Sorcerers are meant to protect us, not harm us, but well...things have not worked out that way." He was looking at Colin when he was speaking these words. Cornelius then got up and stood behind Victoria, putting his arms around her and interlocking his fingers in hers.

Thomas began again, this time in a bit softer tone. "As you know, Victoria, Kybon is ruling instead of Marcus. What you do not know is that the law is written stating the oldest child of the king is the heir to the throne. The oldest child, not oldest son. 'The first offspring of the Ruler is to assume the role of ruler when the Ruler passes away' is the exact wording. It says nothing about the offspring having to be a boy or that the child had to be born into a legitimate marriage." He stopped and took a deep breath. Then he continued, looking only at his niece.

"Your mother, my sister, was Marcus's mistress. You are Marcus's child, though he pretends to believe that you are dead to appease the queen who found the wording of the old law offensive since you are six months older than her twin sons. Which makes *you* the rightful heir to the throne."

Victoria stopped listening. Cornelius's arms tightened a bit as she felt herself going numb. She was sure that Thomas was still talking, but she was no longer able to concentrate. This couldn't really be happening, could it? This was supposed to be a conversation about her becoming betrothed, not about being the long-lost heir to the throne!

Then it hit her. She remembered the dream she had been having for years. It all made sense now. The intense blue-gray eyes were her father's. The large chair started to take shape in her mind. It was a throne. In the dream, she had known she was the princess. She had known that someday she would return to the king to appease his tears. There had been other dreams—all of them about her getting back to the man she now realized was her father.

Cornelius rubbed his hand down her back. Then he whispered in her ear, "It will be all right, I promise."

She took in his words with a deep breath. She pictured her father's tear-filled eyes again. There was a weakness and pain in them that broke her heart. She would take this mission with all her strength. It was clearly time to return to her father. The entire kingdom knew the king was weak and under the control of evil. She would be strong enough for both of them.

The years she has spent in Thomas's care had given her a mental strength that she knew would prove useful.

When her focus returned, Thomas had unwrapped the sword, and he handed it to her along with a cloak. She unfolded the cloak carefully. It was emerald green and unadorned except for a family crest on the left breast. She knew at once that it was the family crest of Thomas and her mother because it matched the faded painted one that hung above Thomas's bed in the other room. She ran her fingers over the embroidering. The shield-shaped crest had a soaring eagle in the middle with a blood-red background. In the top-left corner was a crescent moon, in the top-right corner were three sprigs of wheat, and at the bottom was a horseshoe.

Cornelius leaned forward to examine it. Victoria realized he had never seen Thomas's crest. She thought about the days in school when she had learned what all the symbols and colors represented. Cornelius was out of school by then. Rupert had been out recovering for a broken leg.

"Do you know what the color and symbols mean?" she asked Cornelius quietly.

"I know what they mean in my family crest. But I know where to look to find out." Cornelius smiled at her. "The detail work is very good."

"It was my Clara that sewed that crest," Thomas told them. "The king wanted Victoria to have a cloak like all the other children of noble birth, but it is too dangerous to have his crest upon it. His crest is on your sword, however. Go and change from that dress into pants with a belt and put on the sword."

"I can wear it with my dress!"

"Not if you are going to war! Women are not supposed to fight! They are not good soldiers!" Colin's voice was a little higher than it had been before.

All four of them turned and looked at him. Thomas picked up Victoria's sword and quickly pulled it from the scabbard. He pointed it at Colin and walked toward him.

"You are lucky I have been forbidden to kill you!" he said, still pointing the sword in Colin's direction.

Victoria realized that no one but she was confused by Thomas's actions. She looked around and realized Rupert had drawn his own sword. She had no hate for this man, but Thomas and Rupert both did.

Cornelius leaned in and whispered in her ear, "Colin has made a few bad decisions that will cost him dearly one day. Today is not the last we will see of him, and we will not be glad to see him again. But let it be for now. He is here for a reason."

Victoria nodded and tapped her uncle carefully. "Uncle Thomas, we have business to finish here."

Thomas shook his head as if he had been in a daze. Then he returned the sword to its scabbard. Rupert did the same.

"Colin, I told you to keep your mouth closed. You will do what I ask in my house. You owe me at least that." Thomas's voice was now calm and almost emotionless. "Victoria, go and change your clothes! That dress is not appropriate for your journey."

Everyone was silent as Cornelius slowly loosened his arms and helped her up. She walked to another room alone though she wanted him with her to steady her. Her legs were shaking.

It took her longer than usual to change. She was distracted by the shock of the news she had just been given. She, of course, knew the stories. Everyone knew the story of the lost child of the king who would one day conquer Kybon and restore peace and happiness to the kingdom. She had heard them as a young girl right along with the rest of the kids in town, even dreamed of what it would be like to be the lost child of the king. But now she had been told it was actually her.

She wanted to scream. Her thoughts were flying into her head faster and faster. She felt like she was spinning. Then she felt dizzy. All the while she was changing her clothes, using the part of her brain that was habit and didn't require real thoughts. At the realization that she was putting her pants on backward, she snapped herself back to reality. She was suddenly determined to keep herself together and resigned herself to take things as they came. If she let herself get flustered, she would spend the next few weeks needing help getting dressed correctly. What good would that do, anyone?

She took a deep breath and glanced at herself in the tarnished- looking glass. She wondered if she looked at all like her father. She sighed at the thought of what Cornelius would think of her now very masculine attire as she went back into the main room. This was not how she had pictured her birthday. She forced her panic and fear to the back of her mind. She was afraid that panic and screaming would come, but she was able to keep it at bay for now.

Cornelius smiled at her when she walked back into the room. Not even tattered men's clothing could destroy her beauty in his eyes. She smiled in spite of everything. His smile let her know everything would be all right in time. They would get through what was to come.

Cornelius glanced at Rupert to see what he thought of Victoria's attire, but Rupert had not even noticed her return. He was staring at the sword that lay on the table. It was a magnificent weapon, nearly three feet long. The hilt was a golden cross with decorative knobs on either sides. In the center of the hilt was the king's three-colored crest. The sword at Rupert's side, which had been his father's, looked the same, except it was his own family's four-colored crest in the center. The four colors were blue, yellow, red, and green. Each color represented a trait of the family. That was all he knew. He knew from the way people spoke to him in town that he was supposed to live up to his father's name. But since had never known his father, he did not know how he was supposed to do that. He decided that his family crest would help him learn how to act as he became an adult.

When he looked up, he saw that Victoria had returned, and she looked very strange. She was wearing her uncle's shirt, which was a little big on her thin frame, and a pair of his own pants that were torn in both knees. She had meant to sew them for him, but she never did. Thomas handed her the sword and scabbard. She attached it to a belt loop, then threw the cloak over her shoulders and tied it under the collar of the shirt. The cloak fell to her ankles revealing only the black-stained hide of her boots. Her hair fell past the middle of her back.

"You almost look the part of a great nobleman's son ready to defend his land, but I am afraid we'll have to cut your hair," Thomas said.

"So you are sending me off to war alone and dressed as a man, with a cloak bearing your family crest and a sword bearing the king's." She tried to keep her voice steady. "I am a decent swordsman, but I fear that in battle, I will not know what to do." Victoria stopped because her eyes met Cornelius's. Her heart sank. They would not be married anytime soon.

"I am not sending you alone, and you are not going to battle. You, my dear niece, are the rightful heir to the throne. Cornelius knows these lands better than anyone in the kingdom. He will be your guide. And Rupert is going to be your sorcerer and high counselor when you are queen, so he will need to learn to counsel you now. So I send the three of you off to save us all."

Thomas gave Colin a look of warning and got up and walked back over to the chest. It was still open in the middle of the floor. He picked up the last of its contents, which was a tattered book. He handed it to Rupert. "This will answer many of your questions. I won't answer anymore. I leave my last heir in your hands. Protect her."

Rupert nodded. He looked curiously at the worn leather cover that was marked only with a staff, the symbol of a sorcerer.

Thomas picked up another book from the pile he had removed from the chest and handed it to Cornelius while he pulled him out the door to stand under the small snow-covered overhang.

"This is a book of blank pages. Record your journeys so that the world will remember the great things you and your future wife will do," Thomas said in one breath. Then he inhaled the cold air and uttered with a sigh, "Cornelius."

Cornelius looked up eagerly.

"I know that you will lay down your life for her, the woman you love, but you must be patient and wait a bit longer before you can take her hand. When the time comes, I give my blessing." He hugged Cornelius and went back inside, leaving Cornelius alone on the small, weathered porch.

Leaning against the wall, Cornelius sighed and turned the book over, taking out a small piece of coal he often used to label and trace maps from inside one of the many pockets of his cloak. He opened the book to the first page. In his small, neat handwriting, he wrote the date and the words, "Our journey begins." He closed the book and placed it carefully in a different pocket of his cloak. It made a thudding noise as it collided with the ring he had intended to give Victoria as a birthday and betrothal present. Tears began to well up in his eyes both from fear and sadness.

The fears that he kept buried were beginning to surface. What if he couldn't protect her? Just then Rupert opened the door and stepped out quickly.

"Corn, come back inside. It's very cold." He stopped when he saw the look on his friend's face. He closed the door and walked up and put his hand on Cornelius's shoulder. "I am scared too. But now is not the time for that."

"Rupert, the fate of the whole kingdom is now on the three of us. I am not sure I am strong enough."

"What?" Rupert said. "You are stronger than me, and besides, we'll have help when we need it." He thought again of Thomas's conversation with Ashel. "It will be a great adventure, I think. And besides, you get to be king one day. I am stuck with the stupid job of being your high counselor for the rest of our days!"

Cornelius laughed. Rupert opened the door, and they walked back into the house. Thomas and Victoria were sitting at the table, waiting for them. Colin was sitting stone-faced by the fire.

"Come now, there is much to do," Thomas said quickly as he beckoned the boys back to the table to look at the map spread out upon it. He glanced back at Colin, who was watching them intently. Rupert glanced back too. He wasn't sure how to react knowing that Colin was a spy.

Thomas walked up to Colin and handed him several coins. "Go into town to the market and buy some meat for supper tonight. I will not have time to do it!"

"I am not your servant, Thomas," Colin said forcefully.

"You have no food with you! If you plan to eat tonight, then you will go. I have no problem with letting you starve!" Thomas said as he pulled Colin toward the door.

Colin sighed as he opened the door and walked outside. Thomas held the door open and watched him go. He closed it when Colin reached the gate.

"I can't allow him to know your plans. Rupert, you have to be careful. Until you are eighteen, there are men who can hurt you if they know your weaknesses."

Rupert smiled warily and held up his book. "I will be all right, Uncle Thomas," he said, trying to convince himself as much as Thomas.

"Why can't you come with us?" Rupert asked, already knowing the answer to that question.

Thomas had taken Rupert's father's place as town guardian. Every town in the kingdom had a guardian who protected the town and made important decisions regarding the well-being of the townspeople. The role was traditionally held by a sorcerer, but there was no one to take over for Oberon because all the sorcerers were in hiding even at the time of his death. Thomas was given the job by Ashel. Rupert now realized that Thomas probably had her protection and maybe even a bit of her magic.

"You know I can't leave this village for more than a week. I am afraid you three are on your own."

"We still have nearly a year before Rupert is eighteen. I will try to keep us out of trouble until he can protect us all," Cornelius said, casting a sideways glance at Rupert and smiled broadly. "The Lord knows he can't fight without tripping on something!" He jumped out of the way as Rupert lunged toward him in an attempt to shove him. Rupert fell forward from the momentum of missing his target. Cornelius leaned over and stretched out his hand. But Rupert stubbornly got back to his feet on his own, pretending to be angry.

"The book I gave him will help, but if he is to be truly powerful, he will have to find his own way," Thomas said, stifling a laugh. "But about your way, do you have a sword or a weapon of any kind?" he asked Cornelius.

"I have a knife in each boot."

"Does a knife really protect you against a sword?" Thomas asked. "I don't know. I have never actually been in a fight. Truthfully, I am well protected by the highwaymen since they are my kin."

"Yes, the highwaymen are no friends to Kybon after the way he has treated them for years. They know these lands well enough to stay out of Kybon's sight, so they will be great allies," Thomas said.

"Thank you, Thomas, for your blessings and your advice," Cornelius said sadly. He knew that the conversation was over.

CHAPTER 7

The First Journey

By midday, everything was ready for their departure. Thomas had to go into Bale to solve a dispute and to check on Colin. Cornelius needed to get a few things from his parents' house.

When they arrived, Rupert did not go inside. Instead, he took the horses to the town stable, where he had them brushed and their hooves cleaned. He also bought some oats and hay to bring with them.

"I will be inside at lunch time, all right?" Rupert said to Cornelius as he took the smaller path off the road.

"Aye!" Cornelius said distantly.

Cornelius's father, Malcolm, was out of town working, but Genevieve, his mother, was sitting in the entrance hall when they arrived. Cornelius looked a lot like his mother. Her hair was longer and a little darker brown, but they had the same bright blue eyes.

"Hello, Mother," Cornelius said happily as he opened the door. "Hello, I have already packed your things for your journey."

"Umm.. .thanks?" Cornelius's astonishment showed on his face.

"Well, Thomas said you would have a lot to do. Now come inside before you two catch fever from standing in the cold," she said, hugging Victoria as she entered behind Cornelius.

The house was the largest in town with five rooms and a detached kitchen. There was a main living area, with two doors on the two sidewalls leading to four other rooms. The biggest was Malcolm and Genevieve's room. Cornelius's bedroom was the smallest. It was large enough to house a small bed and a few cherished belongings. He had been the town messenger since he was eleven so he spent little time in his room. The rooms on the other wall were the same size. One room housed many books that Genevieve and Malcolm had collected over their twenty years together. The other was the bedroom of Cornelius's seven-year-old sister, Mary.

Genevieve walked to the hearth opposite the front door and picked up a well-worn leather pack and handed it to Cornelius. "Make sure everything you need is in it," she said.

Cornelius opened the pack and looked through it. "I want to grab a couple of books from your study too," he said.

Genevieve called it a study, but it was more like a library. The walls were lined with shelves full of books. Over the arched doorway was a small tapestry of Malcolm's family crest. On the other side, above an identical archway leading into a small window, was another embroidered tapestry of a genealogy table.

Victoria noticed that there was a small shelf above the window that did not have books on it. Instead, there was a small painting of Malcolm and Genevieve and Cornelius as a small boy and another that she had not seen before of Mary and Malcolm. Next to the paintings were some figurines very much like the ones Thomas had. If she stood on her tiptoes, Victoria could see the figure of the tall-cloaked woman. She wondered who made these magnificent mini statues.

"Mother?" Cornelius asked quietly.

"Yes?" she said and set down the book that she was reading on the chair as she stood up.

"May I have the book on family crests?" he asked.

"Yes." She walked to a shelf near the window and pulled a book out without really looking at it. She handed it to him and continued across the room and left without a word.

Cornelius thumbed through it, then he closed it carefully and put in his pack with the rest of the things he needed for his trip.

"Aren't you going to read it?" Victoria asked quietly.

"No. It is for Rupert. He is the one who really needs to know what they mean. He thinks he has to live up to his family history."

"Yes, I suppose he does," Victoria said thoughtfully.

Genevieve walked into the room with a pair of cross-bladed shears in her hand. She opened the curtains and light flowed into the room. Then she moved the chair near the window. "Victoria, sit down, please, dear. Cornelius, put down the pack and stand next to her—and hold her hand too. This is going to be difficult on Victoria. Her long hair means a lot to her!"

Genevieve gently led Victoria to a chair. Even knowing it was coming and that it didn't hurt at all to have her hair cut, Victoria still felt a shudder run down her spine. This was really happening! She closed her eyes.

"Don't worry, Victoria. It'll grow back," Cornelius said tenderly, seeing the tears welling in her eyes.

She smiled back at him. "I know, and that means you will have to do this again pretty soon!" Victoria shut her eyes tightly and squeezed Cornelius's hand for the ten minutes it took to cut off sixteen years' worth of hair.

When Genevieve finally declared Victoria's hair done, Cornelius let go of her hand and stood back and looked at her. "You look different, but you are still beautiful!" Then he turned and grabbed two books off the shelf. "Mother, I am taking these two books also!"

Victoria was glad he changed the subject so quickly. She knew she could not dwell her thoughts on the things that were happening. She had to stay focused on the task before them.

"What are they, dear?" she asked.

"The book of maps of all the towns and cities and a book of our country's history."

"Good choices, son!" she said with a smile.

Rupert came inside just as they were finished preparing lunch. He looked at Victoria but said nothing about her hair. They ate lunch and listened to Mary ramble on about the things she was learning in her first weeks of school. It was a pleasant distraction from their coming departure.

They arrived back at Thomas's house a few hours later. Just after dark, Rupert's mother, Katherine, arrived for one last visit before her son and his two best friends left. She ate supper with them and told a few stories that the three of them had enjoyed hearing as children. Katherine often gathered the children of Bale and told them stories and rhymes to help them remember the long history of their country and so they would understand the magic that many people in the kingdom possessed, whether it was used for good or evil.

Thomas had been standing against the wall by the fire. After about two hours of storytelling, he let everyone know it was time to sleep. Katherine hugged each one of them. Victoria saw her slip a piece of paper into one of Cornelius's pockets. A look passed between them that Victoria was not sure of the meaning. Cornelius winked at her, and she decided not to ask what that was about just yet.

Rupert walked his mother to the door and out. He hugged her a second time. "Are you gonna be all right here without me?" he asked.

"Rupert, I will be fine. Don't worry about me."

"But what if the highwaymen that robbed us come back?" Rupert asked, his voice almost as scared as he had been at twelve when the robbery had happened.

"They will not come back. That clan is under control now. Besides, they got all the valuables the first time!" Katherine grinned at her son and continued speaking, "Your father used to worry about me when he was off on business. I can handle myself. And Thomas has promised to look after me. I want you to concentrate on helping Victoria."

Just then Cornelius walked outside. Katherine looked at him and smiled. "Cornelius, make sure you write down the events of this journey. I want to be able to tell this story in a few years."

Cornelius smiled back and agreed by shaking her hand. Then he looked at Rupert. "It is time for us to sleep. We have to be well rested if we want to start this trip out well."

"Good-bye, boys!" Katherine said. Then she turned around and walked down the small path and up to the road, carrying a lantern as she went. She did not look back.

Rupert could see the lantern light shrink until the lantern was on the porch of his house. He and Cornelius stayed on outside until the light on Katherine's porch moved up in their view and then disappeared behind her door.

Victoria was well enough to sleep away from the fire, so she slept in her room, while the two boys slept on the floor by the fire. Colin had been relegated to the stable much earlier in the evening.

CHAPTER 8

The True Journey Begins

The next morning dawned colder than the day before. The snow was thick on the ground, and there was a steady flow of snowflakes falling from the sky. Rupert wondered where they were going because Pallen was at least a week's ride and Thomas gave only enough dried meat for two days of the journey. After a hearty breakfast, the three of them told Thomas and Colin good-bye and departed.

Thomas watched them leave. Colin was next to him, ready to make his ride back to the hidden council. Both Victoria and Rupert looked back when they heard Colin's angry voice break the silence of the crisp morning.

"Thomas, I think the high sorceress will be less than pleased that you sent Victoria and Rupert off with a messenger kinsman of thieves."

"He is of high birth on his father's side. He is very well bred, indeed. And he loves Victoria. He *will* protect her." Thomas's voice was louder than normal, and there was a hint of reassurance in it.

"If he is of high birth, then why was he not betrothed at birth?" Colin said definitely.

"He was, but the girl's family got themselves on the bad side of Kybon. She and her family were killed a few years ago. Victoria is betrothed to no one. It's the only advantage of 'dying' at two and half years of age. Now go, Colin, while the snow is still falling. It will be harder to track you that way."

Colin mounted his horse and left without another word to Thomas. He did not like being alone with a man that he had betrayed. As he departed in the opposite direction of the others, Thomas watched him leave. Victoria and Rupert both now knew Thomas would a have look of hatred in his eyes if they had been close enough to see his face.

Victoria was thankful for the new cloak as they rode through the thick snow. Even with its added warmth, she was still very cold. The well-maintained main road was broad enough for them to ride three abreast. She had not seen much of the kingdom, but Cornelius had told her about it, especially about Pallen and about the king's palace, which was quite beautiful. She finally realized why she was able to picture it so well when he described it. She had seen it all before.

After nearly four hours of silent riding, Cornelius spoke, "We need to get off the road soon. There is a town a few miles ahead. If we can get across the river, we may encounter spies there. Thomas said we should keep our departure from home a secret as long as possible. We should find some of my kin in the woods and maybe better food than what is in our packs."

"Aye, we'll follow you," Rupert said through gritted teeth, not because he was mad but because his face was very cold and it hurt to talk. Victoria said nothing.

Cornelius pointed to the woods that flanked the west side of the road and spoke again. "All right, there is a small path that leads into the forest that starts just up ahead. The path is very narrow, so we will have to ride single file. Victoria will be in the middle. Keep your eyes open both of you. The highwaymen control those woods, and they are not trusting people. Especially of anyone who has, as they call it, the curse of magic." He gave Rupert a warning look.

"I thought you said you are their kin?" Rupert said.

"I am, but you two aren't. I have only even been among them while on delivery missions. They usually offer me food and a place to sleep, but since you two are with me, they will know I am not on a delivery," Cornelius said as he carefully pulled the reins on his horse.

"If they ask us what we're doing, what do we say then?" Rupert looked intently at his friends.

"I think we should tell something close to the truth that we are headed to Pallen to join the war effort against Kybon. We're trying to help make a life better for our families," Victoria said quietly.

"I agree with Victoria. They will give us advice and food if we take the side they want us to, though fighting for one of the princes is a lost cause, and they know that," said Cornelius.

"I'll let you do all of the talking, Cornelius," Rupert said.

"All right. Victoria shouldn't talk at all. We really must hide the fact that she is a woman. Not many people will approve of a woman going to the war, plus we don't need people talking and altering suspicion."

"I'll stay silent, but what shall you two call me? *Victoria* is not a boy's name."

"I've been thinking about that since we left Uncle Thomas's house. I have decided to call you Mark," Rupert said.

"Why Mark?" Cornelius asked in curiosity.

"Because there is a symbolic mark on her arm. It means something, but Thomas would not say what. And since she keeps it covered most of time, I have never gotten a good look at it, but I think some of it matches part of the marking on my medallion and the family's crest. The ones that mean magic." He pulled a small round piece of metal on a thick string out from under his shirt.

The medallion had on its face five circles one inside the other. Each circle contained a series of symbols going around. In the very middle of the fifth circle was the same staff symbol that was on the book Thomas had given Rupert.

"It says I'm a sorcerer and what family line I am from I think. It is written in the old language. I haven't translated it all yet." As he finished speaking, he put the necklace carefully back under his shirt and out of sight.

Both Cornelius and Victoria had seen and heard that before, but they knew it made him feel important so neither of them mentioned that they knew all of this already.

"Mark is as good a name as any," Cornelius said.

"Aye, I'm now Mark, and we will discuss what the mark on my arm means later. It's freezing, and the horses want to move again. Corn, lead the way to this forest, and let's hope if we meet anyone, they have a warm fire going and food they are willing to share."

The journey to this point had been easy except for the extreme cold. They had been following the wide well-kept road. It was the main road between the cities. There were men employed to keep the road clear of debris and keep it safe for the carriages that transport food and other goods to the towns. Victoria knew that traveling would become much more difficult very soon.

Cornelius turned off the road and made a beeline for the thick, dark forest ahead. Victoria followed him closely. Rupert took up the rear, going a bit more slowly because he was riding such a large horse with no saddle. There was a special bridle on the horse's head, giving Rupert reins, but reins don't help with balance. He looked back over his shoulder. The snow was still falling, so their tracks were well covered.

As they entered the woods, Victoria got the feeling they were being watched. Cornelius had turned to look back at her just before he passed into the trees. She knew him well enough to know that he knew something she didn't. She began to brace herself for anything sudden. She had only ever ridden a horse from Thomas's house into Bale. If anything startled her horse, she was afraid she would not be able to hold on. She wished Cornelius had told her what to expect. He sometimes forgot minor details. She gave him credit for putting her in the middle, though.

Rupert was prepared for anything. He had a feeling in his gut that they were being followed and had been for a long time. It takes great skill to track someone out of sight when the snow fell so thickly on the ground. Anyone with that kind of skill was not someone that would be easily beaten. Whoever was tracking them was not on Kybon's side. Rupert knew that. He did not yet have the powers of a sorcerer, but he had a heightened awareness and acute senses—small powers he was born with. He could not tell, however, if the tracker was on their side.

After about ten minutes of riding on the uneven narrow path, Cornelius made a low noise, pulled up on Kob's reins, and stopped. Victoria did the same, followed by Rupert.

It took about ten seconds for Victoria to see the man walking toward them. The trees were thick around them, dimming the already muted sunlight. Only a little of the snow was making its way onto the forest floor, so the narrow path was visible.

The stranger didn't seem hostile, but he was very solemn and haggard looking.

Cornelius dismounted Kob and greeted the man with an extended hand. "Hello, John."

"Cornelius, you have been sent out again? You just passed through two days ago!" John's voice was jovial and bright. It did not match his tired face at all.

"I am on a different sort of trip this time. My companions and I are trying to reach the capital. We wish not to be followed! I am hoping for passage through these woods."

"Raven 'as been expectin' this. He wishes counsel with you and your friends. It's not yet noon, but you will travel no farther today. You'll make your camp among us tonight. It's already too cold to camp without a fire." John smiled at them warmly. The smile took years off his face. Victoria realized he was not much older than Cornelius.

"We'll follow you," Cornelius agreed.

John led them slowly through the woods. They were not on any distinct path at all. After only about ten minutes, they came to a clearing in the trees. The snow was falling lightly, but there were several small fires burning with two or three people sitting around each one. John led them past all of those people to a large tent.

The tent's roof was tied to two large trees about ten feet in diameter about thirty feet apart and two wooden posts nearly as thick as the trees that were braced with planks for balance. There was a hole in the top of the cloth that had been fitted around a stone chimney that led down to a stone fireplace in the middle of the tent. Five smaller poles were around the fireplace for support. Victoria wondered how well the tent would keep out rain.

The front and one side of the tent were rolled up and tied so that the inside was open to the air. A small amount of smoke from the stone fire pit was pluming out of the open side. Other than the fire pit, however, the inside of the tent was sparse. In the closed corner was a medium-sized wooden box that looked very similar the one Thomas had. There were also a few extra blankets folded next to it and two bed rolls neatly placed next to the blankets.

Sitting inside on a blanket was a large man with long black hair and a black beard and the same haggard look as John. He was cooking a small piece of meat in the fire. Sitting next to him was a woman with much lighter hair and bright blue eyes. They both stood up as John and the company arrived. In the far corner of the tent, another person was wrapped tightly in a blanket, sleeping very deeply.

Cornelius jumped to the ground a few feet from the tent and ran to the man and woman, hugging them both at once. Victoria was much slower at her dismounting. She wondered if anyone noticed how awkwardly she got to the ground.

Rupert slid down to the ground and walked past her slowly and whispered a reminder to her. "Don't forget to let Corn and I do all the talking. If you must talk, try to disguise your voice. I think they are friendly, but we are among thieves and vagrants. I will be on my guard."

"I will be careful, but Corn is related to the woman. She is his cousin on his mother's side. You forget that he and I are going to be married by our own choice, not by arrangement. He has told me all about his friends here. We are safe here, Rupert. They will help us if they can.

"I still don't trust them. There are spies everywhere," he retorted.

"Fine, I will stay quiet, at least for practice."

Rupert shrugged at Victoria. He turned back to the tent and walked quickly to Cornelius. Victoria came in more slowly. She was trying to look as much like a boy as possible, but she was not used to wearing pants or having a sword weighing heavily on one side. When Victoria joined the others, the man motioned them to take a seat on the blanket. Victoria watched Rupert carefully as he sat and pushed his sword up and off to the side. She did the same with modest success.

The man did not sit on the blanket like before. While Victoria was fumbling a bit with her sword, a young boy walked in and placed a chair in front of them and walked out again without a word. The dark-haired man sat and began speaking.

"Welcome, all three of you. Cornelius, I know well." He smiled warmly. Then he looked closely at Rupert and continued. "You must be Oberon's son. Your name is Rupert, is it not?"

Rupert only nodded. He was not expecting to hear his father's name or be recognized as Oberon's son in such a crowd.

"You must be Victoria that I have heard so much about. You look bit like your Uncle Thomas in that disguise. You are taller than I expected as well. Your mother was not tall."

"You knew my mother!" Victoria burst out. He already knew who she was, so she didn't even bother to mask her voice.

The man only laughed. "There is a lot Thomas didn't tell you, but first things first. I should introduce myself. I am called Raven. I am the leader of this clan of outcasts. This is my wife, Kenna," he said, motioning toward the woman behind him who was doing several chores at once. She stopped for just a moment to acknowledge them and then went back to her work. Raven then turned and pointed to the sleeping person in the corner.

"Over there, asleep, is my daughter, Kylan." Then he turned back to them. "Welcome to our home." As he finished talking, Kenna handed each of them a cup of soup. The soup was hot and warmed them, but the cups were very small, and the soup was not filling. She handed Raven a plate with the meat he had been cooking and a cup of soup.

Rupert ate his soup quickly. When he was finished, he got to his feet and turned to leave the tent.

"Rupert, where are you going?" Raven asked.

"To tend to the horses, they must be feed as well."

"Your horses are well taken care of! I promise you that."

"And I should trust the promise of a thief, why?" he said in his toughest voice.

Raven laughed heartily. "Rupert, I know that you do not trust thieves. Your mother never trusted us an inch, but I will not hold that against you. At seventeen, you know of the world only what you have been taught. I am expecting that you three will stay with us for several days. You are just in time for our festival, so you can be taught to think better of us."

"Sir, I was thinking only for the rest of today and tonight. A festival will draw unwanted attention to our departure from Bale," Rupert said.

"No, you will stay at least two weeks. There is much you need to learn. You will not make it far while the snow is so thick. And as for your departure, those who care already know."

"The falling snow is an advantage. It will cover our tracks." Rupert didn't like having other people make important decisions for him.

"You are as stubborn as your parents, boy! The snow will cover your tracks as well as your bodies when you freeze to death. It would be a great loss for us if you die before you reach your full powers. You will be a great man when you are a man, Rupert." Raven laughed again.

Rupert said nothing, but he could feel his cheeks getting hot with frustration. It had been a long time since anyone had chastised him. He realized that this would probably not be the last time. Then his stomach growled loudly, and he knew that he could no longer hide his hunger from the others. Even after the soup, he was still cold and hungry. He was hoping for hot food, not the stuff in their traveling gear that was salty and dry and cold. He thought that this was a boyish desire. He got angry with himself for having such juvenile thoughts.

At the moment, Raven looked from one to the other of them. "Where are my manners, you three have been traveling nearly half the day. It is time for good hot food. That desire is not a childish want, Rupert. It is human."

Rupert was struck dumb. Was this man a mind reader, or was he just very intuitive to other people? Rupert pushed the thought from his head for the moment. He would worry about mysterious magic after they ate a real meal.

The meal was hot and good. It was mostly meat. Vegetables were hard to come by when the snow is so thick. There was enough food to fill everyone in the tent. Victoria thought of the others out in the clearing sitting by fires.

"Why are all the others not eating with us?" she asked Raven.

"Because there is only room by each fire for four or five people to be comfortable. Don't worry about them. They have enough food."

"Why can't you build a larger fire so we can all sit together?" Rupert asked quietly, knowing that he should know the answer.

Raven smiled. "If the fire is too big, then there is no warmth. One side is too cold, and it is too hot on the other. A small fire puts out enough heat to keep a few people warm on every side of it. Which is good for us. A huge fire might catch the trees. If the forest burns, we have no shelter from the heavier snow—or Kybon."

CHAPTER 9

The Winter Festival Begins

When they were done eating, they found themselves walking from fire to fire meeting all the people in the clearing. The snow had stopped falling, but the temperature was not rising.

By midafternoon, people began coming into the clearing from many sides of the woods not just the road as Rupert had expected. Soon there was barely enough room to stand. A large table was brought in from somewhere. There was a buzz of conversation and laughter that echoed off the trees. Musicians came in lugging their instruments, and music began to fill the air, making the conversations louder. Smells of cooking food and burning wood filled their noses.

Victoria had never been to a festival before. She found herself getting lost in the whole experience of it. She walked back to Raven's tent and sat down to watch the merriment though there was little joy in her heart.

She had a lot to think about. Her heart was heavy as she thought of the days to come and the possibility see would have to be separated from Cornelius or Rupert. They were now all she had left of home, which she had never been away from for more than a week. She loved them both in very different ways. She had hoped Cornelius would be her husband one day when all this adventure was over and Rupert, as the high advisor, would be the protector of the kingdom. She knew now for sure that her destiny was leading her toward the throne, but she was not sure they would succeed. She sighed.

Kenna walked over and sat down next to her. "I know that look. Tell me, child, what you are worried about?" Kenna said in a soft, motherly voice.

"If we succeed, I will be queen in less than two years. I know nothing about how to rule anything."

"You will have help. Rulers always have advisors. From what Raven was saying, you have brought yours with you."

"Rupert is brave, but high advisor at eighteen? I can't image the clumsy and reckless boy I grew up with being that wise and powerful."

Kenna laughed for a moment. "The reckless ones make the best leaders if they grow up. Plus his magic will teach him discipline and honor. There was a time when I thought the way you do about Raven and your Rupert's father. Oberon proved to be a great leader for the short time he had before he was betrayed."

"I keep forgetting that everyone here knows our parents. I am not sure how to feel about everyone knowing my life before I do."

"Yes, that is unfortunate, but you can't change things now. Be assured, child, that Cornelius will help you along the way. I have watched him grow into a wonderful young man. He will be a good ruler."

"He is still young, though. I can see him there talking and telling stories to his family. He has a boyish innocent grin, which I love and I know he will lose one day. He has seen nearly all the kingdom on his journeys, and he hears and knows more than he lets on, even to me, but I know in my heart that he is still not prepared for what lies ahead of us."

"No one is ever prepared for what is next in life, dear, but you will find a way to get through. All of us will," Kenna said and stopped abruptly.

"All of us?" Victoria asked because there was sadness in Kenna's voice when she said the word *us*.

"One day, you will understand. In two weeks, when you and your friends leave, my daughter will leave too. But it is the natural course of life. Children must make their own path. Sadly, it is not something a mother can ever really prepare for." Kenna looked at the crowd of people sadly, and then she patted Victoria caringly on the hands and got up and walked back to a small pile of clothes she had been mending. Victoria watched Kenna's retreat and then looked back at the crowd.

Rupert was a little uneasy among a large group of thieves, beggars, and vagabonds. Initially, he felt he needed to protect the things of value he had with him, but soon he learned that everyone knew him. It was bad luck to steal from the family of someone who saved you. It became clearer as the day progressed that his father had saved nearly the entire population of highwaymen from Kybon. It was hard for him to be revered by everyone because of a man he never met, but deep inside his heart, he began to hope one day he would be as brave as his father had been.

He listened to many different versions of the story of how his father had warned them that Kybon had set an ambush for them all. His favorite version was the one that had his father fly in with a magical cloak and defeat Kybon's fifty soldiers with only a shovel and few a small rocks. Raven told him that Oberon had gathered the best and biggest of the clan (well over one hundred men) and lead them to the soldiers' hiding place. The fifty soldiers surrendered immediately. Oberon would not let them be executed. They were sent back to Kybon unarmed. What he did to them was his business, but Oberon would not harm defenseless men.

Rupert decided that Raven's story was the closest to the truth, but he held on to the picture of his father flying in to save the day unassisted. He liked imagining his father as a great hero. The fact that Kybon later destroyed his father was irrelevant to him now.

He crossed paths with a very old man who looked at him and said in a high, scratchy voice, "Boy, you are the splitting image of your father, except when he was with us he never wore that expression on his face. That is a look you got from your mother."

"You know my mother?" Rupert asked, a bit confused. No one except Raven had even acknowledged that he had a mother.

"Yes, a worthy and wise woman she is, but she never trusted us. Not that I could blame her—only the very wise and the very foolish trust thieves."

"But my father trusted all of you. Did that make him very wise or very foolish?" Rupert asked, truly wondering if his father had made a mistake in trusting these people.

"Your father was revered even before he saved the clan from Kybon. As a powerful sorcerer, he could tell who was trustworthy and who wasn't. He had very sharp instincts, and he always caught anyone trying to pick his pocket, but it was his powers that kept most people away. Fear will keep even the best of thieves honest," said the old man quietly.

"What about you? Did you fear him?"

"Yes, I saw firsthand what would happen if someone committed an truly evil act. My brother Baoth was among the worst of us. He tried to steal from your mother while she was here in the care of Bale's guardian because her father was away from Bale on business. When she defended herself, Baoth hit her hard across the face. He was a stout man. She fell to the ground. Your father taught Baoth the consequence of hitting an innocent woman in his presence. He must have been about your age then, so he could not have used magic, though I think he would not have anyway. Baoth never mistreated an innocent person again."

"Wait, why was my father here as a boy? My grandfather had no use for thieves, nor was he of any relation to any of you," Rupert said smugly.

"All of the sorcerers are of one bloodline. Your father was here to learn with an orphaned young sorcerer who lived among us. There are incantations you need to know before some spells will work and other details young sorcerers need to learn. Your grandfather found it easier to teach them both at once. He was Bale's guardian back then." The old man's voice had grown quieter, but it was still shrill.

Rupert kept a steady gaze on the well-aged man. "Thank you for your honesty, sir. May I ask your name?" Rupert asked, stretching out his hand in greeting.

"I am Garbhan."

"I am Rupert. I am glad to meet you." Rupert knew that Garbhan knew his name, but he wanted to formally introduce himself out of respect. Garbhan accepted Rupert's hand. They both walked back to the nearest fire together.

Rupert looked back at Raven's tent and saw Victoria sitting on the ground. She looked strange to him in her uncle's clothes. He knew she was thinking about their journey and what lies ahead for them. He excused himself from the man he had just met and walked back to the tent on a path over a hundred sets of feet had cut through the fallen snow.

He sat down next to her but said nothing. He took the book Thomas had given him out of his pack that someone had removed from his horse and left for him in the tent. He began to read. He was years behind in his knowledge of sorcery.

Cornelius found his mother's five brothers standing by a fire on the edge of the clearing. He knew his uncles, but it had been three years since he had seen them. As Bale's messenger, he had not been there the past few times one or more of them visited his mother, nor had they been there the last few times he stopped at Raven's camp during his missions.

"Welcome, Cornelius, we are glad to see you again." It was Benjamin who spoke. Cornelius shook their hands one by one, starting with Benjamin, Byron, and the twins, Daniel and David, and then Bastien. All five men looked very much like Genevieve. There was the same light-brown hair and blue eyes, except for Benjamin, who had gray eyes. Byron had a small scar on his left arm.

"How are your parents?" Bastien asked.

"They are well despite the hard times. They will manage. They always have."

"Yes, getting by on very little is in your mother's blood. And Malcolm is a reasonable man. He will listen to Gen."

"How is Grandpa? Mom has been worried about him."

"Well," said Benjamin, "there is not much money to be made in running an inn these days. The king levied steep taxes on the innkeepers. And he has to rebuild rooms every few months, but he is getting by."

"Kybon is constantly searching for sorcerers and their power keepers. So he will destroy furniture, walls, everything, if he thinks there is someone hiding. He has no mercy for people trying to run a legitimate business," Byron added with a snicker in his voice.

"I know. I have stayed at the inn many times. Grandpa always has a room for me when I am on a delivery."

"He has a cousin there, helping him when we are away," said one of the twins.

"You and your friends will be safe enough there. Father has special rooms for people in hiding. By the way, who are your friends? And where are they?"

Cornelius looked around, pointing to Raven's tent where he could just see the figures of Victoria and Rupert sitting on the ground. A pang of jealousy ran though him. He didn't like Rupert sitting next to Victoria if he was not there. He pushed the thought from his head. He was being dumb. There was nothing but friendship between them.

"They are sitting there in Raven's tent." He pointed to the two of them. From that distance, they could not tell that Victoria was a girl. Rupert stood up to stretch his legs just as they looked at him. Benjamin jumped.

"Why, he looks like Oberon!" he exclaimed.

"Oberon!" they all said together, turning quickly to look at Raven's tent.

"His son, actually," Cornelius said.

"Oh yes, Rupert, I believe is his name," said Bastien. "How old is he now?"

"Seventeen," Cornelius said.

"If I remember correctly, his birthday was a few weeks ago," Bastien said with a note of sadness in his voice. "I had hoped it was his eighteenth."

"How do you know when his birthday is?" Cornelius asked Bastien in a very decisive tone.

"Calm down, Cornelius, I know that tone. I have not been spying on your friend. Rupert was born around the time I got married. His mother and Thomas were absent from the party in Bale. I found out later it was because Rupert was born and Thomas was taking care of them both," Bastien replied calmly.

"You have very powerful friends! Who is the other kid?" asked Byron politely.

Cornelius wanted to tell them everything that had happened so far, but he thought better of it. He didn't know whom to trust anymore. Even though they were family, he was not sure that they would not play spy for Kybon if the price was right. He thought out his words carefully. "The other is a kid from Bale. He is along to help us, Rupert and I, on our journey."

He knew they could tell he was lying. They pressed him for the information, partly out of curiosity and partly because they knew that the knowledge would be valuable to them.

"Do you not trust your own family?" asked one of the twins.

Cornelius was still not sure who was who. It appeared to him that they wanted it that way because David and Daniel were dressed exactly the same way. It was probably an advantage in their thievery. "In times of trouble, it is unwise to trust anyone but yourself," Cornelius responded.

"I suppose you think that you are a wise man?" asked the other twin.

"No! In my travels, I have discovered that speaking the wrong thing can get you killed! I would just as soon be silent and stay alive. If no one knows you, they cannot betray you, can they?"

"You are a wiser man than you think!" said Bastien quietly.

Just then, Raven walked up, carrying a bundle and a sword. "Cornelius, I have brought you some simple armor and dull sword. I want you to learn to use a sword."

"I know how to use a sword. I was trained in fencing as a child."

All five of his uncles laughed together.

Raven thrust the bundle and the practice sword into Cornelius's hands. "You have never actually been in a sword fight, have you?" he asked in an almost sarcastic voice.

"No. Not a sword fight, but I could beat all of you in a knife fight," Cornelius said in a harsh tone.

"I know that, but there may come a day when someone challenges you to a duel with a sword, and you need to be ready."

"Fine! I will learn to have a real sword fight, and I suppose my uncles would like to help me." Cornelius looked closely at the men by the fire. He felt that this would be an exercise in futility. If anyone ever challenged him, he planned to refuse.

"I will at least," said Bastien. "Let us get you dressed in that armor. My sword is a bit sharper than that one. But I will go easy on you… at first."

"Thank you, Bastien. I have seen your exploits with a sword. The boy should have great skills before the end of the festival." Raven smiled broadly.

Cornelius felt a little better about his uncles' company because Raven trusted them. Raven would know if there were double-crossers in their midst, but nonetheless, he would be cautious. If they betrayed him, that was one thing, but he knew he needed to protect Victoria's and Rupert's secrets too. He looked back over to Raven's tent. They were still sitting in the tent, and Raven was walking toward them carrying another bundle.

Victoria saw Raven coming. She had been watching Cornelius as he talked to his family. She wanted to go and join him but thought better of it. As Raven approached, she caught Cornelius's eyes. She knew that he was as unsure as she was. He was thinking that they should be cautious but open to learning what they could. He winked at her and turned quickly away to face his uncle. She stood up and then pulled Rupert up with her.

"I suppose Raven will be wanting you to learn to use your sword properly," Rupert said.

"Well, since I have a sword now, I guess I should learn to use it. There is so much I don't know. Do you really think we can handle this?"

"We have to handle this. You will be queen one day, and I will be the sorcerer in change of protecting you. But don't forget that Corn will be there too! He will guide us both." Rupert stopped speaking when Raven was only a few feet away.

"It is time we start teaching Victoria to use that sword of hers. I have Cornelius working with his uncles. Rupert, you will work with Victoria, though I am guessing that Thomas taught you both a great deal."

"He taught me some but not nearly enough to win a fight. Rupert taught himself a lot more than Uncle Thomas could," Victoria spoke quietly.

"I bet he has a great talent for it. His father did. But enough about the past. It's time you two to start looking to the future. Practice with these swords for a while. The festival starts at sundown, so you have only a couple of hours left today. All three of you will be sleeping in my tent tonight. You will need to be well rested when the real journey begins.

CHAPTER 10

The Old Storyteller's Story

Victoria and Rupert practiced until the sun fell behind the trees. They worked mostly on Victoria's footwork. She had the strength to swing the sword. Rupert was a good teacher because he knew Victoria well enough to anticipate her movement. She learned quickly not to make her moves predictable. By the end of the lesson, they were both very hot and sweaty despite the extreme cold.

Cornelius walked up only moments after they finished. He looked very tired and a little frustrated.

"I guess your lessons didn't go as well as mine," Victoria said as sympathetically as possible.

"No! Swords are awkward. They are so much longer than knives! I held my own, but my uncles found it funny to watch me fall and hit me with the sword in places the armor didn't cover. I got Bastien, though. He disarmed me, but while he watched the sword flying out of my hand, I pulled my knife and ended the fight with him flat on his back and a knife at his neck."

"What did he say?" Victoria asked.

"He said, 'You win!' but I would really like to practice a bit more."

"Well, you can work with us tomorrow but leave the knives out. Now let's join the festivities." She took his hand as they turned toward the large stage that had been set up during the day.

"Yeah, we should. Uncle Ben told me there is a storyteller here to kick off the festival."

"I suppose we should go and listen then. I am exhausted."

So the three of them gathered with the rest of the people to listen.

The storyteller walked across the makeshift platform. He stood well over six feet tall. As he began the story, his voice flowed deeply.

"Four generations ago, in this very land, there lived a young woman named Asheenial." As he spoke, silence spread, and by the time he finished the first line, the only sound was his voice in the air. "Asheenial was the youngest child and the only girl of a very special family."

"Special indeed!" came a few voices from the front row.

"Her father and her brothers and she possessed the power of sorcery."

"Magic!"

"Now she watched quietly as her father, Rodrick, and her brothers—Laurence, Nolan, and Lake—perfected their magic and power."

"Watched and waited!"

"She was careful, as she grew older, not to let on that she was more powerful than all of them."

"All of their power together was weaker than hers."

"The three boys competed all the time and would not have been happy to be shown up by their baby sister."

"How embarrassing that would be!"

"As the years went on, the four men took on the task of advising the king and the other powerful people in the kingdom."

"People not as powerful as they!"

"But Lake became greedy and wanted to be king himself since it was after all his family that was protecting and advising the king. He began to torment the mortals. Now his father tried to stop him from his evil ways, but Rodrick grew mysteriously ill."

"It is only a mystery if you want it to be!"

"Asheenial was left to care for him because her brothers thought she had not inherited their powers."

"That is what they got for thinking when they weren't used to it!"

"They believed that only men were entitled to these powers, though the laws at the time were not as they are today. Women could hold as much power as they wanted."

"Right, they should."

Victoria noticed that most of the voices in the front row were female.

"While Asheenial took care of her ailing father, she confided in him her great powers. Together, they worked out a way to stop Lake and any other sorcerer to become corrupt."

"To this day, they did!"

"As she thought, Lake had cast a horrible spell on his father. She was able to counter it and secretly returned her father to his full health."

"Smart girl, she was!"

"Meanwhile, Lake became more and more corrupt. He had begun to kill innocent people."

"Powerless more than innocent!"

"Laurence and Nolan realized they were no match for Lake so they tried to help the mortals in his wake instead of combating him."

"Cowards!"

"Rodrick and Asheenial took a similar approach."

"Well, not quite!"

"Together, they cast the most powerful spell that has ever been cast! Even today, it remains unbroken."

"Two is better than one!"

"This spell was cast out over the whole of the kingdom."

"Even the mountain people!"

"Brave and loyal families found themselves possessing a sacred mark on their upper forearm."

"Secret mark!"

The storyteller pointed to the leather band around his right arm. Victoria glanced at the long sleeve of her shirt to see if the leather band around her arm was visible through the thin sleeve. Rupert and Cornelius glanced over at her.

"The mark is, I am told, a square with a staff on top and three sprigs of wheat on the bottom."

"Check your arm if you are unsure!"

"The staff is a symbol of the magic and the wheat of mortality."

"Power, but always a need for food."

"What this spell did was to make the mortals with the mark the keeper of powers of a sorcerer."

"Theirs forever and always!"

"You see, if this mortal dies of an unnatural cause, the sorcerer whose powers he protects will lose his magic and become fully mortal." "How sad that would be!"

"Lake was never told about the spell. He was only warned by Asheenial that he should be protector of mortal men because without them he would be nothing."

"As nothing as they were!"

"But Lake only scoffed at her and belittled her because she was a young and silly girl."

"Young, yes! Silly, never!"

"Asheenial just walked away from him and did not speak to her brother for many years."

"As if he noticed!"

"The day they spoke again was the day that Lake killed his own power keeper."

"Oops!"

"He realized why his sister had warned him years ago, and he returned home and begged her to undue the spell and restore his power and his much longer life span."

"*Groveled* is a better word!"

"She refused, but she did take pity on her brother as she had a very kind heart and gave him and his young daughter Alexa a job in her manor."

"How sweet!"

"Now there was more to the spell as Alexa's grandson, Korgan, discovered two hundred years later when he attempted to kill another powerful sorcerer, the great Oberon in cold blood."

"The saddest day in history!"

Rupert jumped at the sound of his father's name. The storyteller looked out at the crowd, and his eye met Rupert's. There was a pause as the man on stage caught his breath, and then he finished the story. However, it appears that Kybon finished off Oberon.

"It has been said that Oberon's son and his friends will defeat Korgan's oldest son."

"There is still hope!"

"Yes, the evil man who oppresses us all"—he raised his hands in the air and his voice grew deeper—"Kybon!"

"Ahh!"

Then the storyteller made eye contact again with Rupert. "As long as Oberon's son keeps a kind heart and strong will, we all will live to see the day when Asheenial's dream of peace and prosperity for this kingdom comes true.

"Thank the heavens for Asheenial and Oberon's son!"

"Peace is on the way!"

The storyteller bowed, and the people in the front row cheered. Someone in the back yelled for more stories.

"I will tell no more stories tonight! Raven has signaled that the meal is ready! So let us all eat and be merry. This is a great celebration, maybe our last in hiding!"

There was a roar of cheers from the crowd. The storyteller bowed again and walked off the stage. He walked to the table and began to gather his food; the rest of the gathered people began to head toward the large tables.

A stranger walked past the three shocked teenagers still sitting in their chairs. He looked at Cornelius, whom he was closest to, and said, "Come on, the feast has started!" The man hurried off, still smiling happily. "Ya do not want to miss the food, do ya?"

Rupert and Victoria both stared at the now empty platform.

Cornelius spoke softly. "Come on, I know that is a lot for both of you to take in, but I promise we will all think better on full stomachs."

Victoria turned and looked at Cornelius. "I am a keeper of powers."

"I know," he said softly.

"How do you know?" she said still in a bit of shock.

"I figured it out," he said, then turned to Rupert to change the subject. "What about you, Rupert? Are you all right?"

"I am destined to kill Kybon! Other than that, I am great," Rupert said in a strange, dejected voice. Then his stomach rumbled loudly. He got to his feet. "But you are right. We should eat first, and then we will think this over."

The food was hot and delicious. After they got their food, they wandered through the crowd back to Raven's tent, careful not to drop it in the thick snow.

The storyteller came into Raven's tent to eat with them. He sat next to Cornelius and faced Rupert.

"Hello, young ones," said the storyteller, who was very old, "mind if I join your group here?"

"Not at all," Rupert said. "Please join us. We have questions."

The storyteller sat down slowly. He glanced at Raven who nodded. "I suppose I should introduce myself. I am Cadmus." He extended his hand out to Rupert first and then the other two.

Cornelius said his name, but Victoria remained silent.

"Now, young Rupert, what are your questions?" Cadmus asked.

"Well, um, how do you know who I am?"

"Except for your eyes, you look like your father."

"No, there is more than that. You would have known anyway."

"Ahw. I see you have inherited your father's extra sense," he said quietly. "Yes, I have it too. So I simply knew it was you."

Rupert wanted to argue, but he understood what Cadmus meant. There had been moments when he knew things, and he could never explain how. "So I really do have an extra sense?"

"Yes, and you should trust it. Any other questions?" Cadmus asked, looking at the disguised Victoria and Cornelius.

Victoria leaned over and whispered in Cornelius's ear. She was afraid to give away her identity.

"Can a power keeper find out whose powers they keep?" Cornelius asked.

"I don't think the keeper is supposed to know just as the sorcerer isn't supposed to know, but years of evil sorcery have corrupted the spell. I have heard that there is a sorcerer who knows all the power keepers and whose powers they keep. But I don't know for certain. We have had to be so careful with information these last several years since Oberon's death," Cadmus said.

Rupert froze. "Do you know how my father actually died? My mother never talks about it," Rupert asked.

Cadmus sighed. "That I cannot answer. I was not there, and no one who was there ever told anyone what actually happened. I know the rumors."

Cornelius stood up and took a very deep breath. He reached into his pocket and pulled out a folded piece of paper. "Rupert, your mother gave me this letter the night before we departed from Thomas's house. She asked me to give it to you after we heard Cadmus speak. It is the only account of your father's death that we know about. Cadmus, would you like to read it to us? I think you are the only person here who is not directly affected."

CHAPTER 11

The Account of Oberon's Death

Cadmus took the letter and scanned the writing quickly. He looked around. Raven walked up and looked at the letter.

"Yes, Cadmus, please read it. I cannot tell this story again." He looked a Rupert and then to Victoria. "I wrote his letter, but I shall not listen to it read. I have already lived through it once that is more than enough for one lifetime." Raven's voice cracked at the last words, and he shook Cadmus's hand, clapped Rupert on the back, and quickly left their table.

Cadmus cleared his throat and began to read.

Dear Katherine,

I am sorry to write about such news with your small boy, but since you sent the inquiry to the castle, I felt that I should reply straight away. I am sad to say that Thomas's dear sister, Kate, passed away due to the complications of giving birth. It seems her Keeper status was passed on to the baby, Victoria. Thomas is racked with grief. I am afraid that his sister was the latest of his friends and family to fall in this...war...I guess that is what this is.

He will be here for a few weeks, I think, before he will return to resume his duty as town guardian. I was asked to tell you that because your late husband asked him if he would take on the job. Ashel will protect him since he is not of the sorcerer bloodline. I hope that information helps you cope somehow.

I suppose now is as good a time as any to answer your second question. I was there when Oberon fell. It is hard to write it all down, but I suppose since Thomas and I were the only two to survive, one of us has to tell the story.

As you know, we had all gone to the capital to find out why the supplies had been cut off to Bale. Looking back now, I realize it was a trap.

We got into the palace and waited to see the king. When we finally got into the throne room, we knew something was wrong. The king was not on the throne! He was in a curled heap on the floor. Kybon stood next to the throne, looking at the king with a wild smile on his face.

Oberon stepped forward. "I should have known the king would not cut us off!" he yelled. "It was you. You will not get away with hurting the innocent!"

Kybon did not respond except with a laugh. Several soldiers in the king's guard came into the room from behind the throne and surrounded us. Then five more entered each holding onto an innocent one. The fifth soldier had Clara!

Thomas screamed and rushed passed everyone toward the soldier! Kybon laughed, stepped forward, and threw Thomas to the ground. From the ground, Thomas yelled something about war. It was muffled from where I was standing.

"You're wrong! This is not a war. Wars mean there are two sides fighting. By the laws of magic, I cannot officially be a part of this fight." Even now, the evil in Kybon's voice is with me.

Clara and the four others were marched out of the throne room, and the rest of the soldiers followed. One stopped and grabbed Thomas and took him. So Oberon and I followed.

We ended up outside on the palace grounds near the stables. There were soldiers everywhere, but we decided that they were no match for us. Oberon led off the fight without magic. He drew his sword and ran for the solider that had Clara. Thomas got free from his holder at the same time. He ran to Clara from the other side.

I drew my own sword and ran into the fight. Many of the soldiers ran toward us. That is when Oberon and I used our powers. We were able to stun nearly all of the men. Except, of course, the men holding the innocent ones. Clara was free.

Then there was a crackling sound near us. We all looked at once and saw the stables were on fire. We could hear the horses whinnying inside.

Without thinking, we all ran to try to save the horses. Thomas and Clara and I ran to the first stable, and Oberon ran to the second. The stable boy was tied to a wall. He was screaming, but Clara got to him first. Just before Thomas and I got there to untie him, a large beam from the ceiling fell on Clara and the stable boy. I tripped and fell. I jumped back to my feet and tried to use magic to put out the flames and move the beam, but my magic was gone.

Thomas and I were able to move the beam, but the stable boy was dead. Clara hurt very badly. Thomas picked her up and carried her out.

"Go and help Oberon! There is nothing we can do here!"

So I ran to the second stable. Oberon was putting out the flames. His horse was next to him. In less than a minute, the flames were out. We ran back toward the first stable.

When we got there, Colin was standing in front of it, barring our entrance. He released the horses, and they ran off in fright toward the soldiers that held the four people we did not know. As the horses ran, the soldiers threw the people down in their path of the spooked animals.

It was an awful sight.

All four of them were killed. We turned away and rushed to help Thomas. Clara was shaking in his arms. Oberon tried to help, but his powers were gone too!

The soldiers grabbed us and began pulling us away from Thomas and Clara. Kybon was now outside. He ordered us to be brought to the dungeons for setting the stables on fire.

In the confusion, Thomas and Oberon charged toward Kybon. He threw a flame at them, but Oberon's horse ran in front of them and took the brunt of the impact. I will never forget it as long as I live.

The horse was badly hurt, but he kept running in front of them as if to protect them. Kybon made a strange noise and ordered them to be killed. Our stun spells had been broken, so all of the soldiers ran in with their own swards drawn.

Kybon disappeared.

Thomas and Oberon and I began to fight hand to hand. Ashel appeared with soldiers of her own, but we were still out numbered.

Thomas was hit in the head and knocked unconscious. Oberon ran to help him and was struck down by a soldier. There was a large bolt of lightning and then blinding rain.

But it was too late! Oberon was dead, and so was Clara.

I figured out that the stable boy was my keeper and one of the people killed in the stampede was Oberon's.

I feel as if I failed because I could not save them. I have been rendered helpless to stop Kybon. But there is hope. Kenna says that our job now is to protect and rear our daughter. You must do the same with your son. They are our hope now. I know in my heart that we will live to see the day that our children stop this evil that has taken hold of our land.

Your friend,
Raven

There was silence. Rupert took the letter slowly as Cadmus handed it to him.

"I will not soon forget your father's story, and I hope to complete it one day with your triumph over Kybon." Cadmus nodded and left Rupert to ponder what he had just read.

Rupert wiped tears from his eyes. Then he put his head down on the table and sighed.

Victoria got up and walked away from the others. There was enough light from the fires and the moon, which she could see a little way into the forest. She sat down in the snow behind a larger tree and listened to the murmur of voices.

Cornelius followed her a few minutes later and wrapped her in her cloak. He sat down next to her. She said nothing but put her head on his shoulder. He ran his fingers through her short hair.

They just sat there for an hour or so in silence. Finally, Cornelius whispered softly, "Come on, it is time for sleep." She got up slowly and walked back to Raven's tent. Cornelius followed her at a slight distance.

CHAPTER 12

Mastering Weaponry

The next morning, the snow had begun to fall again. Rupert and Cornelius both awoke stiff and cold. Raven was already awake. The two boys could see him cooking at the fire again, just as he was when they met him the day before. The heavy snow was making the top of the tent sag from its weight.

The smell of the food let them both know instantly that they were both very hungry. They listened to the other's stomach growl. Raven looked over at them and laughed.

"I am cooking enough for both of you," he said in a very jovial tone.

"Do you need some help?" Cornelius asked quickly.

"No, but you should both come nearer into the warmth of the fire."

They both hastened closer to Raven. Victoria's sleeping form was just visible in the growing light. Cornelius wondered if she was as cold as he was. Without thinking more about it, he walked back over to the pile of bedding he and Rupert had left in a heap and shook out his blanket. He walked quickly over to Victoria and carefully placed the blanket over her.

She turned her head slightly and smiled broadly at him and whispered so that only he could hear her. "Thank you, Cornelius. I was starting to shiver. Don't tell them I am awake yet. I want a few more moments of peace before this adventure starts again."

He smiled back and kissed her forehead. Then he walked back to Raven and Rupert. Cornelius inhaled deeply, taking in the smell of the eggs and thinly sliced meats cooking on the flames. The oak wood always gave a distinct flavor that he had grown fond of.

Rupert, on the other hand, didn't like the oak flavor. He realized that there was going to be a lot of things he was going to have to get used to. He was grateful that the food was fresh and hot and that there was enough to go around. The letter Raven had written to his mother was still in his pocket. His father had lost his life to help the kingdom. Rupert decided that the least he could do was to be thankful for having the things so many others around him had lost.

"Rupert," Raven said when the breakfast was nearly ready, "please go and wake Kylan and Victoria. It is time for breakfast and then more learning for you three."

Rupert gave no response to Raven's request; he walked over to where the girls lay. He had not yet met Kylan. He had been told she was asleep when they arrived because it had been her turn to take watch the night before. She was not at Raven's tent during the festival feast. He leaned over Victoria and gently pushed on Kylan's shoulder.

She was sleeping on her side with a blanket covering her face. He could see her long dark hair creeping out from under the cover.

"Kylan, it is time to wake up. Your father has breakfast ready." As the girl began to stir through the blanket, Rupert looked at Victoria and laughed. "Get up, Victoria, if I can't pretend to sleep under two blankets and be comfortable and warm, then you can't either," he said with jest in his voice.

"Well, I am warm, but this little piece of ground is not all that comfortable," she said with her eyes still closed tightly.

"Well, get used to it. A bed will not fit in our packs, though I bet Corn would carry one for you on his back if you asked him to." Rupert laughed again.

"I would never ask him to, and besides, I would make you do it. He is going to be king one day. You will be a lowly sorcerer of no importance at all," she said with a laugh as she slid her leg over into his legs. He was still leaning over, so he fell to the ground as she rolled away so he would not land on her. She got quickly to her feet still, wearing her boyish outfit from the day before. Rupert lay on the ground, laughing careful not to roll into Kylan as he tried to get back on his feet.

Kylan got to her feet much more slowly. She sat up and stretched and yawned. Rupert looked at her. He realized he had seen her the night before. She had been in the front row calling out with a few others during the story. She had been sitting next to Kenna. He should have figured it out.

A pang ran through him. He realized that she was quite beautiful. He felt that she was powerful. His extra sense hit his gut. She was a sorcerer or would be very soon.

She caught his eye. Instead of turning away, she looked unblinking and steadfastly at him. She could feel his powers too. Then she reached up her hand. Without thinking, he reached out and pulled her to her feet. She walked quickly away from him. He could tell she was as shaken as he was by their connection.

Victoria saw their exchange but said nothing to either of them. Cornelius had been too intent on his breakfast to notice anything at all. He idly rubbed Victoria's hands as Kylan set out plates for everyone at the small table Kenna had just set out. They ate their breakfast in silence. Everyone was lost in thought.

As they ate, Kenna walked around the tent with a large stick, pushing up on the roof. The snow fell to the ground with a soft thud, making mounds of snow around the tent. After assuring her guests that she had already eaten, she began shoveling the snow away from the tent. Victoria watched the few remaining people left in the clearing shovel snow away from the stone fire pits and from the sides of smaller versions of Raven's tent that had been put up when the snow began to fall.

When all the food was gone and the plates were cleared away, Raven brought out the practice swords from the day before as well as a map of the kingdom.

"I want you three to practice more with these swords. Rupert, you should practice with Cornelius today, and Kylan will teach Victoria."

"Why can't I practice with Corn?" Victoria asked.

"Because you would both practice too easy, so as not to hurt the other at all, not to mention that it is difficult to concentrate when you are doing anything with someone you love. You must work hard and learn. There will be plenty of time later, once your skills are improved, to practice together," Raven said. Then he turned to Cornelius and continued. "Later tonight, Cornelius, you and I will sit down together and look over this map. I want there to be a plan to get to Pallen.

Before Raven could finish, Kylan spoke. "Father, where do you want us to practice? The snow is getting deeper by the minute. It will be impossible to move around if we are standing two feet deep in snow."

"The four of you are quite smart. I am sure you will figure something out. I need to help your mother shovel the snow," he said to Kylan, giving her a quick hug as he hurried off to his wife's side.

Rupert had been thinking the same thing but quickly formulated a solution. He pulled the armored shirt over his head and ran off into the woods hollering over his shoulder. "I'll be right back."

Just as he had hoped, there were a few spaces between the trees that would allow ample movement for them to practice. The trees were large enough to block a lot of the snow, so it was only a few inches deep on the ground.

He ran back to the others. "There is room to practice in the forest. The snow is only a few inches deep. Unless anyone else has any other ideas."

No one did, so they told Raven they would be in the forest and headed into the thick leafless trees.

By noon, they were once again covered in sweat despite the bitter cold. Victoria's hands were so cold she found it very difficult to swing her sword properly with gloves on. It was impossible to tell the position of the sun because of the trees, but Rupert knew it was nearly noon. He always knew the time of day. The hunger they were all feeling helped as well.

"It is nearly noon. We should head back to camp and have some lunch," Rupert said boldly.

"Who put you in charge?" asked Kylan in a defiant tone.

"Fine, I am heading back for lunch. The rest of you can join me if you would like."

Without another word, he shouldered his dull practice sword and walked in the direction of the clearing. Cornelius picked up his and Victoria's swords and followed. Victoria smiled broadly and jogged to catch up with Cornelius and took him by his free hand. Kylan turned and walked slowly, taking up the rear of the party. She shuddered at the strange feeling in her heart.

After lunch of the same meat they had the night before and would have that night, they felt that they needed to relax a bit. Rupert sat down in Raven's tent next to the fire to read more of the book Thomas had given him. He wanted to find out if there was anything in there about clairvoyance to another sorcerer.

Cornelius went to talk with his uncle Byron, who was the only one of his uncles to stay on after the main feast. The other four had things to attend to. Cornelius wasn't sure he wanted to know what the men were up to. Victoria sat down on the other side of the fire from Rupert. She watched for a moment as Kylan cleaned up after the meal. She glanced at Rupert. He was engrossed in the book. So she got back to her feet slowly.

"Do you need some help?" she asked Kylan. "Sure, if not just to have someone to talk to."

"I am good at talking!" Victoria said.

Soon after, Cornelius walked into the tent carrying a small wooden box. He set it down on the low table where they had eaten their lunch. "Uncle Byron gave me this game. Would you guys like to play?"

"Sure," the other three said at once.

"How do we play?" Victoria asked, looking at the rectangular board and the small leather bag of different colored stones.

"I am not quite sure actually. I played this a few times as a boy, but I don't remember all the rules," he said sheepishly.

"I think I used to play this too. We can figure it out," said Rupert happily. He was ready for a bit of distraction.

They spent the next few hours playing and discussing the rules and making up a few. The sun had begun to set when Raven returned, and they ate the evening meal.

After the meal, Raven requested counsel with Cornelius about the maps. Victoria seized that moment to talk to Rupert. She pulled him by his shoulder out of the tent. They walked together to another part of the clearing out of earshot of everyone else. They stood next to an abandoned stone fire pit still containing the remnants of a smoldering fire. She had brought some kindling and three small logs from Raven's woodpile with her. She placed it in the smoking coals and blew on it. A small flame sprang up and caught the small dry wood.

When the flames where burning almost a foot high, she motioned Rupert to sit down. He brushed the snow off of a rock in front of the fire pit. Victoria did the same.

"Do you have any idea what is going on with you and Kylan? And I get a strange twinge in my arm when she is near me. I felt the same strange twinge around Colin."

"I guess a keeper knows when a sorcerer is around," Rupert said. "But I don't think I feel it around you. I thought at first that I would only know a full-powered sorcerer, but Kylan isn't eighteen yet."

"I think maybe you do feel it when I am around too. You just got used to it. I am not sure what is going on between Kylan and I. But according to Raven's letter, she is part of this adventure."

"Yes, Kenna said yesterday that Kylan was leaving at the same time we are. Do you think she is coming with us?"

"I hope so!" Rupert said without thinking. Then he added, "There is so much she can teach me. I am pretty far behind where I should be on my training."

"Yes, it would be good to have her around. Can I see the letter to your mom? I never knew how Aunt Clara died."

"Yeah, I want to read it again too. I wish we had known this sooner, but I guess we would not have really understood it as children."

They stood there by the fire for a few more minutes, taking turns reading parts of the letter out loud. When tears began to well up in Rupert's eyes, he folded the letter carefully and returned it to his pocket. He took a deep breath, wiped his face with his cold hands, and turned back toward Raven's tent.

Victoria used a long stick to separate the wood in the fire so it would go out. She had to jog to catch up to Rupert.

The next week went on in much the same way. They practiced in the mornings before lunch. After lunch, they played games or told stories. At night, they would dance and sing with those who came to the festival. There was a storyteller every night. Kylan sat with them and told them what to say during the stories. She knew them all. Raven told them of the old days when the whole kingdom came for the festivities. What was then called the midwinter festival was the biggest holiday in the kingdom. Now it was just the outcasts and beggars and thieves who came to the forest. It was nearly impossible to go anywhere now because of the armies in every city. Kybon had banned festivals in cities and towns. He had never given a reason why.

Rupert read as much as he could every night, but there was so much in the book that he had to take in that he spent a lot of time rereading the beginning sections. He and Kylan were still having moments of clairvoyance, but it was clear now that it was not all the time.

Two days before the end of the two-week festivities, Victoria found herself alone again with Rupert. Nothing more had been mentioned about Kylan leaving with them. She was acting as if she was going to stay with her family.

"I think you should go to Raven. Kenna seemed to think that she was leaving. Maybe she has changed her mind, though."

"No, it is her parents' place to decide if she goes."

"You have to do something, Rupert. She can read your thoughts. She can help us. I think she should come with us."

"I agree that she can help us, but her duties are here with her family. It should be her choice to leave."

"What? It wasn't our choice! We were sent here because it is our destiny or something like that. Why is her life any different? She is a sorcerer, or at least she will be when she turns eighteen. Therefore, this affects her as much as it affects us."

"Vic, what do you want from me?"

"You are going to be my high counselor one day! Grow a spine! If you are too afraid to go to Raven, then talk to her! Or I will do it for you. I am tired of waiting on Raven or Uncle Thomas, to make decisions for us. This is our journey, not theirs. She can help us, and I want her to come with us."

"Fine! I will talk to her then! I am not scared!" Rupert took a deep breath and then continued calmly. "I am confused. I know I am going to be high counselor and all that, but, Victoria, are we ready for this? The lives of everyone in this kingdom are at stake here. Can we handle it?"

"We have to handle it. You told me that! We will handle it better if Kylan is with us."

"I will talk to her," he said quietly.

Cornelius walked out of Raven's tent just then and bounded toward them. "Hey, do you guys want to play colored stones again?"

Rupert stood up, shook his head quietly, and walked away into the woods.

"Is he all right?" Cornelius asked.

"He has a lot on his mind. I don't want to play, either."

"Are you all right?"

"I have a lot on my mind too."

He sat down behind her and took her into his arms. She would have protested, but there were very few people around, and if there were spies about, they knew who she was already. Then he took out the blank book Thomas had given him. Together, they began to write down an account of what had happened so far. Victoria fell asleep long before Cornelius was done writing.

The firelight was nearly gone when Rupert returned. He sat down next to Cornelius, who said hello without looking up from his writing.

"What are you doing?"

"Writing our story like Thomas told me."

"Good, aw.. .is Victoria actually asleep?"

"Yes, she is. Why?"

"She hasn't been sleeping much. I think you should do this more often."

"Do what?"

"Sit by the fire with her in your arms and write down our adventures. You are the only one that can get her to sleep."

"Really?"

"Yes, Cornelius! Are you that oblivious? She loves you, and you comfort her even if you aren't trying to."

"I know what you mean! I have not been this comfortable since we left home."

"Come on, it is late. Let us try to get some sleep as well. Who knows when we will have peace again."

Rupert helped Cornelius stand without dropping Victoria. Together, they walked back to Raven's tent. The boys laid Victoria next to Kylan, who was sound asleep.

Raven appeared next to them. "The two of you should sleep here tonight. The ground is softer, and it is warmer. You have learned a lot in a short time. Rest tonight."

Cornelius and Rupert lay down next to the girls. The ground did seem softer, and they were warm enough that they did not shiver. They were both asleep within minutes.

The next morning after breakfast, Rupert pulled Kylan away into the woods to talk to her.

"What is going on between us?" he asked rather hastily.

"I am not sure, Rupert," she responded in a whisper.

Rupert leaned forward and whispered back. "Victoria thinks you should come with us. You can help us."

"I know what Victoria thinks. What do you think?"

"I think you should come too."

"Why?"

"Well, because you are going to be powerful and because I would like to have you around," he said sheepishly.

"I would like to go, but I can't. I have to return to Pallen tomorrow. I work at an inn there. The one that Cornelius's grandfather owns actually. I have to return as soon as the festival is over, or it will arouse suspicion. There are soldiers in every town. They will be stopping everyone on the way. I have a pass to get me back to Pallen."

"You will not be going alone?"

"Of course. My parents will be with me. We are only here for the festival. Do you really think we live in a tent all winter?" she said, laughing.

"I hadn't thought about it, I guess," Rupert said, shrugging his shoulders.

"Don't worry about us. You three are the ones in danger, and without you, all will be lost."

"So I will see you again in Pallen?"

"Yes, the inn is the safest place I think. I will be waiting to hear all about your travels." She kissed his cheek. He hugged her and then took her hand. They walked back to the clearing together.

The rest of the day was spent preparing for their departure. The snow had finally stopped falling, but it was still very cold. There was still a half a foot of snow on the ground. All the fire pits had been dismantled and the stones placed under trees until next year's festival. There was only a handful of people who remained in the clearing.

Cornelius and Rupert packed up their bags while Kylan cut Victoria's hair even shorter.

"Your hair grows very fast. You need to keep it short. They will be looking for a girl," Kylan warned.

"I will. I don't mind it short. It is easier to manage, but Cornelius likes it long. He likes to run his fingers through it."

"I'm sorry," Kylan said abruptly.

"Why?"

"Because you will be with the man you love, but he won't be able to hold you. You will have to pretend to be his cousin or something."

"I will be all right. There won't be much time for affection anyway."

"Why not?"

"Rupert will be with us."

"That would make him feel a bit awkward."

"You are a good friend."

"I hope so."

By sundown, everything was ready. This time it was Cornelius's turn to talk to Victoria in the woods. He pulled her by the hand. There was no moon that night, so it was very dark.

"What, Cornelius, it is very cold out here in the—"

Before she could finish, he kissed her. "I don't know when we will be able to be ourselves again, and I wanted one last kiss." He started to walk back to the clearing, but Victoria stopped him.

"Wait, hold me for a minute."

Cornelius wrapped his arms around her. She looked at him intently. She could barely see his face in the dark, but she could tell he was smiling brightly at her. He whispered "I love you" in her ear. She tried to whisper back, but there were unexpected tears and a lump in her throat. She tried to sob quietly.

"I am scared too. But we will be fine. We will protect each other." He held her as tightly as he could without hurting her. She said nothing.

After a few more minutes, Cornelius loosened his hug and took her gloved hands. "We need to go back. We have to depart before dawn."

"Only if you kiss me one more time."

He kissed her again, took off his glove, and ran his fingers through her very short hair. He frowned a little. Then he put his glove back on, and they walked carefully back into the clearing in the darkness.

CHAPTER 13
The Second Departure

The next morning, Raven woke them before sunrise.

"Wake up, you three. It is time to get a move on." Raven's voice sounded harsh in the stillness of the cold night.

Rupert felt something strange in his gut. He looked straight into Raven's face. There was a fear and sadness in his eyes.

Rupert stood and grabbed his arm. "Raven, what is it? What is wrong?"

"I have word from a trusted source! Kybon knows you're here. He wants you dead, Rupert, and Victoria in his dungeon. I am not sure if he knows that Cornelius is with you or not," Raven said, a little distracted by the afterthought.

Victoria stood up and put her sword at her hip. Her clothes were baggy and patched. She wore a shabby wool cloak that was unadorned. Cornelius was wearing his riding coat with many pockets. He was well known in the area as a messenger, so he decided that he would look as if he were on a delivery. Rupert was dressed all in black with Victoria's emerald-green cloak. They had decided the night before that they would pretend to be riding together by chance, and Victoria would be Rupert's servant.

"Mark, ready the horses," Rupert barked out in Victoria's direction.

"Yes, sir, right away," she said in a low and steady voice.

"I think we know our parts. Corn, you are the famous one, so you do most of the talking. I will be a bit meaner to our servant than you since most people know your cheerful disposition. But we have to pass her off as a servant or this won't work." Rupert's tone was firm but kind.

"I know. I will remember. It may not work anyway." Cornelius took a very deep breath as he finished speaking.

Victoria cleared her throat. "Sirs, it is time we get a move on."

Raven laughed. Victoria was going to do fine as their servant.

They departed just as the sun began to tinge the sky a lighter gray at the horizon. They were again riding single file with Cornelius leading the way, but this time, Rupert was second in the procession. It was the custom for servants to ride last and several feet behind. Victoria was more comfortable on her horse now, so she didn't mind as much.

Every so often, Rupert would turn around and bark out to Victoria to keep up, usually followed by an unpleasant insult. He again had the feeling that they were being watched and followed, but this time, he knew the person was not on their side. After nearly five hours of riding, they finally made their way out of the forest.

Rupert pulled up alongside Cornelius and shouted, "I thought you knew these lands! Why did it take that long to get out of the woods? I think you are leading me astray, message boy!" He winked when he finished.

Cornelius realized instantly that Rupert thought there might be someone tracking them in earshot. "Look, I am being paid to take a message into Pallen from Bale. I said you could ride with me since you have urgent business in the capital! But I suggest that you treat me with more respect than you do your servant. I know the safest ways around here. You, sir, do not. Without me, the soldiers will kill you for sure."

"I offered to pay you well!"

"And I refused your fair! I am messenger for the king. I will not take money that is not due to me from that station! I am an honest man. But as I am not excepting your money, you can go on your way if you so choose."

"But I don't know the way to Pallen. Why do you think I asked for your help, dimwit!"

"If you don't know the way, I suggest you shut up, or I will ditch you the first chance I get."

With that, Rupert pulled his horse back in line behind Cornelius. He glanced back at Victoria, who was stifling her laughter.

By dusk, they were tired from the long hours riding. There was nothing on the road ahead of them for many miles. They made a camp not far off the road under a small clump of trees. They huddled together for warmth and so they could whisper without being heard unless someone was very close.

"You were brilliant earlier, Corn," Rupert said.

"Thank you. I take it you think someone is following us."

"Yes, though the feeling is less intense than it was in the forest. Probably because whoever it is has to stay far behind us and off the road, or we will see him."

"I looked back a few times, but I didn't see anyone. I agree that we should stay on the side of caution. Do you think we will actually meet soldiers soon?" Victoria asked.

"There is a huge camp of them up the road a ways. It is just past the village of Kelter. Kelter is about another two days' ride, at least. If there is any more snow, it will take even longer."

"I think one of us should stay wake for a while and keep watch. Corn, I will wake you in a few hours. I think it is better if every night one of us gets a full night's sleep. Tomorrow Mark will take the first shift."

Rupert watched the sliver of the waxing moon as the hours past. It was freezing out, and they had opted not to build a fire. The light and the smoke would draw unwanted attention. Rupert wondered if Kylan was sleeping and whether or not she missed him. He couldn't sense her at all. He lay in the dark listening to the quiet stillness of the night. There was nothing moving in the darkness, but his uneasy feeling remained.

Thunderstorm blew warmth on his neck as he sat in the dark. Rupert had managed to acquire a raw carrot before they left the clearing. He broke it in half and gave his horse one of the pieces.

"I know it is cold, and the hay is stale. I could only get you one carrot. I will give you the other half tomorrow. I will try to get you some more when we get to Kelter," he said, rubbing his horse's nose. When the late-night constellations were up, he woke Cornelius.

The next two days were spent in much the same way as the first. It was hard riding in the snow. They were on the main road through the kingdom, but it was not well traveled when the snow was thick. There were sections that were nearly impassable. Rupert's feeling of being watched and followed never went away. He grew more unhappy that they were out in the open.

On the fourth day after they left Raven, they came to an icy bridge that lead across a large river called the Kelter Way. The small village was visible from the landing of the bridge.

"There is Kelter. We should be able to get shelter for the night there. I know the innkeeper well enough," Cornelius said more enthusiastically than he planned. The others were just as keen on sleeping in a warm bed and having a hot meal.

Victoria was beginning to wonder if she would ever be truly warm again. "Why are we standing around? Let's go across. It is already starting to snow again," she said in as deep and raspy voice as possible.

"I am not sure we can cross it. The wood looks iced over," Rupert said quietly.

Cornelius nodded. "It is not a sturdy bridge as it is. I usually ford the river if I can when I am traveling through these parts."

"So the river is not deep?" Rupert asked, surveying the area around the bridge.

"It comes up to Kob's stomach in the late spring and summer. Early spring, it would be over his head because of the runoff from the hills up stream. I have never crossed it in the winter."

"How do you get to Pallen in the winter then?" Victoria asked emphatically, knowing full well he had delivered messages at all times of the year.

"Well, there is a different bridge about a day's ride from here. I take that one. It is newer and sturdier. And there is a bridge tender there, so if anything happens, he can get help."

"Maybe we should go to that bridge," Victoria said as much as she wanted a warm bed that night. This way didn't look safe.

Cornelius agreed that it would be safer, but Rupert stopped them. "Wait, we should talk about this. How far is it back to Kelter from there?"

"Probably a day and a half in this snow. I don't come to Kelter in the winter. I usually only have two weeks to get to Pallen, so I ride without stopping except to sleep. I will admit I would have to follow the river to get back here."

"Are there any other towns near there?" Victoria said.

"No, the road to Pallen from there is uninhabited except for an old hermit."

"I think we should take our chances and cross here. I really would like a warm bed tonight, and we are out of hay and grain. We can't ride another three days without feeding the horses!" Rupert yelled.

Victoria and Cornelius knew he was right.

"I suppose that settles the matter then. We will cross here," Victoria said.

They spent the next few minutes surveying the area. They dismounted their horses. Cornelius felt it would be easiest to use the bridge. The river was frozen, and the ice was slick. He wasn't sure if the horses could walk across without slipping. So he went first taking his horse by the reins and leading him across the narrow creaking bridge.

Victoria followed Cornelius. She made it safely to the other side. Rupert and Thunderstorm took up the rear.

Rupert looked at his horse, who was much larger than the other two horses, and then he looked at the bridge. "Be very careful boy. This bridge is not safe," he said in a shaky voice.

As the two of them started across the bridge, there was a great crack. Rupert and Thunderstorm both knew instantly that the bridge would not hold them. Thunderstorm shoved Rupert with his nose, trying to push him across the bridge to safety. Rupert lunged forward with the reins still tight in his hands. He was determined to get Thunderstorm across the bridge with him.

Two thirds of the way across, the bridge gave out entirely. Rupert and his horse plummeted nearly ten feet into icy riverbed below. Thunderstorm managed to pull himself forward in the fall so that he hit the ice first and Rupert landed on the horse's torso, breaking his fall.

The force of the bridge, the horse, and his own weight broke the thick layer of ice. Rupert found himself covered in a frigid combination of ice and water. Rupert's body seized up from the shock of the extreme cold. He felt a deep pain in his skin and breathing became instantly difficult. There was blood in and on the ice. He did not know if it was his or his horse's.

Just as he realized the amount of pain he was in, he heard voices calling to him. He suddenly remembered Victoria and Cornelius. He looked around through his daze and saw them on the bank. The river was not flowing at all, and the break was only where he and Thunderstorm lay.

Cornelius got to him first. "Are you hurt?" he asked with panic in his voice.

"There is blood. I don't know if it is mine," he said weakly.

"No, it is Thunder's," Victoria said more calmly than the boys. She had watched the fall as if in slow motion. She saw the horse move to break Rupert's fall.

"Get Rupert out. We have to tend to the horse," she said to Cornelius.

"We should leave the horse for now and get him to Kelter, to a doctor." Cornelius was concerned for Rupert much more than the horse. It was Rupert that needed to live to be eighteen.

"No!" Rupert and Victoria said at once.

"Thunder will be all right. He is a strong horse," Rupert said just as he blacked out.

Cornelius pulled him to safely. Discovering that he was soaked through, he removed most of Rupert's wet clothes and wrapped him in dry blankets from his pack. When he was done, he ran back to Victoria who had managed with the help of her horse Joyful to get Thunderstorm out of the icy water. There was a large gash across his stomach, but he was able to stand.

"Put Rupert on my horse and take him into town. I will lead Thunder. It will take a while, but we will get there," Victoria said.

"I don't want to leave you," Cornelius squawked.

"Go, you silly man. I will be there soon. Remember, my name is Mark, and I am Rupert's servant!"

Cornelius smiled weakly, kissed Victoria on the cheek, and ran to Rupert. Just as he was getting him onto Joyful, a few townspeople approached them. One of them was the innkeeper. He was a short, pudgy man, but he was quick on his feet. Cornelius knew him well, though today the innkeeper was not smiling as he usually did when meeting travelers. Instead, he had a look of great concern and fear. The man was called Mr. Ganther.

"Cornelius, what happened?" Mr. Ganther asked as several people surrounded the three wayward travelers.

"My traveling companion, Rupert, was crossing the bridge with his horse when it collapsed."

"It is remarkable that they are both alive. Why where you trying to cross the bridge in this weather? You should be at home warm and safe." Mr. Ganther had never liked that Cornelius was a messenger so young. He said boys should play, not work.

"Well, I have fallen into some financial trouble. Rupert here needed to get to Pallen on business for his family, but he did not know the way. He found me in Bale and offered to pay me a hefty sum if I would be his guide to the capital. I really need the money, you see, so I took him up on his offer."

"You should have gone to the other bridge," Mr. Ganther said sadly.

As the other people from the town hurried Rupert off on Joyful, Victoria, quietly and carefully, explained her station as servant but told them that she would lead the horse. A dark-haired man told her he would lead her to the stables where he could examine the horse.

"I suggested the other bridge, but Rupert insisted that it was too far. He wanted a warm bed and hot food tonight. And we are out of supplies!" Cornelius explained.

"Well, he is paying for his poor judgment for traveling in deep winter. Who is the boy with the injured horse?"

Cornelius nearly corrected the innkeeper but caught himself. "He is Rupert's servant. His name is Mark."

"He is very good with animals," Mr. Ganther said, noticing that Victoria was stroking the horse's nose as she led him to town. He knew of only one other person who could lead an injured horse.

"Yes, I think it was his family who raised the horse." Cornelius knew that Thunderstorm had grown up in Thomas's stable. Thunderstorm was the last colt born to Oberon's horse, Black Shadow. Thomas raised the orphaned horse just as he had raised his niece. Black Shadow died trying in vain to protect Oberon. Cornelius realized how naive he had been suggesting to leave the horse.

CHAPTER 14

That night, Cornelius found himself in the tavern connected to the inn. Victoria sat at a corner table alone and quiet. He walked across the room full of curious people to join her.

"What did the stable keeper say about the horse?" he asked more gruffly than he expected to. He didn't want anyone to figure them out, but he didn't want to be mean to her, either.

"Well, sir, he was able to stitch up the deep gash, but he also said that three of the horse's ribs are broken where Master Rupert fell on him."

"Is the horse going to live?" he asked, pretending that he knew very little about horses.

"He said that is up to the horse. He will keep him stabled there as long as we need him to."

"Is there a price for that?" Cornelius asked.

"No, he does not charge travelers to stable injured horses. If the horse recovers before we leave, he may need compensation for the food."

"Your master is going nowhere for a while." Cornelius knew that Victoria had been at the stable most of the day, so she had not been told of Rupert's condition. Though she knew that he was not hurt much in the fall, there was still reason for concern.

"How is he?" she asked.

"He is sleeping now. Even though he wasn't hurt in the fall, the doctor said he contracted a fever. Probably from the amount of time he spent in the icy water. We will have to watch him and the horse closely." Cornelius finished and stood. He wanted a drink from the bar.

"They will both be fine. They are strong."

"I agree. Would you like anything to drink while I am up, Mark?" The name felt wrong and cold as it came out. He wanted to hold her. He knew she was scared for her friend.

"Yes, an ale would be nice. Thank you."

They sat quietly for a few more hours, watching people come in and out. Cornelius set to work recording the day's events in his book. Victoria sipped the ale and read parts of what Cornelius was writing, but she was still too numb from the day's events to say much.

Mr. Ganther gave them the room adjacent to Rupert's. There was a door from inside their room that led to his. Some of the blood Rupert had seen had, in fact, been his own. His arm had been cut deeply when he hit the jagged ice. The dressing needed to be changed every few hours. Victoria and Cornelius took turns that night and all the next day.

Rupert was very sick. Victoria had taken some of her uncle's sleeping herbs with them in case this very thing happened. She ground up two of the eight leaves she had and mixed them in a glass of water. Rupert drank a little every time he woke up. He knew that sleep would cure his fever the fastest.

On the second day, Victoria kept him awake long enough to tell him that his horse would recover. After that, he slept as much as he could. Cornelius made him eat dried meat and some dried fruits they had for the journey. "You need food to keep up your strength so you can heal more quickly," he said, when Rupert, in his daze, did not want food.

It was nearly two weeks before Rupert recovered to his full strength. When Cornelius woke up that morning, he, like every morning, went to Rupert's room. Rupert was not there. Cornelius smiled and went back to his room. Victoria was still asleep on the bed. He had been sleeping on the floor. She wanted to take turns sleeping on the floor, but he wouldn't hear of it.

He woke her gently and told her that Rupert was up. "I am going downstairs to look for him. There are some decisions we need to make."

"I am willing to bet that he is in the stable with Thunderstorm," Victoria said through a yawn.

Cornelius went downstairs to the tavern. Rupert was not there, so he went to the stable. When he walked in, there was Rupert rubbing Thunderstorm's nose and whispering to him. The huge gash in the horse's side had been very skillfully sown. It was nearly completely healed.

"I'm glad to see you up and about, Rupert."

"Hi, Corn. I feel much better. How long has it been since we fell?"

"Two weeks tomorrow."

"It felt longer, we'll go and get Vic...um...Mark. Meet me at the wrecked bridge. I want to see the wreckage, and it should be a quiet place to discuss what we should do next."

"I agree."

Twenty minutes later, the three of them were sitting on a blanket in the snow by the frozen river. There were planks and boards jutting out of the ice and covered with snow. The entire bridge had collapsed and was now in the frozen water. It looked as if two or three beavers had fought about the correct way to build a dam and then abandoned the project halfway through.

Rupert looked at the wreckage for a long time. The other two were quiet.

"I could have died. I guess we should have gone to the other bridge," he said at last, breaking the silence abruptly.

"No, that way may not have been any better. I have never trusted the bridge keeper. I think he would have killed us if the right person paid him to. Plus, I saw one of Colin's men come into town two days later. I think he was the one following us. I am guessing he used the other bridge since you cleverly blocked his way from this bridge." Cornelius laughed at his own joke, but then continued somberly. "He is no longer in town. I am not sure how long he stayed. Colin is not going to show his face here, so his man probably got word of your condition and left to report it."

Rupert said nothing to that but took comfort in knowing that he had not made a completely stupid decision. Then he broached the subject of their next move. "Okay what do we do now? My arm is nearly healed, but Thunder is in no condition to travel."

"I think we should stay here until spring." Victoria said, making a minimal effort to disguise her voice.

"What?" Rupert and Cornelius both said at once.

"Yes, Mr. Ganther has offered me a job. Besides, we aren't going to get far anyway. I have heard that the army we talked about is camped out a few miles down the road. They are waylaying any travelers who pass. I don't think they will let us have passage to Pallen. If we stay here, we have a place to sleep, food, and we won't have to deal with the army just yet.

"But we need to get to Pallen!" Rupert said nearly in a scream.

"And what are we going to do there? You can't avenge your father until you are eighteen anyway. I think we are safer here," Victoria said. "Thunder will be healed by then, and we won't have to sleep in the freezing snow with no fire."

"What if Kybon finds out we are here?"

"How can he? The prince's army won't let anyone through to Pallen. Lucas, the stable keeper, was telling me that they are having trouble getting supplies into town. He said he is not surprised at all that the bridge collapsed. Many supply wagons have been crossing it from Bale. They can get nothing in from Pallen or any other town from that direction. Uncle Thomas is going against royal orders to get supplies here."

"How are they getting supplies now that I killed the bridge?" Rupert asked quietly, hoping that the townspeople would not blame him if there were no supplies.

"There is a place a little ways up the river where the water is shallow. Whenever a supply wagon comes, they go there. They break the ice first and walk across the still water. It is better, Rupert, that we were the ones that broke the bridge. Not the wagon holding food for the winter that came the next day."

"The spring equinox is in seven weeks," Cornelius said. "Victoria is right. We will be safer here then out there on the road.

CHAPTER 15

Life in Kelter

After Rupert got well, he spent a week in the stable with his horse. Victoria stayed with him when she wasn't working for the innkeeper because she was keeping up the act as his servant. Cornelius knew a few people in town, so he spent much of his time in the tavern talking with the townsfolk. Had he been able to take a different side than his own, he would have been a great spy. But as fate had it, he had to spy only for himself. So he got what information he could about the soldiers up the road. No one in town knew much of what was going on, but there were soldiers that came to the tavern from time to time. Cornelius listened to them when he could, but they didn't talk much.

He had his own line of credit with the butcher. Every night, the three of them had a nice hot meal of fresh meat. They didn't eat much of the vegetables that came on the supply wagons. They wanted to leave those for the townspeople.

Their rooms at the inn changed as well. The innkeeper could only afford to give them one room because of the influx of soldiers coming into town to escape the bitter cold. They took turns sleeping in the one bed in the room. The boys tried to give Victoria the bed every night, but she refused. "We are all in this together, and we are going to share the luxuries as well as the difficulties," she said. That was the end of the discussion.

Eight days after the three decided to stay until spring, Rupert went to the stable after breakfast, as had become his routine. When he got there, he had a strange feeling in his gut. He was being watched again, but there was a familiar pang that did not go along with only being watched. It was someone he knew.

He looked around the dark enclosure. The sun had not yet risen to its full brightness. He heard her laughter before he saw her sitting against the far wall. Her sword was at the ready in case of danger.

"Did you laugh out loud, or am I hearing your thoughts again?" Rupert said to Kylan in a strangely scared voice.

"I don't know. I did laugh, but I am not positive it was audible," she said quietly.

"Great! So why are you here?"

"I have a cousin in Prince Bartholomew's army. He sent word that he will be staying at the inn, and he wishes me to stay with him. He and I have not seen each other in a few years, and he wants to catch up. Really, he wants to get close to me so that he can inherit from my father since Dad has no sons. If I don't marry, then my father's things go to the next male kinsman. My cousin, Nicol." Her voice full of fake contempt.

"Your father has money to leave?" Rupert asked, truly curious.

"He has wealth stashed away somewhere. I don't know or care how much. I will not inherit it. I will get my true inheritance on my eighteenth birthday."

"Your powers, you mean?"

"Shh, keep your voice down. And yes, my powers. I will not need much of my father's money."

"Well, I, umm, do you want to help me feed Thunder?"

"Sure, I heard about your fall at the bridge. I am glad you are both alive," she said in a nonchalant voice.

"Yes, it was a minor fall. And Thunder got only a flesh wound, right, boy?" he said as he rubbed his hand up the horse's head.

Kylan laughed and rolled her eyes. They gave the horses fresh hay and stayed with him a few more minutes. Then Kylan broke the happy silence.

"Come on, let's go back to the inn and get the others. I have information about the soldiers and Prince Bartholomew that might help you on your quest, but I haven't got much time. Nicol will be here by noon."

A few minutes later, the four of them were back out in the cold by the collapsed bridge, partly because Kylan wanted to see the wreckage and partly because they could see if anyone had followed them.

"Are you sure that no one is listening, Rupert?" Cornelius asked, looking around, still in doubt even though he could see no one.

Kylan answered before Rupert could. "It doesn't matter. If someone is hiding well enough to overhear, then they already know who we are and why we are all here."

"Aye, start talking. I am cold, and Mr. Ganther will be wanting my services soon," Victoria said, making little effort to disguise her voice.

"Three days ago, the king issued a decree that all males between the ages of fourteen and twenty must join the army."

"Wait, I thought the king was ill," Victoria interrupted.

"He is. Father says all orders actually come from Kybon. Anyway, this means that all three of you have to join the army."

"But, Kylan, there are two armies," Rupert said.

"Yes, which side you join depends on what town you live in," Kylan said.

"So Kybon is trying to divide the country and the princes," Cornelius said in a thoughtful voice.

"Maybe so, but I have heard a lot about Prince Bartholomew. He does not want to take the throne. He says it is not rightfully his, even if he wins the war."

"Then whose throne is it?" Victoria asked quietly.

"Yours!" Rupert and Cornelius said together.

"So how long before they make us join the army?" Cornelius asked.

"I don't know," Kylan said. "I will ask my cousin in a couple of hours and let you three know as soon as I can get away."

"I think making all the boys between fourteen and twenty join the army is foolhardy. Kybon knows that the war will solve nothing. Why run the risk of destroying the entire kingdom by killing off so much of the population. And why now?" Rupert asked mostly to himself.

Cornelius laughed a sad sort of chuckle. "He is trying to flush out the lost princess. If all the boys between fourteen and twenty join the army, that leaves her unprotected because you and I will be off fighting a war. He won't have to search as hard to find her."

"What?" Rupert said.

"He is right. It means that he knows I am no longer with my uncle. I am assuming that he knows I am with you"—she lowered her voice to a barely audible whisper—"Oberon's son! If you leave to join the army, then he can find and kill me much more easily! And hopefully kill you in the war before you turn eighteen!"

Rupert laughed at his own naivety. "Well, I guess that means all three of us will have to join then," Rupert said.

"Yeah, that will show him right," Victoria said.

They returned to the village and resumed their roles. Victoria went back to work. Cornelius spent most of the day in the tavern, talking to the locals about anything they would talk about. Rupert sat in the stable reading the book that Thomas had given him. It was the only thing he had that came through the fall unscathed. This confirmed his suspicion that the book was enchanted.

By the end of the week, word of the decree had reached everyone in town. All the boys of eligible age gathered in front of the town guardian's house in the cold morning air and waited for a lieutenant from Bartholomew's army to come and tell them what to do.

Cornelius, Rupert, and Victoria (dressed as Mark) stood in the middle of the group. Cornelius found himself sizing up all the boys. They all looked as if they would fall over if the snow fell too hard. Rupert saw this too. He knew that he and Cornelius stood out. Victoria, however, fit in well. Rupert caught Cornelius's eye. They both had the same thought.

Rupert leaned toward Cornelius and whispered to him, "We will have to leave her on her own, or they will figure us out. You and I stand out. The lieutenant will know we are outsiders."

"I don't want to let her go!" Cornelius said.

"Cornelius, we may not have a choice."

"I can handle myself, but I would prefer not to have to! I think we should wait and see what the lieutenant thinks of us," Victoria whispered to both of them.

They both stared at her.

Rupert suddenly heard his name called in Kylan's voice. He looked around and saw her standing a little ways down the street where a few other women had gathered.

"I will be right back."

"Where are you going?" Cornelius and Victoria asked together.

"Kylan wants to talk to me. I think she knows something we don't." With that, he pushed his way carefully through the crowd. Most of the boys let him through easily. He was nearly a head taller than most and much stronger.

When he got through, he walked casually toward the crowd of women. He didn't dare let on that he was excited to talk to Kylan, whether or not it was important. He also needed time to think of what to say when he got to her. He couldn't exactly say that he read her mind. He decided on saying that he noticed her in the crowd and came to say hi because he hadn't seen her in a few days, which was mostly true.

"Hey, where have you been? I was starting to worry about you," he said, sort of harshly. He could say nothing else.

"I told you I was visiting my cousin, but I must talk to you. I have just received word about your family. It is to do with your sister."

Rupert stifled his laugh as she took his arm and led him away. They walked out of earshot of the crowd, but they could still see when the lieutenant arrived.

"I have a sister. That is great! What is her name? Does she look like me?"

"Shut up and listen," she said without making any effort to hide her laughter. "I managed to get out of my cousin that the lieutenant is going to get names and ages and that's it. No one will have to leave town until spring, the day after the equinox festival. He said they are also looking for you. You shouldn't give them your real name. And when the festival comes around, leave and go to sorcerers in hiding and learn your powers. I will go too! But I don't think we can go together."

"Why not? It would be an easier journey, and we wouldn't have to talk!" Rupert said, trying to hide his disappointment.

"One person is harder to follow. They are in hiding for a reason."

"How will I know where they are then?"

"I don't know! I don't know the way, either!"

"We will cross that bridge when we get to it, I guess."

"Well, you may fall though the bridge!" Kylan said through girlish giggles.

"Very funny!" Rupert said, but he was smiling too.

"Now back to business. Cornelius should be all right. Everyone knows his identity, but Victoria will be a problem. She will need a surname to go with Mark. She cannot give Thomas's name. She is his only heir, so they will know what family line she comes from."

"I know, but what do we do?"

"We need more time. I need to talk to my father and see what he says. I can ride out tonight, but that will be too late."

"Wait, I have an idea. I have to get back. Don't worry I've got this worked out. Let me know before you leave. I should be at the inn."

Rupert hurried off but not to the guardian's steps with the others. He ran in the opposite direction to the stable where he had been keeping what was left of his things. His book was with him, so he already had it open to the right page when he got to his pack. He quickly found his small leather sack of assorted herbs. In the book, it said, "Mill grass and coal together would rid the system of poison by causing its expulsion from the stomach." There was a large pile of coal kept in the stable for the inn so that it would stay dry for the fires. Rupert mixed a small amount of coal dust with the mill grass and water in his canteen.

He flung the full canteen over his shoulder rushed back to the courthouse. He pushed his way back though the crowd. Cornelius looked at him with questions in his eyes. Victoria knew something was up.

Rupert said in as casual a voice as possible, "Mark, you need to drink some water. It will help you feel better."

"Thank you, sir," Victoria said quietly. She took the canteen, opened it, and took a large gulp. The smell hit her nose just before she tasted the concoction. She knew immediately that in a matter of minutes she was going to be very sick. She didn't know why, but she trusted Rupert.

Nearly a minute passed before anything really happened. Then she looked at Rupert with contempt. "Sir, the water didn't help. I actually think it may have made me feel worse." Then she started to turn very pale.

Cornelius began pushing boys aside and calling, "Out of his way."

Victoria made it to the edge of the crowd before she began vomiting violently.

Rupert quickly grabbed her. "Cornelius, I am taking him back to the inn. Mark is too ill to stay. Tell the lieutenant he can find me at the inn.

Mr. Ganther will let me know if he arrives." Then he pulled Victoria's arm around his own neck and helped her walk the one hundred yards back to the inn. They had to stop every few feet so she could vomit.

When they got back to the inn, Mr. Ganther helped Rupert carry Victoria up the stairs. He left them at the door. "I will be back later to check in on him. I hope this doesn't last very long. He is a great help to me," Mr. Ganther said over his shoulder.

Rupert unlocked the door and pulled Victoria inside. He laid her facedown across the bed and dragged over the heavy metal bucket that should have contained a plant. Before he could do anything more, he realized suddenly that they were not alone in the dark room. Even though it was morning, the small windows were covered so they would not be seen by spies.

"Who is here?" he asked, fumbling with the lantern on the wall. He heard a matchstick, and a flicker of light appeared. Then the room was filled with golden light that grew whiter and brighter and then filled the room with white light. When there was enough light, he could see that it was Kylan holding a lantern.

"Kylan, what are you doing here? How did you get in?" Rupert stammered.

"First things first," she said, turning to Victoria. "Here, Mark, drink this it will help."

"What is that? What are you giving her?" Rupert asked.

"It is the antidote to what you gave her. I figured you were not going to remember that you would need to neutralize the serum you made."

"I feel stupid now!"

"You shouldn't! I have had a bit more training in the ways of wizards than you. Besides, there wasn't really time for you to make both. And you didn't have the right ingredients anyway."

Just then there was a coughing and sputtering from Victoria. Then she stood up and looked at Rupert directly. "There had better be a good reason why you made me violently ill."

"You and I have to keep our names off of the army's list. I hope Cornelius figures that out and doesn't tell them who I am."

"Give him some credit, Rupert. He knows more about life than both of us. He will figure it out. Thank you, Kylan, for making that vomiting stop."

"You are welcome, but quickly change into your sleep clothes and get into the bed. You still have to pretend to be sick. We may have to give you more."

"We? I thought you were leaving to go see your father tonight," Rupert said, not at all wanting to see her leave.

"I got word that he will be here tonight. So I will stay here a while and help you take care Mark. Most people consider it a woman's job, so it will look better for us if I am here with you. My cousin will understand."

"How did you get in?" Victoria asked, remembering Rupert's question.

"I grew up among thieves. Do you really think that I need keys to enter a locked room?"

"I suppose not."

"I am going to go downstairs and wait for Cornelius to come back," Rupert interjected.

Rupert left the room before Victoria could ask him one final question, so she asked Kylan instead. "Is Cornelius going to be able to come back? I mean, he is there being dragged into Bartholomew's army."

"No, they are only taking names today. He will not have to leave until spring. It is fully intended for you to go with him, but we have to find Mark a surname first."

Three hours later, Cornelius and Rupert returned. The two young women were sitting in the small room waiting for them. Kylan was stoking the fire.

"Aye, what was that all about earlier?" Cornelius asked after he carefully shut the door.

"Possibly an overreaction. What did you tell the lieutenant about Rupert and Mark?" Kylan said.

"I told them nothing. They asked for names and checked them off a list. My name was not on the list because I do not live here. I told them I was passing through on business to Pallen."

"So maybe they don't know that Rupert and Mark are here," she said.

"Well, I certainly didn't tell them. As far as they know, Mark does not exist and Rupert will be on the list for Bale. As will my name. Bale belongs to the Prince Mathew."

"Why does Bale belong to Mathew? Who made that decision?"

"I don't know. I saw the list of which prince had what town. It makes no sense," Cornelius said, very sadly.

"This will truly be a civil war soon!" Rupert said from the corner.

"I don't know. I think Kybon may be bluffing. But we will finish this discussion later. I have to check in with Nicol soon, or he will get suspicious," Kylan said.

They decided that Victoria should stay upstairs because everyone thought that Mark was very sick. Rupert and Cornelius went down to the tavern together. Kylan stayed with Victoria several minutes more.

"I am afraid that we are going to have to separate soon," Victoria said sadly.

"Yes, I get the worst of it. I have to go to the sorcerer's council alone," Kylan said.

"I thought you and Rupert would go together."

"No, we can't. He will go later. You will be all right, though. You and Cornelius will at least be together."

"Yes, but we cannot even hold each other. I think that may be worse than being apart!"

"I never thought of it that way," she said with a sigh. *It must be truly terrible,* she thought to herself.

"I know, but you had better go. I hope your father can give us insight on what is really going on. Because the decree and the armies building but not fighting makes no sense. There is something going on that we don't know."

"I agree. Are you going to be well enough up here alone?"

"Yes, it will be nice. I have not been by myself since this journey began. I love them both, but it will be nice to think for a while and sleep without Cornelius's snoring or Rupert's constant shifting."

They both laughed. Kylan nodded and then left the room, closing the door quietly behind her. She locked it and put the key Rupert had given her in her pocket.

It had been nearly an hour before the door to the tavern opened from the outside. The bell on the door rang into the murmuring voices. The boys did not look to the door. Cornelius was telling a few other men about some of his travels. Rupert was reading his enchanted book. His reading was interrupted by Kylan's gasp. He looked at her and then at the three people walking toward him. Kylan grabbed his hand and held it tightly. Rupert turned back to his drink, took a sip, and then turned around again and watched as Raven and Thomas and his own mother walked up to Kylan and sat down on the other side of her.

The door opened again just as they were sitting down and in walked a tall man in a traveling tunic. He was jovial and smiling with the same brightness as Cornelius. He nearly ran across the room as his son was turning around to face the door. They hugged joyfully.

"Father, what brings you here?"

"Business, my boy, business. I am glad to find you here. Let us go and talk awhile."

While Malcolm spoke loudly, the other travelers and Kylan and Rupert quietly left the tavern through the rear exit. They walked down to the remains of the bridge as the sun began to sink in the sky. Malcolm and Cornelius joined them a few minutes later.

"Where is Victoria?" Thomas asked Rupert.

"She is in a room in the inn. We had to pretend she was ill to hide her from the lieutenant of Bartholomew's army. The true question is, why are you and Mother here?"

Thomas responded, "Your mother can answer that question."

Rupert hugged his mother. Thomas went back to the inn to check on the situation there.

"Rupert, honey, you forget that I was married to a powerful man. I know a good many things about the world of sorcery, and I am not safe with that knowledge. As far as I know, your father kept no secrets from me. It is because of my knowledge and memories that Kybon wants me dead."

"But Dad died seventeen years ago. What could you possibly know that would be relevant now?" he said warily.

"For starters, I am your mother, and by getting me, he will get you. He is trying to get you and Victoria into the open."

"So he doesn't know where we are?"

"Not really."

"I figured he somehow knows everything that is going on."

"He is not clairvoyant. That is a rare gift. He can see things using a crystal bowl and other wizard tricks, but really he is forced to rely on spies."

Cornelius heard the other's voices, but there was something nagging in his mind. They were discussing the war and how things didn't fit. Then suddenly he realized what was bothering him. There was a teenage boy stooping low in the darkness on the wreckage of the bridge. He was wearing army uniform pants that were blue with a thin black stripe down the legs, which was the uniform of an officer. His shirt was plain white. It had long sleeves, but the material was thin. His eyes were the same green and the same shape as Victoria's. The boy was trying to listen to their conversation.

Cornelius leaned over to Rupert and whispered in his ear. "Hey, there is a kid on the bridge listening to us."

"Do you think he is a spy?" Rupert whispered back as he made a sign to the others to stop talking.

"No, he is not a spy. He looks like Prince Bartholomew," Cornelius whispered back.

"What?" said Rupert out loud.

Raven looked around and saw Bartholomew. He did not know what the prince looked like, but he could tell that the boy had been eavesdropping. He got up and walked to the wreckage and carefully grabbed the onlooker. Raven took him by the arm and walked with him back to the group.

"I think we should finish this with Mark and Thomas here," said Raven, holding the eavesdropper tightly. The boy squirmed a bit but said nothing to defend himself.

"I agree," Cornelius said. But there was no sign of them. "Thomas may have found him in the inn. We should go and find them," he said to Cornelius.

Raven and Katherine nodded at them. So they hurried off to the inn, leaving the others standing silently in the cold. When they reached the inn, Thomas was talking to Mr. Ganther. He nodded toward the stairs, so Rupert and Cornelius hurried up them to collect Victoria.

"Are you sure that boy is the prince?" Rupert asked as they ascended the stairs.

"Yes, I have been the messenger of Bale for seven years. I have met Bartholomew many times."

"I thought they were twins. Are you sure you have the right one?" "Yes, Mathew has a scar on his chin that he got in a knife fight when he was eleven. He is quite proud of it."

"Who would get in a knife fight with an eleven-year-old?" Rupert asked.

"I don't know! Mathew has been in a lot of fights. One day, he will learn his lesson!" Cornelius said as he stopped walking.

They stopped in front of Victoria's door. Cornelius went to open the door.

Rupert grabbed his hand. "Shouldn't we knock first?"

"Yes, we should," Cornelius agreed. Then he added with lament, "I am waiting for the day when I can walk into her room without the formality of knocking." He knocked on the door but barely waited for the words "Come in" before he opened the door.

Rupert waited outside because he was still thinking about what Cornelius had said. He wished in that moment he could help them both. He realized just how hard this journey would be for them.

Victoria was sitting quietly at the table in the room writing in her journal. Without looking up, she spoke. "I wish you didn't have to knock, either, but it is the proper thing to do. We are not married yet, so it is still not our room." She tried to hide any emotion in her voice. "That is not my choice. If I had my way, we would have been married before we left Bale." She laughed and put down her pen. She stood and kissed Cornelius, then went to the door. "Rupert, get in here before someone sees or hears you too," she admonished.

"It doesn't matter now. Things have changed a bit. Prince Bartholomew is here, and he heard some of what we were discussing," Cornelius said from behind her.

She grabbed a cloak, her sword, and her boots. In less than a minute, she was dressed as Mark again and pulling the boys to the door.

Thomas was waiting for them at the bottom of the stairs. "I am sorry I was unable to get her. Mr. Ganther needed to be updated on what is going on. He is a talker!"

"Prince Bartholomew was listening to our conversation. We are headed back out there to see what he knows."

"Bartholomew? Very good!" Thomas said, and then he continued because of the confused looks on their three faces. "He knows about Victoria, and he wants to help her take the throne!" Thomas said in a whisper. He turned and headed for the back door. The other three followed, stunned after a second of hesitation at the shocking news.

In five minutes, they met up with the rest of their party, who were still standing in silence. Raven was still holding Bartholomew's arms, who had long since given up fighting Raven's grasp. Katherine was rummaging through her bag for a blanket she had brought with her from home. She was fussing about him being so young and alone out here. It was well known that he was able to walk about unguarded; he had dismissed all his guardians years before, and his mother had not protested.

Kylan was balancing on one of the stones that had supported the bridge. When the four of them got close, she jumped to land and ran to Rupert. She looked into his eyes for a moment and then looked at Cornelius. "Are you sure?" she asked quietly.

Cornelius only nodded. He was not sure how to react to Kylan knowing things she had not been told.

Raven spoke next. "All right, what do you know about this boy who was spying on our conversation?"

Cornelius walked up to Bartholomew and spoke directly to him. "Why are you here?"

Bartholomew was silent for a moment and then seemed to decide that it was in his best interests to respond. "I am trying to oversee the army that is assembling in my name."

There was a gasp from Raven and Malcolm who did not already know that they were talking to the prince. Raven let go of the boy's arms and turned him around, keeping tight hold of his collar. He looked at his face as Bartholomew rubbed his arms where Raven had been holding them.

"I should have known. You look like your father when he was young. I take it you are Bartholomew. Mathew would have told us before now who he was."

"My brother is too outspoken for his own good." Bartholomew looked at Raven. "Sir, please let go of my collar. I won't run. I came here to find my sister. I heard from my lieutenant that Cornelius was in town. So I figured I would start with him since he is from Bale, and that is where my spies say my sister lives."

"Why do you want to find your sister?" Victoria asked. "Because both Mathew and Kybon are looking for her. She is the key to stopping the tyranny in this country. I will start by saying I have no desire to be king. The throne is not rightfully mine."

Victoria spoke again, careful to disguise her voice. "Why is Mathew looking for her?"

"Because he wants to kill you, Victoria," Bartholomew said calmly. "Don't be upset," he added quickly. "Your disguise is actually quite good, but you are my half-sister, and our family crest is on your sword. It looks just like mine. Don't worry, I am on your side," he said as Cornelius grabbed him and pinned his arms behind his back.

"Cornelius, let him go! He will be your brother-in-law soon enough. I would hate for you two to be on bad terms."

Rupert and Kylan laughed. Cornelius let go and quickly put himself between Bartholomew and Victoria. Katherine quickly stepped in and put the blanket around the boy's shoulders. He looked at her and mumbled "Thank you."

"Speak your mind then, but I will admit I will not trust you yet. Everyone in that castle has wanted her dead for many years," Cornelius said hotly, looking at Thomas who stood in silence. Thomas knew something they didn't.

"Not everyone!" Bartholomew put in. "Kybon wants her very much alive. So much so that he is assembling his own army to combat Mathew. Mathew and I both know that Victoria is Kybon's keeper of powers, of course. If she dies, then Kybon loses his power, and one of us becomes heir to the throne all in one moment."

Rupert suddenly remembered what Colin had said in the barn to Thomas about there being another way to stop Kybon. Rupert looked over at Thomas and his mother. This was not news to either of them.

Bartholomew continued. "That is why I had my lieutenant do a count of the boys in town. I am trying to find out who is loyal to my father and who is loyal to Kybon. Mathew is trying to flush out Victoria. If he controls Bale and all the people in it, he should be able to find her. I am glad you left before he got there."

Rupert broke in, "But if there is a war, wouldn't there be the risk of Victoria getting killed in the process?"

"No," Bartholomew said, looking at Thomas. "Her uncle will never let her be killed."

"I do my best!" Thomas said. Then he stepped away from them with Katherine. She had wandered to the wreckage of the bridge that had nearly killed her son. Thomas was talking so quietly that the others could not hear them.

"So what do you propose we do about your brother wanting Victoria dead?" Kylan asked, pulling Rupert back to the conversation. "I am not sure. But I don't want her to be killed. Mathew would get the throne and would not be a good king. He is highly ambitious and power hungry. He will not be fair to the kingdom. He has too much of our mother in him."

"So you believe that we have a chance at defeating Kybon?" Rupert asked quietly. He knew that he would have to confront Kybon face-to-face, and it may happen before he was ready.

"I do," said Bartholomew. "Kybon has gotten sloppy. He thinks he is invincible. He doesn't believe that anyone can kill him. So he is not really trying to protect himself." Bartholomew looked up at Kylan and then at Raven. "You must be Raven, the leader of the clan of outlaws, and she is your daughter, that is obvious, which means she is a sorcerer too. Are you older than Rupert?" he asked her directly.

She looked to Rupert and then at her father. Raven nodded. "Yes, by four months."

"So you will have your full powers pretty soon. You can help us! I will do my best to help too." He removed his sword that looked identical to Victoria's.

"Mr. Thomas, take this and hide it. What are they calling you, Victoria?"

"Mark!"

"Aye, I gave my sword to Mark, and he has agreed to be a spy for me." The shivering prince sighed and continued. "I am in a bad position. I have to be on both sides of this, but I don't feel I have a choice. Can we go back to the tavern now? I need to meet with some of my officers, and I am freezing."

"You should have worn a coat," Katherine said as she walked back to the group. She forced him to close the blanket around himself like a robe.

"I don't have a coat," he said sheepishly as he began to walk briskly back to the tavern.

"What has this kingdom come to? The prince doesn't have a coat!" she said harshly.

"It is a long story!" said the prince.

Malcolm took off his heavy coat and handed it to Bartholomew. He gave the thin blanket back to Rupert's mother on the way back to the warm comfort of the Tavern.

Rupert, Cornelius, Kylan, and Victoria took up the end of the line. They walked more slowly, whispering as they followed at a slight distance.

"Do you believe him?" Cornelius asked.

"Yes," said Kylan. "So far, Rupert's are the only thoughts I can read, but feelings are easier. He was not lying."

"That settles it then! Come on, let's get back inside and plan our next move," Victoria said quickly. She was overjoyed at the thought of finally getting to know her brother.

CHAPTER 16

The Next Move

That night all of them gathered in the room Victoria, Rupert, and Cornelius were now sharing. Bartholomew joined them when he was done with his meeting.

"Victoria, we must return to Bale," Thomas said. "I cannot leave Bale unprotected for long. The five of you are on your own now. With God's will, I will see you as queen in a year's time."

They said their goodbyes. Malcolm hugged everyone in the room, including the friends he was leaving with.

"Malcolm, we are going with you!" Katherine said, smiling at him.

"I know, I guess I got caught up in the moment." Laughter exploded around the room.

Thomas smiled. "I guess magic has not taken everyone!" he said to no one in particular.

When the laughter dissipated, Thomas led his friends out the door. He took one last look at the teenagers he was leaving behind. "I will see all of you soon!" His voice was reassuring as the door closed.

The five of them stood quietly for a moment. Victoria took Cornelius by the hand and pulled him closer to the only chair in the room. She sat down, and he stood next to her.

Rupert began to pace. "Um, so what do we do now?" he asked.

"I don't know. This is something we need to think through," said Cornelius, squeezing Victoria's hand gently.

"Our duties take us to different places. I have to leave on the equinox and go to the hidden council. Bartholomew has a war to fight. The rest of you must head out to Pallen. Rupert, I think it is best if you three stay together," Kylan said quietly.

"Who put you in charge?" Rupert and Bartholomew asked together.

"I am not giving orders. I am stating what is happening!" Kylan said defensively.

"She is right. It looks as if that is the way things will happen. Rupert and Bartholomew, it does none of us any good if we start fighting over who is in charge. We all have to stay here for now because the armies have the roads blocked," Cornelius said.

"So we are staying here until spring," Victoria said in a firm tone. There would be no more discussion on that subject. "Bartholomew, are you staying here in Kelter, or are you staying at the army camp?"

Bartholomew said sadly, "I am to stay here out of the cold. I get sick easily, a condition I got from my father."

Victoria sighed and cut in, "I got it from both my mother and our father." She laughed and stood up, walked to her younger brother, and hugged him. "We will have to learn to live with this. I refuse to let my sicknesses get in the way."

"So we have a few weeks to get better acquainted. I have always wondered what my sister would be like."

"Unfortunately, whenever I leave this room, I am Mark! I can't even dance with Corn down in the tavern when there is music being played!" she lamented.

Cornelius grabbed her hand again and pulled her to him. He kissed her. "While we are in this room, we are betrothed!" he said firmly.

"Great, I am stuck in a room with two people in love! I may start sleeping in the stable," Rupert said half-jokingly. Kylan laughed. Rupert turned and looked at her.

"What? It's funny," she retorted. She was careful to guard the thought that she would like to dance with Rupert if they ever found themselves in the tavern at the same time. He tried to hear what she was thinking, but he found nothing there. He wondered if he could block his thoughts from her mind too. Was this clairvoyance going to be consistent?

Victoria looked out the window at the moon. It was already high above the houses of the village. It was late, and she would have to be up at dawn to help Mr. Ganther with the daily chores, as was the arrangement to keep the room. Rupert and Cornelius promised to help when they could.

Victoria sighed and said through a yawn, "It is late."

Kylan left for the night to sleep in her cousin's room. Bartholomew left as well because he had his own room and servants.

It was Victoria's turn to have the bed, but she told Rupert he could sleep in the bed. She lay on the floor with her head on Cornelius's chest. He put his arms around her, and they drifted into sleep together. They were both determined to enjoy the little time they would have together before Victoria would be in her disguise all the time.

They got up at sunrise and Victoria transformed into Mark and headed off to work, Cornelius followed her down to get breakfast, and Rupert made his way to the stable. The morning was clear and cold. There was snow on the ground from the night, but none was falling from the sky. He cleaned and brushed Thunderstorm. The horse's wounds were nearly healed.

Rupert examined the bandages and realized they were not the work of the town doctor.

"Who has been here, Thunder? Who did you let near you?"

"It was me," Kylan's voice broke the silence.

"You scared me! How did I not hear you come in?"

"Do I need to remind you again about the people I grew up with."

"Yes, I know you can come in a door silently, but I can usually hear you thinking, as strange as that sounds."

"I am guarding my thoughts. You need to learn how. Our thoughts can betray us if we meet others that are clairvoyant. I could read your thoughts before I even entered the stable. You have to learn to be guarded at all times."

"Aye, I will try. Thank you for helping my horse. How did you get near him? He trusts very few people."

"I am good with animals too! And I gave him a carrot. They are his favorite! I have a pretty extensive knowledge of medicine. Your horse will need his strength to guide you all over these lands."

"How did you know that carrots are his favorite?"

"He told me," she said in a very matter-of-fact way.

Rupert decided that nothing was impossible these days, so he did not question her further. He asked a question that was much more pressing to him. "Can you teach me some of this knowledge of medicine? You will not be with us all the way."

"Of course, I will teach you, but it will take years to learn it all."

"Well, I guess we will have to spend the next few years together."

Kylan blushed and turned away, hoping he didn't notice. "We haven't got a few years. We may not even have all day, so close your mouth and pay attention!"

They spent much of the morning together. She taught him the names of many herbs and their medicinal properties. He learned a few of the more practical ones by heart. Around lunchtime, they took a break from their studies and found Mark and Cornelius eating together at a table in the tavern. Mark did not speak.

"May we join you two for lunch?" Kylan asked as she and Rupert walked up with plates of food from the inn's kitchen.

"Sure," was Cornelius's response. Mark only nodded.

Kylan told Cornelius she was teaching Rupert about healing herbs and where to find them. She told them these were lessons she had been taught by her father. Cornelius told them what he knew from his travels. Mark only listened.

After lunch, Mr. Ganther told Mark that he would not be needed for the rest of the day. So the four of them wandered outside. It was a beautiful day. There were few clouds, and the air was cold but not frigid as it had been. Rupert took a deep breath of the air. He drew his sword and whirled around to Kylan who was behind him.

"I challenge you to a duel!" He laughed and jumped back a foot or two to give her room to draw.

She laughed and drew her own sword quickly. As she swung her sword into a fencing position, she yelled through her laughter. "Hey, Mark, help me out here! I am only a girl. He will beat me!"

Victoria laughed and drew her masterpiece of a sword and got into fighting position.

"I will fight you both and win! Haha!" Rupert hollered with mock maniacal laughter.

For a moment, Cornelius looked on in disdain. This was silly and childish. But the urge to prove to them that knives were better weapons came over him. Besides, this might be their last chance at any real fun for a long time. So while Rupert tried in vain to fight the two skilled girls by himself, Cornelius pulled his knives from his boots. He walked up behind Rupert, placed one arm at his throat, and the other around his right arm. Cornelius then, being careful not to actually cut his friend, pulled one of Rupert's legs out from under him and pulled up on his arm so that the tight grip was lost. Cornelius shook the sword from Rupert's hand and laid him on the ground.

Without breaking his motion, he slipped his leg out and pulled Kylan's foot forward. She went off balance and he jumped up and disarmed her. Then he spun around and grabbed Victoria's sword arm so that her sword went over his shoulder, and he mocked stabbing her in the stomach and then pushed her gently to the ground. Then he backed up, bent down, and picked out their swords. He was expecting some praise from his defeated friends.

"I have been saying for years the knife is a bet—"

But before he was done with his triumphant speech, a peach-sized snowball hit him on the forehead. Then Victoria's disguised voice rang out in the still day. "Never drop your guard before you are sure the battle is over!" Then she hurled another snowball at him. This time, he ducked, and it hit over his shoulder. He leaned over to grab some snow to fight back when two more snowballs hit from the directions of Kylan and Rupert, who were now both on their feet.

Cornelius pelted all three of them with his own gathered snow. Soon snow was flying in all directions, and the three were no longer after Cornelius, but they pelted each other and laughed and ran around in circles trying to dodge in coming blows from everywhere. They sang and laughed.

A few minutes later, Bartholomew came up as asked what they were doing. They all answered by throwing a snowball at him. He quickly retaliated, and soon he too was lost in the fight.

The free-for-all fight continued for nearly an hour until they were all exhausted and hungry again. Then Rupert made his way over to the stable while the others gathered their abandoned weapons and followed. The five of them sat against the wall for a few moments to catch their breath.

Rupert got up first and walked over to Thunderstorm in his stall. "Hey, boy. I know you heard us out there laughing in the snow. I promise as soon as you are all healed, I will take you out for a good ride." He took the pieces of a broken carrot out of his pocket. "Sorry, Thunder, it got broken in the shuffle."

The horse ate the carrot pieces carefully out of Rupert's hand. When he was done eating, he nudged Rupert's face gently, letting him know he appreciated the carrot no matter how many pieces it was in.

Just as Rupert turned to get the horse's brush, Lucas and the town doctor walked into the barn. The doctor gave a start when he saw Rupert and his friends standing in there. Lucas, however, gave no reaction to seeing them. He had done his job around Rupert many times now, though he had never given more than a hello or short responses to questions.

"Ah, Doctor, this is Rupert. Thunderstorm there belongs to him," Lucas said in a clear but low voice.

"Nice to meet you, Rupert, I must say that your horse is a magnificent one. What is his parentage?"

Rupert was about to tell the doctor Thunderstorm's linage when he heard Kylan's voice in his head. *Do not give away that your father was Oberon. The less the town knows about us the better.*

So Rupert responded with the best lie he could think of. "I got him in Bale from a horse breeder there. The breeder Mr. . . ."

Kylan's voice broke in again. *Sumner.*

Rupert continued. "Sumner told me when I bought him that he came from a line of wild horse tamed by magic."

The doctor's eyes widened. "Yes, of course, the great Sorcerer Oberon lived in Bale before he was killed. This horse must be from the line of Black Shadow, Oberon's horse! You are a lucky man, Rupert! Thunderstorm should be brave and loyal. Take good care of him. I see you or one of your friends has been aiding in his recovery."

"Yes, sir, he has already proven to be a great and powerful friend! We will do our best for him," Rupert said, hoping that the doctor didn't figure out that he as well as the horse was connected to Oberon.

A few minutes later, the doctor spotted Bartholomew and asked him to come with him to check on some of the army's horses. Bartholomew begrudgingly agreed. So he and the doctor and Lucas all left together. Lucas lingered for a few seconds before he walked out past the prince, who was holding the door for him.

Rupert sat down again next to Kylan as Bartholomew closed the door tightly when he followed the doctor and his helper. He looked at her questioningly. "How did you know the name of the horse breeder in Bale?" he asked quite bewildered.

"I didn't! Victoria was thinking it, and I picked it up."

"I was hoping I could tell you without speaking," Victoria said happily.

"It seems the closer I get to my eighteenth birthday, the more I can pick up thoughts! Have you tried to tell me things before?"

"No, I have been consciously blocking you and Rupert from reading my mind. But I dropped my guard to tell you the horse breeder's name. Rupert has only met the man once in passing. He inherited his horse, but I, on the other hand, have had many dealings with Mr. Sumner. It took me several hours to convince him that I was capable of riding my horse without hurting myself when I was eight."

"So wait, you have been blocking me? Cornelius, have you been blocking me too?" Rupert asked.

"I don't think so."

"You shouldn't have to block Rupert. His power to read minds is not as strong as mine! He can read my mind because I can read his, but I don't think it will work transversely! Sorry, Rupert, I think your greatest power is something else!" Kylan said.

"So when you turn eighteen, you will be able to communicate with Rupert wherever you are?" Cornelius asked.

"I hope so!" Kylan said.

"That will be very useful," Cornelius said. "Since it will get harder to know who we can trust!"

"Who can we trust?" Rupert asked.

"I trust Bartholomew. He wants to have friends. Cornelius, you told me once that you felt sorry for the princes because they really have no one but Kybon and their mother to talk to. I think we can trust him just because he wants to be part of our group so much that he will never willingly betray us," Victoria said.

"I agree, but he may unwillingly betray us. Be careful what you tell him. I know he is your brother, but he is young and he could say the wrong things," Cornelius said sadly.

There was silence.

Rupert broke the silence. "I am taking Thunder out of here. He has been cooped up for a month now. A horse from Black Shadow's line should run free."

The others watched him go. Kylan pulled out a small knife and mumbled something about trimming Victoria's hair. Cornelius took out his book and began writing.

After nearly an hour, Rupert and Thunderstorm returned to the stable. The horse began eating hay at once. All four of them realized that it was getting close to suppertime.

Rupert rubbed Thunderstorm's nose once more before they left. "At least you will never be forced to betray us," he whispered to the horse. Kylan took his hand and softly pulled him to the door.

As the days went on, the snow became more sporadic and less deep. Victoria had less free time as the spring approached. She worked alongside Mr. Ganther to make the preparations for the festival. Rupert spent those weeks riding Thunderstorm all over the town and its outskirts. Sometimes Kylan rode with him.

Cornelius spent the days drawing maps of the land he had ridden or walked on his missions. He was planning different routes to Pallen. He thought up different scenarios and planned routes according to the time it would take depending on the roughness of the trail.

Victoria and Cornelius only saw each other at night because they were still sleeping in the same room. She was usually so tired from the day's work that she would fall straight to sleep. Cornelius lay each night with her in his arms, dreading the fast-approaching day that they would have to sleep apart.

CHAPTER 17

Spring Begins

Finally, the day of the equinox was upon them. Victoria was busy all day getting the inn ready for the festival that kicked off at dusk.

Just before sundown, Kylan found Rupert sitting just inside the gates of Kelter on a stump. He was staring at the ground, lost in thought. She could tell by the look on his face that he was very sad. She couldn't tell exactly what he was thinking.

"Hey, you look sad," she said.

Rupert looked up slowly before he responded. "My grandfather planted this tree," he said, patting of the side the stump.

"How do you know that?" Kylan asked.

"An old man in town told me. He said it was a magical tree and the leaves from it could save lives. Kybon cut it down just before he killed my father."

"It makes sense. Your grandfather was a powerful sorcerer. He was the one other sorcerers went to when they were sick with a poison or a hex from a wizard or something."

"How did you know that?"

"My father told me. I think he knew your grandfather."

"You mean *knows*! My grandfather is still alive. He is in hiding with the rest of the sorcerers. He sends me letters every once in a while."

"Really, how does he get letters to you?"

"Cornelius. My grandfather would somehow get them to the king, and Cornelius would bring them home with him. That is how we became friends."

"So Cornelius knows more about the king than he is letting on. It is weird when I walk by people and I can usually pick up on at least some of their thoughts. I mean sometimes it is just what they want for dinner or who they are mad at, but with Cornelius, I get nothing."

"That is good! He knows how to close his mind. I am glad to know that his thoughts won't betray us. He will be deciding things, like what route we are taking to Pallen. Victoria and I don't know, so even if a clairvoyant spy finds us, all he will learn is that we are going to Pallen, which Kybon has probably already figured out anyway."

Rupert smiled for the first time. Kylan realized he had been worrying that Cornelius would accidentally betray them.

"He has blocked his thoughts," Kylan said. "He probably doesn't even have to try anymore. You don't need to worry about that. So what else is bothering you?"

"Your horse is packed. You are leaving before the festival."

"Yes, Rupert, I have to go. I have to see the council before I turn eighteen."

"I know, but will a few hours really make a difference?"

"All the boys are leaving at sunrise to head for Bartholomew's camp!"

"I know, but well, I..." He paused for a moment and then looked into Kylan's eyes. "I really wanted to dance with you tonight." He looked sheepishly away.

Kylan laughed and then took his hand. "I would love to dance with you too, but I have to leave. I want to get past the army before

I make camp. And besides, Victoria and Cornelius are going to have a hard time tonight as it is. We don't need to throw it in their faces that they can't dance together."

"I didn't think about that," Rupert said sadly, realizing how he might have upset his friends. "How are you going to get past the soldiers tonight?"

"My father is the leader of the most notorious clan of highwaymen. I know ways around them."

"Oh, right!"

"I have to be going now," she said, letting go of his hand.

He took her other hand and pulled her toward him. He kissed her on the cheek and whispered "Safe travels" in her ear.

She laughed again.

"You are not allowed to die because you owe me a dance."

"Yes, I do!" She kissed him softly on his mouth and then got on her horse. He stood there and watched her head into the bright pink sunset. He turned around before she was out of sight. He knew she would not look back.

The sun was nearly completely down when he got to the town square. Everyone was there in their finest clothes. The light layer of snow glistened in the lantern lights. Victoria walked up to him dressed in her green cloak and wearing her sword. Rupert wondered if anyone would notice Thomas's crest on the cloak.

"Where were you? Cornelius wants to talk to you about something," she said gruffly.

"I was seeing Kylan off," he whispered.

"Oh, she left before you could have a dance."

"Yeah. Where is Cornelius?"

"He is in the tavern looking at maps like he has been for the past week!"

Rupert mumbled "Thank you" and started toward the inn. Victoria grabbed his arm. "Are you all right?"

"Yeah, what makes you think I wouldn't be all right?"

"Rupert, I don't have to be clairvoyant to know that her leaving up set you. I know you are worried about her."

"Thank you, Mark, for your concern, but I don't have time anymore to worry. We have to leave for the army camps in the morning. Our fates are now on separate paths."

Victoria let go of his arm. "Fine, go talk to Cornelius. I have to go find Prince Bartholomew. He needs to be at this meeting too."

Rupert continued toward the inn while Victoria headed into the fray of the festivities to find her half-brother.

Rupert found Cornelius sitting at the table in the farthest corner of the room. From where he was sitting, Cornelius could see every part of the room. The back of his chair was against the wall. He glanced up when

Rupert opened the door. All of the other tables were empty. Mr. Ganther was singing in the back room as he filled boxes with clean cups to bring to the town square, where he had set up a small makeshift booth to sell spirits to the townspeople.

"Mark said you wanted to see me," Rupert said, taking note that Mr. Ganther might still be able to hear them.

"Yeah." Cornelius motioned Rupert to an empty chair at the table. Rupert sat down. Cornelius pointed to a pile of papers on the table. "How good are you at memorizing?" Cornelius asked.

Rupert looked at the papers again. It looked to be directions. "No! I am not going to learn the way to get there. My mind is too open."

"What?" Cornelius looked confused.

"Kylan can read my thoughts and most other people's too, but she couldn't read yours."

"I know. I learned how to block the clairvoyant when I was little, but what if we get separated?"

"I will find my way if I need to, but for now, you are the only one allowed to know the way."

"Aye, but look here, I have directions written down. If anything happens to me, use them to get to Pallen safely. There are further directions at my grandfather's inn."

"Do you think you won't get there with us?" Rupert asked very concerned. He was not ready to lose his best friend, not to mention what it would do to Victoria.

"No, I mean I plan to be there until the end, but it is not my job to save the kingdom. I don't think sh—he and you can do it without help. Not yet. I just think it is better to be prepared for anything."

Rupert agreed. They listened as Mr. Ganther's singing grew fainter, and then they heard the back door close. Rupert got up and walked to the kitchen. He closed his eyes and stood silently. He didn't feel anything in his gut. "Okay, Ganther is gone. I think we can be less candid now."

Just then the front door opened. Rupert had to turn around to see who was at the door. Victoria stopped in the doorway with Bartholomew next to her. He was dressed in an officer's uniform. His eyes were shining and bright. He walked in after Victoria.

Victoria sat down next to Cornelius. She took his hand under the table. Bartholomew stood.

"Sit down," Rupert said, pointing to a chair.

"No, I can't stay long. There is a lot to do before morning when my new recruits head to camp. Speaking of which, have you three gotten your uniforms yet?"

"Yes," Rupert and Cornelius said at once.

"Well, I wanted to ask you, Barth, if you know how long we will be at the camp," Cornelius said.

"Well, you three are officers, so there is no telling. I mean, I may need you to go to Pallen with me on a top-secret mission."

"We are officers?" Rupert said, questioningly.

"Look, I am in charge of my army. I am the prince! What I say goes, and I say that Mark is my personal bodyguard. I mean he looks enough like me that we could pass as relatives. So I have decided he is my cousin, and family should protect me, right? And you two get to protect Mark." Bartholomew winked at them. He was proud of the clever story he had told his lieutenants.

"I don't know if that will work, but since none of us have a better plan, I am willing to run with the idea," Rupert said.

"Great, I have to go. I will see you guys at sunup at the city gates." Bartholomew turned on his heels and rushed out of the empty tavern.

Victoria watched him go. "I don't think it will work for long. I met his lieutenants. They see him as a silly boy. He does not have the power he thinks he does," she said sadly.

"No, he doesn't have the power he pretends to have. He knows that as long as Kybon is in control of this land, he or his brother will never really have control of any army. The lieutenants work for Kybon, whether they want to or not," Rupert said.

"I think you're right, but we will have to wait and see what happens. I think we should head upstairs and try to get some sleep. I have a feeling we won't be getting to sleep much in the coming weeks," Cornelius said. Victoria let go of his hand as they stood up to leave.

When they got upstairs, Cornelius and Rupert realized that Victoria had packed everything. All they needed to do in the morning was put on their new uniforms and they would be ready to leave.

Rupert surveyed the room and then picked up his pack. "I am going to sleep in the stable tonight. Thunderstorm has been on edge lately, and I need to calm him before tomorrow."

"But, Rupert, we need a good night of sleep. We have to be at our best tomorrow. We have to be ready for anything," Victoria said, following him to the door.

"I know. Thunderstorm has to be at his best too. He is a very special horse, you know," he said. "Besides, I think that you and Cornelius should have some privacy on your last night together before you have to pretend to be a boy all the time. I will see you both in the morning." He looked at Cornelius.

Cornelius smiled and mouthed "Thank you" as Rupert left the room. They both washed. For the first time, they lay down in the soft bed together alone. Cornelius pulled Victoria close to him and kissed her lips softly in the dark.

Rupert made a nice bed out of hay in the stable, right in front of Thunderstorm's stall.

"All right, boy, things are going to change tomorrow. We are heading out at sunrise to join Bartholomew's army. I know you have been itching to get out of here!"

Thunderstorm whinnied softly in approval.

"I am sleeping in here tonight. Mark and Cornelius have a lot to talk about," he said with a smile in his voice.

He got out the grooming brush and began to brush the horse slowly. He could feel the anxiety that was building in both of them. As he brushed the horse, he tried to clear his mind of all the things he was worried about. He told himself that Kylan was fine. She was out on her own, but he knew that her father would have spies on watch for her. He felt better. Raven would make sure that his daughter was safe, whether she wanted him to or not.

He thought again about the night this all started when Ashel had appeared out of nowhere to Thomas. She must be watching over them too! He recited a prayer he knew in the old language and lay down on his bed of hay. As he fell into sleep, he thought he saw Ashel appear and snuff out the light from his lantern, but he wasn't sure that he was not already dreaming.

Kylan was making camp around the time her three friends were falling asleep. She had not met much trouble so far. She stayed close to the forest as she traveled. She went into the forest when she saw the fires of the army camp. It was a dark night, but her horse was used to the rough terrain inside the forest. They had both ridden through this area before. There was a small clearing just past the army camp that would be an ideal place to make camp. It was well hidden from the road, so they would not be seen by spies. She made camp quickly even though it was dark, having lived in forest camps nearly all of her life.

Her horse kept her ears perked up the whole time she made camp.

"Don't worry, girl, things will be fine tonight. There will be plenty of time to worry soon enough." She was asleep within minutes of completing her camp. She knew her father had men nearby keeping watch over her.

A woman with bright-red hair walked up and gave her two thick blankets, one for her and one for the horse. She was not surprised when the woman disappeared as quickly as she had come.

CHAPTER 18

The Army

Their first night at the solider camp was rough. Rupert tried to find a quiet place to try to listen for Kylan and her thoughts far away. He was worried, and he wanted to be sure she was safe, but there was too much going on.

Victoria and Cornelius knew they would not be able to sleep. Bartholomew decided that they should take first and second watch. Cornelius took first watch so that Victoria could try to get some sleep. She thought that this was a futile effort, but she loved him all the more for it.

The nights were still very cold; patches of snow still lingered on the ground. Cornelius watched Victoria as she tried to sleep on a bed of hay and thin blankets. She had curled up under her cloak. He was watching for any signs of her coughing in her sleep.

She was not asleep but not because of the cold. The cloak actually kept her warm enough. She was not sleeping because she could not snuff out her thoughts. She kept going over the last few weeks in her mind. Then she started to think about the weeks to come. What-ifs started running through her thoughts. She kept thinking that something might happen to Cornelius.

She was okay with putting off their marriage. She was okay with the danger they were all in, but she wasn't sure she wanted a life without him. It was going to be hard enough to be queen. She began to feel a strange ache in her heart. She was about to sit up to get her mind off of her thoughts when she heard footsteps in the snow.

"Hey, Mark"—she heard Cornelius's voice—"wake up. It is your turn for watch."

Without speaking, she got up and pulled her cloak over her shoulders.

"Did you sleep well?" Cornelius asked hopefully.

"I didn't," she said.

"Were you too cold?" he asked, the hopefulness gone from his voice.

"No, there is just so much on my mind."

"Yeah, me too."

"Get some sleep, Cornelius. There is no sense in two of us staying up all night." She leaned in close to him and whispered in his ear, "I love you."

He smiled and took her place on the hay and blankets. She walked over to the tree where the night watchman held post.

The moon was nearly full so she could see the entire camp with little trouble. The road was nearby and flanked with posts, so it could be seen in the snow. She would be able to see anyone coming on the road for miles in either direction. The tree line of the forest was still and quiet.

In the moonlight, she surveyed all the soldiers lying on the ground. These boys and men were going to be in her charge one day. Many were sleeping soundly. A few of them were huddled together in one corner wide awake. She recognized some of them as the new recruits that came with them from Kelter. They looked wide-eyed and very scared. Many of these boys had never been away from their homes before.

Victoria felt another pang in her heart. She missed Thomas! This was the longest she had been away from home too. But she felt lucky that two of the people that meant so much to her were with her on this journey.

As she looked over the group, her eyes landed on Rupert. He was sitting by a small fire in the far corner of the camp. His magic book was open in his hands. She looked down the road in both directions, and there was nothing moving. She got up and walked to where Rupert sat.

"You should be sleeping," she said, still disguising her voice.

"You should be sitting by the tree, watching for visitors." His voice was dry, but not without a sarcastic undertone.

"Do you feel anyone coming?" she asked definitely. They both knew Rupert would know long before the watchmen if anyone was coming.

"No," he said, defeated.

"Then I am fine here. You must get some sleep," Victoria said in a sad tone.

"There are going to be a lot of sleepless nights for me." Rupert's voice was just as sad.

"I know. Corn and I are there with you."

"It is weird to me that one day we will be the protectors of all these boys."

"Yes, but we are their equals for now."

Victoria went back to her post and waited for sunrise. She looked around periodically at the camp. She looked up at the clear sky. She wondered how far off morning was. Cornelius would know. She would have to get him to teach her about the stars. It could be something they could do together without making anyone suspicious that they are lovers.

After a couple of hours, she got up to stretch her legs. She walked around the camp. Everyone including Rupert and Cornelius was asleep. She stopped next to Cornelius's long frame. He was snoring softly. Just then, out of the corner of her eye, she saw movement.

She turned and looked at the boy sitting up and rearranging his blankets. She realized it was Bartholomew. She walked over to him, careful not to disturb any of the sleeping boys.

"Is everything all right, Your Highness?"

"I can't sleep, Mark. I am cold, and the ground is painful to sleep on. I keep rolling over, but I can never find a comfortable position. I don't think I am cut out for this."

"You will get used to it."

"No, I don't know if I will. I am not like you."

"I guess not. I actually kind of like being out here. Have you ever seen the sunrise?"

"No."

She looked up at the sky. It was no longer a deep black. It was starting to gray. She knew that morning was coming. "Well, you are up now, so let's watch it."

She grabbed her brother's hand and pulled him to the edge of the clearing, and they sat down in the middle of the snow-covered road. There, they could see to the horizon. They watched as the sky turned from the dull gray to deep purple then to red then bright pink and orange. The light crept through edges of the trees and made strange images with lights and shadows on the ground.

Bartholomew watched in wonder. He had never seen anything so beautiful in his fifteen years. Victoria realized in that moment that her brother really might not be cut out to be king. He knew nothing of the real world. She admired him for his acceptance of his own ignorance.

She looked at him in the brightest rays of the morning. He was still, and his eyes were closed. "You can't see it if you close your eyes."

"I know, but I want to remember this moment forever." Then he leaned into her and whispered, "I want to be on your counsel when you are queen. I want to lead a great army or something. Maybe even learn magic. But I have been alive fifteen years, only just now have I ever seen a sunrise. How can I be of any use to you if I know nothing about my own kingdom?"

"You will learn. Stick close to Rupert and Cornelius. They will teach us both."

Bartholomew smiled and hugged her. They got up and walked quickly back to camp. Rupert was already awake when they came back. His book was poised in his left hand. His thumb and his forefinger were in the front and his other three fingers behind the book. His elbow was resting on his knee. He looked up as they approached.

"You left your post, Mark!" he said with mock scorn.

"I was showing His Highness the sunrise!" she said defiantly.

Rupert looked at Bartholomew. He had little more confidence in the prince than he had the day before. He looked back to his book. Bartholomew went to rouse his lieutenants.

Victoria sat down next to Rupert. He spoke again without looking at her. "So you took the prince to see the sunrise."

"Yes."

"You are right that I will teach him things. But most of what *you* will learn will be from Corn. He knows more about the land."

"Can you teach him magic?"

"I suppose, but most of mine will be inherent and therefore impossible for him to learn. Kylan might be able to teach him."

They sat in silence for a moment. They both listened to the sounds of the boys around them waking up.

"So what are you reading about in your book?"

"The history of sorcery and how to use my powers once I get them. That's about it."

Pretty soon the whole camp was bustling with the noise of people cooking a breakfast for an army. Victoria felt a little lost among so many boys. She began to miss Kylan almost as much as Rupert did.

After breakfast, training began. All the new boys were put in a group. The older boys who had been there the longest began to test the skills of the new recruits. Rupert, Cornelius, and Mark were among them, but Bartholomew came and got them.

"I told you three that you will be my guards. Leave the others to be trained as solders. You three are already trained, so come with me to meet my lieutenants."

Many of the other boys looked at them with wonder and awe. Rupert took the lead to follow the prince. He was beginning to feel out of place. Many of them spoke badly and looked at his book as if it were evil. As a sorcerer, he was also becoming a scholar. He had only just realized how many of his countrymen could not read. And many of them believed sorcery to be evil based on their limited knowledge of Kybon. This was something he would change when he became high counselor.

Victoria hurried behind him. She knew she would feel more comfortable with Rupert and Cornelius. Even though she barely knew Bartholomew, she felt a great connection to him because he was her brother. She was a little worried about the lieutenants, though. They worked for Kybon, not Bartholomew. He was like his father, only the puppet without real control. She would have to be very careful not to betray her identity.

Cornelius took up the rear as they left. He, on the other hand, was comfortable with the new soldiers. He had spent time with a lot of them on his journeys to Pallen. But he knew that his duty lay in protecting Mark's secret and helping to protect and teach Bartholomew. He did not trust the lieutenants, either.

On the other side of the clearing, near the spot where Bartholomew and Victoria had watched the sunrise, stood five men in full uniforms. Rupert, Cornelius, and Victoria had the same first impression—these men were soldiers!

Rupert realized very quickly that these men were not spies for Kybon. They were not loyal to any man. They were loyal to their kingdom. He smiled a little. His gut feeling let him know these men would not betray Bartholomew.

Bartholomew rushed up to one of them, nearly jumping up and down with a childish enthusiasm. "Malachi, these are the boys I was telling you about—Rupert, Mark, and Cornelius. They will be my guards."

Malachi, who was the oldest of the small group, looked over each of the boys. His thoughts where carefully hidden by an expressionless face. Rupert wished Kylan were there so he would know what Malachi thought of them. Malachi was suspicious by his nature, which is probably why he was still alive. He had been a solider all his life and had lived through most of the country's tumultuous recent history. The other four were Adrian, Nicolaus, Randolph, and Warner. Adrian was second in command behind Malachi. He was taller than all of them, with a taut frame and deep-blue eyes and a bright, broad smile. Victoria thought he was attractive—a thought she was glad Cornelius could not read.

After their introductions, Nicolaus, Randolph, and Warner went off to oversee the training of the new boys and continue the training of the older boys. Malachi and Adrian built a small fire. Then Adrian asked the four of them to sit down for a moment, saying, "We need to assess your skills."

After they were all situated, Bartholomew went first. He wanted to make sure the other three had the same story for Mark and his sword.

"This is Mark, a young man of great stature and a good friend of mine. He is illegitimate, so he has no standing in the royal family, though he is a cousin of mine. I have asked him to be my bodyguard and to carry my sword as a decoy if we need one. He is not much older than me, so unless I or Mathew has met the spy, he can pass up well as the son of the king. The other two are Rupert and Cornelius, both of Bale. Rupert's father, Oberon, was a great ally to my father. His family's crest is there on the left on the hilt of my sword." He pointed to a four-colored crest with a winged horse in the center.

Malachi examined the crest carefully and then let Adrian look. There was an odd look of pride on Adrian's face.

"Oberon was a powerful sorcerer. That crest represents him well. Rupert, am I to understand that you are going to take on what your father left behind?" Malachi said in a slow and steady voice.

"What did my father leave behind?" Rupert asked, wondering if Kylan would be able to read this man's thoughts.

"He left this world before he could bring peace from the evil that befell the king." Malachi had chosen his words carefully. Adrian only nodded in agreement but remained silent.

"I want goodness to reign over evil, and I will do everything in my power to ensure that," Rupert said, choosing his words just as carefully.

"I will help if I can. Let's see, if I remember correctly, you are only seventeen? So your powers are the same as ours for a few more months. We shall see soon enough if you will be as great as your family legacy."

They looked back at Bartholomew, who, after a second, realized he was meant to finish his introduction.

"Oh yes, this is Cornelius, son of Malcolm of the merchant line in Bale. He is also a great ally to my father, and Malcolm was a great friend to Oberon," Bartholomew said, quickly wanting to be done with all this and out of the limelight.

"Yes, Cornelius and I have met several times. He is also the messenger of Bale to the city of Pallen and the king himself. It is good to see you well, my friend. Your skills as a messenger will help us greatly if this conflict actually comes to war."

"Thank you, Malachi. I am glad to be here to help my longtime friend Rupert and the prince." Cornelius was used to being as silent as possible. He only spoke when spoken to when on a delivery. Not being noticed or acknowledged was advantageous to his arriving to and from destinations and delivering his messages safely.

"I, as Cornelius knows, am Malachi, a mere solider. This is my right-hand man, Adrian. He is in charge if I am not around or I fall in battle. Now let us see what skills you have. Mark, you carry the prince's sword, but can you wield it? And, Rupert, you have no magic yet, so we must make sure you can keep yourself alive until you have your full powers. Cornelius, I have no worries about your skills. You are still alive."

"Sir, if these men are from Bale, why are they fighting with us? It is clear that Bale belongs to Mathew," Adrian said skeptically.

"Adrian, these men are not fighting for the princes! They are fighting for the kingdom and all the people in it. Thomas should have been given the choice. Since he wasn't, he sent us his two best men," Malachi said with great pride in his voice.

Victoria was on her feet before Malachi was finished. She pulled her sword into fighting position. Malachi stood more slowly and drew his sword. Before he could swing his sword, Victoria slipped her foot in and tripped Malachi and disarmed him. It was a trick she had learned from Cornelius.

Malachi smiled broadly for the first time and continued. "You will do fine. I think Cornelius was your teacher. Rupert, what has your mother taught you?"

Rupert stood up with a smile. He picked up Malachi's sword from its landing place and handed it back to him. Then he went and stood behind Cornelius and Mark. "She taught me to know my weakness and let those better than me fight and I will run for help."

He dropped his sword and ran quickly to the other end of the camp, grabbed a large tree limb from the ground, and scampered back with it. Then he jumped in front of Malachi as he swung his sword with some force at Mark. Malachi's sword stuck in the wood. Rupert dropped the limb and pushed Malachi to the ground and then sat on him, pinning his hands to the cold, snowy ground. Adrian laughed so hard he fell over.

Malachi laughed too as Rupert stood and helped him up. "Very good. I will leave you on your own then. I need to get these men trained. Adrian, come along. Bartholomew, you have chosen your guards well," he said, messing up the prince's hair as he walked away.

The four of them spent the rest of that day helping with the training. Their skills were very much superior to many of the boys there. Rupert was the best teacher of sword-fighting. He was much better with a sword than he let on earlier that day. Kylan taught him that patience was the most important factor in teaching. Cornelius was the better teacher of strategy. He was proud of the fact that he had never been in a fight. He spent the day teaching the boys ways of talking others out of fighting.

That night, they had a dinner of dried meat and cold beans. The boys told stories and sang songs they knew from home. When the fires began to die out, Malachi made them all quiet down and get ready to sleep. Victoria was exhausted from not sleeping the night before. She lay down next to Bartholomew and Cornelius. She was asleep before Bartholomew could say good night. Rupert took first watch, so he sat quietly by the tree and continued reading his magic book.

Malachi woke Cornelius before the sun was up.

"Cornelius, I have a task for you. The snows have stopped, and the snow is starting to melt. Spring rain will be here soon. You know these lands better than I. Is there a cave nearby we can use as shelter when the rains become constant?"

"There are some in the Foothills three days' ride from here. I am not sure if they are adequate. I have only ever needed shelter for myself."

"I am sending you and your friends and Bartholomew on a scouting trip to find suitable shelter."

"Are you sure Bartholomew should leave his troop?"

"Like you and Rupert, Bartholomew is on a different path. I suspect that Mark is actually the king's older child that was sent away. I thought Thomas once told me the child was his niece, but I could be wrong," he said with a pause and a snicker before he began speaking again. "If Bartholomew is going to help his brother win back his rightful throne, he needs to learn how to find shelter and things you and Rupert and Mark learned by living outside of the palace. I will take care of the troops. Maybe one day, when Kybon is gone and Marcus's heir is on the throne, he will make me a general."

"I think that is a reasonable request. Should I wake the others?"

"Yes, you should leave before the sun is up. I think we have about a week or two before the rains come."

"Yes, two weeks, if we're lucky."

CHAPTER 19

The Hunt for Shelter

The sky was just starting to turn pink when the four of them were on the road heading toward Pallen. Bartholomew was still very tired, but he was glad that he would get to see a sunrise again. Rupert and Thunderstorm were both wide awake. Victoria felt very rested. She was still not completely used to riding a horse long distance, but she was much better than she had been.

"How long of a ride is this going to be?" Bartholomew asked as he fidgeted with his small food pack.

"It will take us about three days to get to the Foothill Mountains from here?"

"I didn't know there are mountains in my father's kingdom."

"There aren't, Barth. The Foothills mark the border of our kingdom. There are very large mountains that run for many miles along the border. Those mountains are natural protection from the kingdoms on the other side. It is next to impossible to get an army over those mountains in good enough health to fight a war," Cornelius said.

"Is that why we are safe from being overthrown from outside countries?" Bartholomew asked.

"Yes, but it is a hindrance too. We have few ally countries. The ocean is the other border. So we are alone. That is why Kybon has such a stronghold here. We can only fight with the army we can provide, and we are a small country compared to the rest out there."

"There are other countries besides ours?" Bartholomew realized this had to be true, but he had been schooled by tutors that worked for Kybon, so he knew nothing of other countries.

"Yes, Barth, the world is much larger than our kingdom. Kybon wants to take over us and then cross those mountains and take over other countries too."

"Why hasn't he yet? I mean, he is pretty much in charge here, why doesn't he start on other countries! Not that I want him to."

"He doesn't have complete control yet. He can't use magical force to take over because there are spells that hinder that. Spells that were cast thousands of years ago to protect mortals against the abuse of a sorcerer's power. So he has to win the loyalty of the kingdom, but as you can tell, there are men like Malachi that keep the peace through loyalty to freedom, not to men."

"So we are fighting not only to protect our kingdom, but the rest of the world too?"

"Yes!" Rupert and Cornelius said together.

They rode in silence for a long while before anyone spoke again.

Bartholomew broke the silence finally. "What is Kybon going to do with the world once he controls it?" he asked.

"I don't know," Rupert answered. "That is a good question."

They rode on and on down the road that Bartholomew could not see. The snow was not as deep as it had been, but there was still enough to cover the road. The prince wondered how Cornelius knew where they were going.

After a few hours, Rupert slowed a bit and rode next to Bartholomew, who had been taking up the rear of the caravan. "Here, have some dried meat. Be careful to hold on with one hand and eat with the other," he said, handing Bartholomew the meat from his much fuller food bag.

Bartholomew reached carefully with his left hand and took the meat as he tightened his grip with his right hand. Rupert wasn't holding on with either hand. "How come you don't fall?" Bartholomew asked.

"Because I know my horse. Thunderstorm will let me know when the road gets rocky. We will eat while we ride. The less we stop, the sooner we will get to those caves and then back to camp."

"Aye, will you ride next to me for a while? I am still afraid I might fall asleep and then fall off."

"Don't worry, I will keep you awake," Rupert said.

The rest of the day, the four of them talked freely about nothing important. Victoria and Cornelius even rode next to each other. Rupert, with the help of the other two, told Bartholomew stories about his family history. They even taught him a few words of the old language. They started with translating the symbol's engraving that ran down the blade of Victoria's sword. One side read, bloodshed in war. by blood of the king. The other side said, blood shed for peace. by the protector of all bloods.

"The old language has fewer words, but many words have several meanings. Blood has two different meanings here. The last word *bloods* really means something like races. Not blood like what is inside our body. You have to infer the meaning based on the words around it," Rupert explained.

The rest of that day progressed with Bartholomew getting a crash course in history. He was glad for it. He was starting to feel that he might now be useful in helping his blood regain the throne.

The road was flanked by forest on both sides the whole time they had been riding. Just as the sun began to set, the land began to change. The trees in the forest were thinning. There was a river and another village in the distance. The mountains were barely visible on the horizon.

"Are we really going to get that far in two days?" Bartholomew asked, pointing to the jagged line of the horizon.

"We are not going that far. The Foothills are much closer. And if we keep moving this quickly, we will get there sooner than two days. I didn't think we would make it this far today," Cornelius answered.

"What village is that?" Rupert asked, pointing with his chin.

"Corslan," Cornelius said in a dry voice.

"Oh, they are not friendly to outsiders," Rupert thought out loud.

"No, we will bypass them. This road doesn't lead there, anyway. They like it that way."

"Are we stopping for tonight? I think we should make camp before it is too dark to see," Victoria said.

"Yes, we should," Cornelius agreed, "and while there are still a few trees for shelter."

It didn't take them long to make camp and start a small fire. Cornelius had been careful to pack dry wood tender to start a fire. There was enough dead wood on the ground to burn all night. The heat from the tender dried the bigger pieces enough so they would ignite easily. All four of them would have preferred a supper of fresh meat, but there were no small animals around to catch. So they settled on a supper of more dried meat and stale bread with some warm beans and water. It wasn't as tasty as they would have liked, but it was filling enough to keep them from going to sleep hungry.

Victoria and Cornelius combined their bedding and went to sleep in each other's arms. Bartholomew was warmer, and the ground was a little softer here. He went to sleep very quickly too.

Rupert, however, stayed up for a while. He took a few sheets of paper from Cornelius's writing book and his writing coal. He wrote out several words in the old language and their meanings. Rupert had a great thirst for knowledge. When he was done with the definitions, he read a few more pages in his book. Then with everyone one else asleep, he cleared his mind to see if Kylan's thoughts would find him.

She was awake and trying to read his thoughts as well. She was alone deep in the mountains that bordered the kingdom. She was not far from the council now. She was able to find her way by telepathic communication with the high sorceress. All she *told* Rupert was that she was fine and not to worry. She could not tell him where she was because it could be dangerous to all of them. Plus she wasn't sure which mountain she was on, anyway.

He was happy with only knowing that she was doing well. He went to sleep thinking of her and when they might meet again. She fell asleep with the same thoughts.

Victoria woke up when it was still dark. Cornelius was still holding her. She woke him gently. "Wake up, it will be morning soon. We should start early."

Cornelius looked at her and smiled. Then he got up and woke Rupert and Bartholomew.

"I like sunrises, but I am not sure I like seeing them three days in a row," Bartholomew said as he watched Rupert carefully separate the coals with the tip of his sword to put out the smoldering fire.

"The sooner we start, the sooner we get there. I don't like being alone on this road. So far, my gut says we are alone, but it may not stay that way," said Rupert in a dry tone.

"Don't worry, Rupert, if anyone comes along, we can defend ourselves," Victoria said with confidence.

"It is better to be on guard. The rest of the way, we are on open road, and it is going to get rocky. We are in for more difficult riding. But we should get to the caves by midday tomorrow if all goes well."

All did go well. The day was uneventful. Bartholomew learned the words Rupert wrote for him. Rupert told them that Kylan was well. Mostly they rode in silence. Bartholomew and Victoria took in the landscape. Neither of them had been this far from home before. Victoria was glad that Cornelius would be her king. He knew the land they would rule together.

At dusk, they made camp in the open land. Corslan was now behind them but not far enough for Rupert's comfort. The Foothills were visible but still a long way off.

"We need to keep watch tonight," Rupert said as Cornelius started a fire. "The smoke from the fire may attract spies. I will take first watch. I will wake one of you when I get tired."

"Aye, see you in a few hours," Cornelius said. Then he took Victoria by the hand and pulled her to his side as they lay down.

Rupert "talked" to Kylan again. She told him she made it safely to the council. She would not be able to tell him anything more for a few weeks. He very sadly wished her a good night.

After a few hours, Rupert woke Cornelius, who very carefully unwrapped himself from Victoria without waking her. "Get some sleep. I am waking everyone before daybreak. I don't like being out here unprotected."

"I don't, either, but the night is still, so we are fine for now," Cornelius said.

As promised, Cornelius woke everyone while the stars were still shining. They all got up, ate a quick breakfast of more dried meat and the last of the stale bread. Rupert gave the horses extra hay. The road was going to be difficult.

They spent the morning picking their way through the loose rocks as the road sloped upward. All the horses but Thunderstorm labored and slowed to a walk. Soon Rupert was far ahead of them. He stopped after a while and let the others catch up. Soon the road evened out a little, but it narrowed greatly. They had to ride single file.

"Are you sure these are hills? They look a lot like mountains to me," Victoria said as she tightened her grip on the reins.

"They are hills. I have been in the mountains. This is nothing compared to traversing those on horseback," Cornelius said.

"So where are these caves?" Rupert asked.

"There are several near here. We have to get off the path, though. I think I should go up and find a suitable one on foot," Cornelius said.

"I am coming with you." Victoria dismounted her horse and started off in Cornelius's direction.

Cornelius didn't try to argue with her. Grateful for her company, he could not let himself think of her as frail and delicate. Yes, he worried about her because her father and mother had been so sickly, but Thomas was strong and had taught her to take care of herself. He pushed the thoughts of her frailty from his mind.

She grabbed his hand as they left the path. Then she reached up and grasped the small ledge next to her and pulled herself up.

Cornelius let go of her hand to use both of his hands to steady her. Then she pulled him up. From the top of the ledge, they both saw several caves carved into the sides of the hills.

Most of the caves were nothing more than indentions in the rock wall. But there were a couple that looked to be deeper.

"Let's check out those two over there," Victoria said, pointing to the two larger ones.

"Aye, good idea," Cornelius said. Then he turned and hollered down to Rupert and Bartholomew. "There are a couple of bigger caves up here. We are going to go explore them. You two wait there."

Victoria reached the first of the large caves first. She thought it would be funny to race, but she didn't tell Cornelius they were racing until she got to the cave. "I won!" she announced triumphantly.

"Sure," Cornelius said, smiling and happy for the first time in days.

The first cave they explored looked promising as a suitable refuge from the rains. It was large, and the ground inside was sloped slightly upward. There were only a few stalagmites inside. Cornelius walked as far as he could before it was too dark to see. There didn't seem to be an end to the cave. Victoria pulled him back before he set out into the pitch-black hollows.

"Come on, we should go look at the other one while we still have bright sunlight," she said.

"But I want to know how far back this one goes."

"We don't have enough wood to make torches. Let's see the other one and then get Rupert and Bartholomew. We can camp here tonight and see if they are truly good shelter.

Cornelius thought that this was a good plan. With only four people and only enough food to get them through four days, they needed to make a decision quickly. Though it was clear to him by now that whether or not the caves where decent shelter, the troops would have to make do. There were not enough supplies to build proper shelters, nor was there enough time to get anywhere else before the rains came.

The other cave was even larger than the first. The light ran much deeper into the cave. They discovered this was because there

was an opening on the other side. It was not a very large opening, but it let air circulate through the cave.

Victoria looked out of the opening and saw a beautiful view of the landscape on the other side. She could see more hills not far off, but there was a very large drop to any sort of ground from the opening.

"That would be quite a fall," she said, showing Cornelius the view from the opening.

"Yes, it would. It is beautiful to look at, though."

"Let's get Bartholomew and Rupert up here. Barth needs to see what his kingdom can be!"

"Our kingdom!" Cornelius corrected her as he pulled her by the hand this time.

Bartholomew quickly ascended the ledge. Rupert, however, climbed up very slowly and carefully, making sure there would be a good way back down that would not require jumping from the ledge. Once they were up, Victoria quickly took Bartholomew into the cave to show him the view from the other side.

Rupert was less concerned about the caves than he was about adequate space for training and supplies and the horses. "There is more to this than sheltering men. We have animals to look after as well. Plus, we still need space to train the boys. That will be difficult inside the caves," he said to Cornelius as he began to walk around the flat land leading up to the caves.

He discovered small paths barely visible in the powdery snow that covered the hilltops. Many of the paths led up to the top of the hills they were exploring. He decided the paths must have been made by animals grazing on the mountain grasses. This meant there would be fresh meat when they needed it.

Cornelius called to him from a different path. "Rupert, come here." He pointed to a straighter and thicker path through the snow. It cut through the rock. He kicked the path with his foot. It made a sharp, cracking sound, a very different noise than dirt makes, under his boots.

"Ice," Rupert said.

"Yes, this looks like the beginning of a stream," Cornelius said.

"We should be careful. When the snow melts, there will be more of these. They may even flood the caves."

"No, I have been up here in the rainy season. I think this is the only stream. It is diverted a little farther down so that the water flows into the river that leads to leads to Corslan. It has been that way for many years. We need to worry more about their scouts and hunters than the water. They are a fierce group, and most of them are loyal to Kybon."

"Yes, his family line starts in Corslan. But our army will outnumber them greatly. Corslan is still very small because they don't like outsiders. Malachi is probably familiar with them."

"It doesn't matter how big the army is if we are cornered in the caves with no way to escape!" Cornelius pointed out.

"I suppose there is a way down that will allow us to escape if we need to. Malachi knows what he is doing. I trust his judgment."

"We will find out soon enough. Come on, let's make camp."

"You three sleep up here tonight. I am sleeping down below with Thunderstorm and the other three horses. We are heading back in the morning, right?"

"Yes, as early as possible, we will make better time back to camp, though. It will be downhill all the way."

"Yes, I know, Cornelius. See you three in the morning."

It was a quiet night for Rupert as Thunderstorm kept watch over his friend for the night. So Rupert actually slept soundly for the first time since they left Kelter.

The other three had a bit rougher night. They decided to sleep inside the first cave to see if it would work as a shelter. It was impossible to light a fire for warmth because the smoke filled the cave. Cornelius spent about an hour trying to find a way to build a fire in different places in the cave, but nothing worked.

They decided to move to the second cave. There was enough light from the moon to see the whole of the cave. Cornelius had noticed early a small circle of stones in the middle of the cave floor. He realized now that it may once have been a fireplace. He found the stones easily and built the fire there. To the amazement of the other two, the smoke went up to the cave's ceiling and dissipated. Cornelius

was not sure why this happened, but he knew it had something to do with the perfect circular hole in the back of the cave. The fire kept them warm, but the ground was no softer inside the cave. They managed a few hours of broken and painful sleep.

Rupert woke just before sunrise and quickly ascended the hills to the cave. "Come on, if we start now, we may be able to make it to the edge of the forest by nightfall," he said quietly. He knew they had not slept well.

"I am all for that. But I am not sure I can feel my feet to walk. I don't think they woke up when my brain did," Bartholomew said in a low voice.

"Once we start moving, the feeling will come back. But you are better off if they are numb," Victoria said in a more cheerful voice than anyone expected.

"Why are you so cheerful?" Cornelius asked in an annoyed voice.

"I had a really nice dream. But you are being mean, so I will keep it to myself," she snapped.

"Guys, fight while you are packing," Rupert said.

They all fell silent and quickly packed their bedrolls. They had very little else to pack. So they headed back down the path as the first rays of sunlight began to lighten the darkened ground. This time, Bartholomew didn't get to see the sunrise because their backs were to the ascending sun as they rode quietly and solemnly toward the soldier camp.

It was nearly midday before Cornelius broke the silence. "After last night, I am not certain the first of the large caves will work well as shelter," he said sadly. "We can build a fire in the second one, but we will need both caves to house all the boys."

"Corn, I am not sure there is much of a choice. The snow is going to turn into rain soon. I would rather those boys sleep in a freezing cave and be dry than sleep out in the cold rain. Besides, three people sleeping in a cave is different than two hundred. My men have many more supplies back at camp. I am thinking that when the rains come, it won't be as cold, anyway," Bartholomew said.

"That is a wise statement, Barth," Rupert said. "Maybe there is hope for you after all!"

The silence returned as they rode. Victoria stared at the path, lost in thoughts of the future. Cornelius watched her closely. He feared that the freezing night before might cause her to get sick. They rode as fast as the horses were willing to go, so they were able to reach the forest before the sunset, where they made camp. Bartholomew watched the sky change colors again. He decided that he could never get enough of the sunrise and sunsets. He was glad that his sister had taught him to appreciate the small beauties of his kingdom.

They all went to sleep quickly. Rupert slept on his guard again, though he had not felt the presence of anyone else for a long time. He was beginning to wonder if maybe he was losing the sense. He fell asleep thinking about what would happen if he didn't get his powers.

The next morning, it was Victoria who woke everyone.

"Get up, boys! We have to get going." She shook Rupert and Bartholomew awake. Cornelius woke up at the sound of Bartholomew's scream and Victoria's laughter.

"Did I really scare you, Barth?" she asked through fits of laughter.

"Victoria, keep it down. We need to stay quiet, in case there is anyone around," Cornelius said through a yawn.

"Corn, you need to lighten up. I haven't seen you laugh in nearly three weeks! You used to laugh all the time. I know that there is a lot on your mind, but I don't think I could bear to watch you lose your spirit. It is bad enough that tomorrow we have to go back to pretending that I am Mark, and I won't be able hold your hand when things get tough!" She was nearly in tears as she finished speaking.

Cornelius got up quickly and hugged her. She sobbed on his shoulder as Rupert packed up the horses. He laughed quietly at the confused look on Cornelius's face.

Just as the day before, they rode most of the morning in silence. Again, it was Cornelius who spoke first. He spent the whole morning thinking about what Victoria had said about him being sad. She was correct, of course. He was scared of what was to come. He came up with the only solution he could think of to lift everyone's spirits.

"Hey, I thought of a way to make us all feel better," he said.

"Really?" Victoria said. She was glad to hear that he wanted to be happier.

"Yes, I think we should sing!"

Victoria laughed so hard she nearly fell off her horse. Rupert, who was in the lead of the group, turned, and looked with mild surprise at his lifelong friend. "And what should we sing?" Rupert asked.

"Well, I don't know, but music and singing always remind me of festivals, and until the last one, I always had fun at festivals."

"Do you remember the song from the festival in the woods with Raven? The one they sang before the storyteller came out," Victoria asked.

"I remember the tune, but not the words," Cornelius said as he tried to remember the words.

"Well, I wasn't there, so I don't even know the tune," Bartholomew said sadly.

"I remember the tune, and so does Rupert. He was humming it a few days ago right before Kylan left for the council!"

"No, I wasn't," Rupert said, trying to sound as if he believed himself.

"Rupert, you know that you can't lie to us. Corn and I have known you much too long!" She laughed at the look of boyish annoyance on his face, then she continued. "Since Bartholomew doesn't know the tune, we can hum it a couple of times and then make up our own words."

They spent the rest of the day arguing happily over the tune and what words would fit best. By the end of the day, they had made up a very long song about trees and caves and wizards and soldiers and traveling in the cold. Victoria made Cornelius write it down so they could teach it to their children. He thought she was silly, but he decided not to tell her that.

They decided not to make camp that night. They were only a couple of hours from camp when the sun went down. So they rode on.

Malachi was on watch when they arrived. "I am glad for your safe return. Did you find suitable shelter?" he asked before they could even dismount from their horses.

Rupert began to feel a bit uneasy. Something was wrong.

"We found two caves large enough to house a large group of people. Something is not right here. What has happened?" Rupert spoke before anyone else could.

"We were visited by soldiers from Kybon's personal army. They were looking for Bartholomew!"

"What did you tell them?" Bartholomew asked quickly.

"I merely said that you left and left me in charge of your army. I made them realize that I am a mere soldier. The whereabouts of a flippant fifteen-year-old is not my concern."

"I am not flippant!" Bartholomew said emphatically.

"I know that, sire, but what else was I to tell them?" he asked sadly. He moved closer to the fire, and the four of them noticed at once that he had a large bruise on his face.

"Did they beat anyone else?" Rupert looked around at the sleeping boys.

"Just me and Adrian, but I would hardly call this a beating! They came last night. Nicolaus was on watch. He saw them coming and woke Adrian and me. I sent Nic into the woods in case anything serious happened. He could head to Kelter for help. Instead, while the ten soldiers were beating Adrian and me, trying to make us talk, he woke a few of the older boys. They were able to overpower Kybon's soldiers."

"Where are the traitors?" Rupert asked.

"Tied to the trees over there." He pointed at the woods not far from the road. Rupert could just make out the figures of sleeping men against the trees in the darkness.

Malachi continued. "I was not sure what their punishment should be. Nicolaus felt we should wait for your return, Your Highness, before we made a decision. He is right that it is your decision."

Bartholomew was honored and horrified at the same time. He was not sure he was ready to make a decision deciding the fate of ten people.

Rupert could tell he was frightened with indecision and said quickly, "There is nothing we can do about them tonight. We need to decide when we should depart for the caves. We are much too vulnerable out here in the open."

"I agree. I vote we begin departure at sunrise," Malachi said.

Victoria knew it was best for the soldiers, but she was hoping they would have one day to rest before they had to turn around and return to the caves they had just left. Rupert saw her face and didn't need to read her thoughts. Cornelius didn't even need to look at her face.

"He is right. We need to leave as soon as possible. It will take much longer to get there with so many boys and most of them on foot. I have been thinking about this on the way here. Maybe we should take the boys in smaller groups. It is a long walk, and there is little space to make camp. I don't think we can take everyone together," Cornelius said as he looked over the mass of sleeping boys.

CHAPTER 20

Journey to the Caves

After several hours of deliberation, they determined that the best way to get all the boys to the caves would be to divide up into smaller groups. Malachi decided that he and the other four lieutenants, as well as Rupert, Cornelius, Mark, and Bartholomew, would each lead a group on the two- to three-day trek to the caves. There were 285 boys total.

"So each of us has to lead a group alone?" Bartholomew asked with fear in his voice.

"Yes, Your Highness, I will give you the smallest group, but you must lead them. You are the prince, and this is your army," Malachi said calmly.

Bartholomew sighed. Rupert put his hand on Bartholomew's shoulder but said nothing. Victoria was ready for the challenge. She was growing tired of being led by Cornelius and Rupert.

It was decided that everyone would get thirty-three boys, leaving a group of twenty-one for Bartholomew. Each group would have some older boys and some younger boys. In case they ran into problems along the way, there would be enough boys to put up a good fight.

By morning, Malachi had divided the boys up. He posted the list he had made on the trunk of the lookout tree. Cornelius was amazed that their leader had been able to learn all the boys' names. As the boys woke up, they were sent to the tree to check the list, and then they were to pack quickly and sit with the boys in their group.

There were many boys who could not read, not even their own names. Malachi didn't help them. "Ask the boys around you for help," he said.

Bartholomew was furious with his lieutenant. "Why won't you help those who can't read? They are slowing us down!" Bartholomew demanded.

"There are enough boys here who can help them. I do not want them depending on me or on you! They must learn to help and trust each other just as much as we need them to trust their leaders. If the leader falls, they must continue fighting rather than run away. That is the secret to a truly successful army. They fight because they are protecting one another," Malachi responded again in a calm, unrattled voice.

Soon all the boys were sitting quietly in nine distinct groups. They were silently waiting for their next order. Malachi praised all the boys for how well and how quickly they followed his orders. He then announced that their departures would be staggered and that Cornelius's group was to be first. He offered no explanation.

Cornelius walked through his group and asked each boy if he had eaten. When they all said yes, he ordered them to line up three abreast eleven boys long. When they had done so, he told them it was time to go.

His group started walking with him in the lead on horseback. He rode slowly so as not to tire the boys out. After about half an hour, he pulled his horse to the side of the line and began riding next to them. As he did so, he asked each boy his name and his age, determined to learn their names by nightfall. He spent the rest of that day answering their questions about the future as best he could.

He also told them stories about his travels as a boy and taught them a few different tunes and had them make up new songs about their new adventure. Somehow he managed to write down the songs while he was riding.

Rupert, Victoria, Nicolaus, Randolph, Warner, Adrian, and Bartholomew drew straws to see what order they would depart in. Malachi's group was leaving last and not until the following morning. He was expecting supplies from Bale that evening so he could not leave. He also kept the extra horse to pack the coming supplies.

Rupert got the shortest straw, then Randolph, then Victoria, then Adrian, then Nicolaus, then Warner. Bartholomew was glad he was going to be the last to leave that day. It would give him time to learn the other boys' strengths and weaknesses before they were sent out alone. Malachi had been sure to give him some of the strongest-skilled boys. Nearly all of them were older than he was.

Rupert had one hour to wait after Cornelius left. He decided to ask them their names one by one. He was bad with names. It had been easier to remember names and other important information when Kylan had been around.

Victoria got her group together with Bartholomew's help. It gave him practice at giving orders and kept Victoria from having to disguise her voice. All the boys in her group lined up and spoke their name as she and Bartholomew walked past. The last boy in line was named Aden. He was the tallest, with broad shoulders. He looked to be a little older than Cornelius. He had a strange look on his face as Bartholomew introduced Victoria as Mark.

It was midmorning when they began their journey to the caves. Victoria had decided that she would talk very little. Few of the boys had ever heard Mark speak. Now without the others, she feared she would have to speak more and maybe give away that she was pretending.

Just after they left, however, Aden came up and began walking next to her horse. She was a little amazed that he could keep up with her, even though she was walking the horse slowly.

"Do you need something, Aden?" she asked quietly, pretending to be hoarse.

"Sir, I noticed that you have lost your voice so I wonder if I might be your second in command and help you give orders. That way, you won't have to speak loudly until your voice recovers." He winked when he finished. She realized he knew she was pretending. But she would not worry about how he knew yet. She merely nodded her head and was glad for the help.

Victoria's boys walked happily most of the day. She told Aden to let them tell stories and talk and sing if they wanted to, to make the time pass. She did want them to be disciplined, but she wanted to get to know her army. She learned that many of the boys in her group actually volunteered to be in the army. They wanted things to change, though few of them had any ideas about how to overthrow Kybon. One of the boys did. His name was Peter.

"I don't know a way myself, but that guy named Rupert, he is going to be a sorcerer. I bet he will be able to get rid of Kybon," Peter said with enthusiasm.

"How do you know that?" Aden asked quickly before Victoria could betray her secret.

"He had a book about sorcery. And besides, he has the look of magic about him."

"What is a look of magic?" a short dark-haired boy asked skeptically.

"It is hard to describe, but I can tell when sorcerers are near me."

"I think you are crazy!" the same boy said.

"Think what you like, but mark my words, Rupert is a sorcerer. And he is going to save us all!"

"Mark my words! You should watch what you say! You can't trust everyone you meet, Peter!"

Victoria thought there was a threat in the dark-haired boy's words.

All the boys fell silent for a while. Victoria wondered if Peter was a keeper of powers. She had gotten a feeling that there was another keeper among the army, but the sheer number of boys and the distractions kept her from figuring out who it was. She decided that Aden would have first watch that night and Peter and the dark-haired boy, who had refused to tell his name, would take second watch so she could find out exactly what these boys knew.

They had made it pretty far into the woods when the sun began to sink in the sky. Victoria motioned Aden to her. She leaned over on her horse and whispered to him to give the order to make camp. She also told him that he was taking first watch that night and Peter and his new friend would have second watch.

Aden gave the orders quickly. He helped the smaller boys make their beds out of the tattered blankets they had carried in packs. Victoria built a small fire for cooking and several slightly larger fires in a circle. She left two unlit and told the boys to make the beds inside the circle to stay warm. She left a small path through the two unlit fire piles.

There was enough salted meat and vegetables to feed them all a meager supper, but the hungry boys were glad for what they had. Victoria found out from their conversations that many of them didn't have much more when they were home. Her father's illness had devastated all the people that were not loyal to Kybon. These boys were hoping to help their families by being soldiers in the war. It was one of the only things that kept many of them from hiding when the lieutenants came to round them up. By joining the army, their parents had lesser mouths to feed, and one day, if things went well, these boys all hoped to be able to support their families because they had been on the winning side.

Victoria thought about Thomas all alone in his house. He hated eating alone. She hoped he was able to find company in town.

After their small dinner, the boys went to sleep rather quickly. It had been a long walk, so many of them were very tired. Peter slept near the path between the fires so he could get to his watch post quickly.

Aden sat quietly outside the circle. Victoria wrote in her journal for a while before she approached Aden. She had thought when she met him that he was handsome. Now she looked at him in the firelight, and she thought him even more handsome.

She thought of Kylan and how she would know what she thought of Aden. She thought about Kylan telling Rupert. Then he would make some candid comment about it to her in front of Cornelius, who would get upset at not knowing what Rupert meant. She thought of the look Cornelius would make! She laughed out loud. Aden looked at her from his post. She knew suddenly how much she missed Cornelius.

She got up and walked slowly and carefully through the path in the fires. When she reached Aden, she sat next to him but far enough away from him that she would not touch him. She spoke quietly, still careful to disguise her voice.

"Aye, what is it that you know? Why did you ask to be my second?" she began.

"Well, Your Highness, first, I would like to say that it is a pleasure to finally meet you. My mother has told me a great many stories about you and your mother and the old days before your father took sick and Kybon took over," he said in nearly a whisper. Neither of them was sure that all the boys were asleep.

"You know who I am then?"

"Yes, your disguise works well. I was fooled by Prince Bartholomew's story that you are carrying his sword. But then I figured out that you are the heir to the throne, and since the missing heir to the throne is a girl, your disguise no longer holds up."

"How did you figure out that I am the heir to the throne?"

"Your sword gave it away. The oldest child of the king is the heir to the throne—no matter who he or she is born by—so your sword is different from those that Prince Bartholomew and Prince Mathew were given."

"How so?"

"The king's crest is in the middle there." He pointed to her sword. "And on each end of the hilt, there is a smaller crest of the four houses in highest favor of the king. And at the very bottom of the hilt, there is a small engraving of two letters. See." He pointed to two tiny letters that Victoria could barely see in the dark. She squinted, and finally her eyes made out a small *Q* with an *A* inside it and the outline of a tiny crown that matched the one on the king's family crest.

"Yes, I see it. I never noticed them before."

"Those two letters are the initials of the craftsman who made the sword. In this case, it was Aden Quidender, my grandfather, for whom I am named. He died just after he completed your sword, so my father made the ones for the two princes. His name is Beck, so on their swords you will find a *Q* with a *B* inside instead of an *A*. The crown under the initials signifies that this sword was given to the future ruler."

Victoria did not know what to say. So she looked back at him and waited for Aden to continue.

"My mother was your mother's best friend, and my father and grandfather and my brother and I are blacksmiths to the king. That is our crest there with the ox in the center. He pointed to the crest on the backside of her sword. She realized she always wore it with Rupert's family crest showing.

"It is nice to meet you too, Aden. And thank you for helping me with my disguise," she said feebly, knowing that there must be something better to say to him.

"You are welcome. Now I think you should get some sleep. I will wake you when I wake Peter for his watch. I assume that you wish to talk to him about his knowledge of Rupert."

"Yes, I do, but I want to know more about your life in Pallen. You are older than I am, so I assume you at least met my mother before she died. And you have met my father as well. I remember neither."

"There will be a time for stories. I know Cornelius as well. He is a good man, and he honors my work. I will be glad when he is your king. My wife likes to tell me that he is cute and it is a shame he fell for you, but she is only joking, I hope."

"You are married?"

"Yes, I am a father too. I miss them very much, but I feel that I am needed here. My mother says it is my duty to help protect you. She and my father swore a pact with your mother and the king to look after you. They knew even then that Kybon had too much power. So we are the blacksmith to the king, but I am more than that.

"And my wife swore that pact with me when we got married. She was a servant in the palace, so she knows a few secrets that can help us. But I am serious, Princess, go and get some sleep. You have to keep your strength up. There will be time to talk later when we get to the caves."

Victoria didn't like it, but she knew he was right. She did not like to admit that she was sickly, but she had spent a great deal of her childhood fighting some ailment or another. Thomas knew a bit about herbs and their medicinal properties so he always managed to keep her well enough for her lessons.

She fell asleep quickly despite the cold and the absence of Cornelius. The next thing she knew, Aden was shaking her awake very gently.

"Wake up, Mark! Peter is on for second watch. The other boy refuses to get up. We will deal with him in the morning."

"Thank you, Aden!" she said as she shook herself fully awake.

Peter was now outside of the fire and sitting on a stump near the forest edge. Victoria felt a connection to him as she walked slowly toward him. Aden came with her.

"I would like to hear this conversation if it is okay with both of you?" Aden asked quietly.

"How do I know you are not a spy for Kybon?" Peter asked harshly.

"If I am, you would be dead already!" Aden said calmly.

"Aye, let's get on with this meeting. Peter, what did you mean when you said you can tell when a sorcerer is near?" Victoria asked quickly.

"Well, I can just tell. It would be hard for you to understand. I have a special power. You would only understand if you had it too, but maybe you do," he said, realizing that he felt a connection to her.

"Yes, you are a keeper of powers!" she said.

"Yes, I am one of the few not in hiding. Why aren't you in hiding? Kybon wants us all dead so he will be the only one with powers."

"Right! Except he has a keeper too! I am his keeper."

"Wow, I figured he had his keeper locked up somewhere."

"He couldn't lock her up as long as she lived under her uncle's roof. That is part of the magic of the high sorceress. Also, he may want all of you dead, but he can't purposely kill another sorcerer's keeper. That is the reason he wants to fight a war. If there is a war and you or Peter fall in battle, he is exempt from the responsibility," Aden cut in.

"How do you know that?" Victoria asked.

"I am the blacksmith!" he said in a hopefully tone. She gave him an I-want-a-better-explanation look. So he sighed and continued. "I work in the palace, and I hear things. There is more magic law than I know or understand. I am not sure what Kybon knows. The only person who knows it all is the high sorceress, and I am willing to bet there are small nuances in magic law that not even she knows."

"Peter, I think you should leave us and go into hiding," Victoria said abruptly.

"No, I want to help you and Rupert. I will be careful not to get myself killed. I can't help you if I am dead!"

Victoria smiled at his statement. "That is my point, but I can't make the decision for you. If you stay, keep the fact that you are a keeper of powers to yourself! I want this to be resolved with all of us alive!"

It was harder for her to go back to sleep. There was more to ponder, but because she was so tired, she fell into a deep dreamless sleep. It was the morning sun that woke her the second time.

"Good morning, Mark," Aden said as Victoria sat up slowly, blinking as her eyes adjusted to the light.

"Why didn't you wake me sooner? We should have left by now. I wanted to make it by tonight."

"We are just about ready to go, but I felt that we should let you sleep as long as possible."

"Whether I am asleep or not, I am in charge here! You should have awakened me!"

"Sorry, but I am under strict orders from Cornelius to make sure you don't get sick."

"Really, he is not in control of me!" She was nearly screaming as rage rushed through her.

"Calm down! He is right not to want you to get sick. Here, have some breakfast. We are leaving in ten minutes." He handed her a piece of bread.

She grabbed his arm as he got up from where he knelt beside her. Because he was not expecting her strength, he nearly fell when she pulled him back toward her. As he steadied himself, she spoke quietly but sternly in his ear.

"You listen to me! I know that Cornelius worries, but I am the one in charge. I will not be treated as if I am second class. I will be queen, but if Cornelius is not careful, he will find himself without a wife or the throne, so you had better be careful who you listen to! I am capable of deciding when and how much sleep I need! So hear this well. I order you to wake me up first, and if you break any more orders, you will find there will be a new family of blacksmiths when I am queen! Understood?"

"Understood!" he said as a reflex from receiving orders for so long. Victoria stormed off into the woods.

Aden was in shock at first, but as he processed what he had just heard, he smiled to himself. "She is tough enough. There is more hope than I thought," he said to himself. Then he pushed himself up from the ground, dusted the lose snow from his pants, and began ordering the boys to line up.

Everyone was ready just as Victoria immerged from the woods. She mounted her horse and nodded at Aden. He gave the order, and they were on their way.

Victoria led them at quite a fast pace, but they were all able to keep up. They made it out of the woods before midday. She kept them going as quickly as they could once they were in the open. They could all see Corslan in distances.

"That is an evil place," one of the boys said as they walked quickly. The sun glittered off the river down below. "It was a beautiful view to look at, but it is Kybon's land. No good has ever come from that place!"

The short dark-haired boy who had argued with Peter the day before was walking behind the speaker. He kicked the speaker in the back of his leg. "What would a country boy like you know of Corslan? You have never been there!"

Before the other boy could respond, Aden jerked the darkhaired boy out of line and pulled him to the front to keep an eye on him. Victoria thought the boy had a strange and familiar look in his eyes.

"What is your name, boy?" Aden demanded. The boy had a strong resemblance to a family from Corslan.

"Jeps!" was the boy's mumbled response.

"I am keeping an eye on you, Jeps! You have a chance at making friends here! So if I were you, I would keep my mouth closed. That will be safest for you!" Aden said. Victoria wondered what those words met. Aden obviously knew something about this boy's identity that she didn't.

As the sun began to set, Victoria told Aden to ask if the rest of the boys wanted to stop or if they wanted to keep going. They were only about two hours from the caves. After a lot of arguing, it was agreed that they should keep going. It was Peter who convinced the skeptics. "If we keep going, we will get to sleep in a cave tonight! We won't have to sleep in the snow. I would be glad to have warm feet tonight!" he had said. There was a resounding sound of agreement.

So they pushed on as the sun set and the cold night air set in around them. Victoria pulled her cloak tighter around her neck and pulled the hood over her head. She thought it best to stay as warm as possible. She did not want to admit that she would easily take ill, but she knew it was better to stay healthy.

It had been dark a little over an hour when Victoria and her crew reached the hills and the rocky terrain leading to the caves. Cornelius had put his oldest boy, Steck, on watch that night. He saw them coming in the moonlight.

"Mr. Cornelius, sir, the second group is in sight!" Steck yelled.

Cornelius ran over to the edge of the hills and looked down. He could tell Victoria was in the lead. He jogged quickly back to the first cave where his boys had set up camp. He grabbed the first three boys he saw.

"Hey, you three grab a torch each and come with me." He grabbed his own torch and jogged down to Steck. "Stay on watch. Those three coming and I are going to lead the next group up. It is dangerous in the dark on those rocks."

Cornelius climbed carefully down the hill with the three boys behind him. They didn't need any more direction; they had already figured out that they were to light the way up the hill. Two of them hustled to one side of the path while the third stayed on the side that Cornelius was on. They made it just as Victoria rode up to the hill's edge. She pulled her horse to a stop and dismounted.

Cornelius reached out his hand to help her. But she ignored it. She would protect herself against the cold, but she would refuse his help. She was perfectly capable of taking care of herself. Her anger with him had only subsided a little since the morning. She walked over and stood next to Aden. The two of them watched as Cornelius and the three boys with lanterns took turns leading Victoria's boys one by one up the hill and to the flat land leading to the caves.

Peter went up last of the group. He introduced himself to Cornelius on the way up. "Sir, I am Peter, and I would like to tell you that I am willing to help you and the other leaders in any way I can."

"Um, thanks," Cornelius said. He returned to Victoria and Aden alone. Before he could utter a word of welcome, Victoria spoke rather coldly.

"How do we get the horses up there in the dark?"

"I don't even get a hello?" he asked, slightly annoyed.

"Answer the question, Cornelius. It has been a long ride, and I am very tired. And since you think I need to get lots of sleep, I want to get my horse *stabled*, so I can do just that," she said in a tone Cornelius had never heard her use before.

"I take it you told her I asked you to keep an eye on her," he said, turning angrily to Aden.

"Oh, so you thought I wouldn't figure it out! I have to be told things. I will tell you the same thing I told him! You are not king yet, Cornelius, and if you keep acting as if you are in charge of my life, you won't be king!"

"Lower your voice! My watchmen can probably hear you."

"You still haven't answered my question about the horse," she said stubbornly.

Cornelius opened his mouth to argue but then thought better of it. He turned and jogged to the edge of the hill. "Steck!" he yelled up.

"Yes, sir?"

"Send Athine down here to fetch Mark's horse."

"Right away, sir."

Cornelius called for the soldier and waited until the smallish boy started picking his way down the hill before he turned back to Victoria and Aden. "Athine is coming for the horse! I want you to go with him. I want to talk to Aden alone."

"Why? So you can plan more ways of having him spy on me and make sure I am being a good girl and not getting sick?" Victoria retorted.

"No, there are other things to be discussed!" Cornelius said harshly.

"You two are to discuss nothing unless I am here. I am tired of the secrets. Whatever you need to speak to him about can wait until tomorrow when Rupert and Bartholomew arrive."

As she finished speaking, Athine arrived in the light of Cornelius's torch. Victoria recognized him as the stable boy from Bale. She didn't remember his name being Athine. He quietly took the reins of the horse and began leading Joyful away from the hard path up the hill. Victoria watched as Athine led the horse to a smaller path that sloped downward. From the torchlight, she could tell that the path curved upward and around the hill.

"There is flatter land that way and some grass under the light snow. Rupert told me to have Athine stable the horses there. He has an amazing ability with horses. Rupert said Thunderstorm was obedient to him," Cornelius said.

"That is great, but you are changing the subject!"

"Maybe the subject needs to be changed. You are mad. We will discuss this when you are..." He stopped because the look on her face let him know that he was only making things worse.

"When I am what? What, Cornelius, calmer, more rational? Maybe when I have had more sleep?"

"I am sorry," Cornelius said in a futile effort to appease her. Aden tried to stifle a laugh by pretending to cough.

"What's funny?" Victoria asked, turning on her heels and glaring at Aden.

"Nothing," he said quickly.

"Aden," Cornelius spoke, "maybe you should head up the hill and check on Victoria's boys, make sure they are settled in and all. Then replace Steck on watch."

"Only if that is okay with the princess," Aden said, winking at Victoria.

She nodded. He laughed again and walked up the hill in the dark. Victoria watched him as he climbed carefully up the hill. He made it look very easy. Cornelius watched her and then Aden. He knew he looked like a klutz even in daylight.

"I hope he doesn't fall!" he said, pretending to be unimpressed by the ease in which Aden climbed and then disappeared up the hill.

"He is much too sure-footed. Unlike you. Maybe I should make him my king," she said, watching Cornelius's reaction carefully.

"He is already married!" he said quickly.

"That didn't stop my father or many other men. Why should I follow the rules because I am a woman? I can marry whomever I want regardless of whether or not he is already married."

"I think this whole queen thing has gone to your head."

"And it hasn't gone to yours?" she said. Then she took a deep breath and continued. "Cornelius, I know that you mean well, but I have to be able to take care of myself if I am going to take care of this country. I can't be in the habit of depending on you."

"But I am just trying to protect someone I love. Is that so wrong?" he said. They heard Aden sending Steck to sleep in the distance above them.

"Very well, I will admit that my health is not as good as some people's, but it is hard for me to admit that. You have known me long enough to know that I don't like being sick. I will take care of myself if for no other reason than that."

"You promise you will not push yourself too far. I know you. You want to do everything. If you promise me you will take care not to get sick, I will promise not to worry or have other people spy on you. And I am sorry. I should have told you my concern, not Aden."

She waited a few seconds before she responded, mainly because she was enjoying watching him try to worm his way out of trouble. But she knew that she loved him even if he was overprotective. "I promise," she said and took his hand as they started up the hill together.

"You don't really want to marry Aden, do you?"

"Well, he is cute, but well, personally, I like the fact that you can't climb this hill without slipping?"

"Really, why is that?"

"Because I like knowing that you need my help as much as I need yours." She tugged on his hand, and he allowed her to lead him up the hill.

Peter had been right in his belief that sleeping in the cave would be better. All the boys slept better that night. Many of them slept in the back of the cave where there was very little light. There was no wind, so they actually stayed warm under their blankets.

Victoria slept alone again, but she felt better, knowing that Cornelius was near. Her anger with him had completely dissipated. She fell asleep with the realization that she could not stay mad at him for very long especially if he were within her reach.

It was after midday when Rupert's group arrived at the caves. Rupert had not slept well the night before. There was something or someone wrong in the group. He told Victoria and Cornelius about it in the second cave that they had decided to use as the officers' headquarters.

"Something doesn't feel right," Rupert said quietly.

"What do you mean? Things were fine when we got back from the cave, weren't they?" Victoria asked.

"Yes, it started after your group left. One of your boys is a spy! Did you tell them anything?"

"Peter announced to the group that you are a sorcerer," she replied.

"Was there an argument?"

"Yes, one of the other boys, Jeps, argued with him. Oh yeah, and Peter is a keeper of the powers, but he kept that quiet and the fact that I am too."

"I will be talking to both of them discreetly."

Just then Aden came in and told them another group was arriving. Victoria left to go help. Cornelius turned to go with her, but Rupert pulled him back.

"Watch out for Victoria. Her life is in danger. We both know that if she dies Kybon loses his powers. I am wondering now who else knows that. It was good that you told Aden to guard her."

"She found out about that and got very angry with me."

"I know."

"How?"

"I dreamed it! I am clairvoyant after all, but it seems only in my sleep," Rupert said sheepishly. "It has happened before but only when the person has stronger emotions than normal. I guess it is part of those gut feelings I get. I only got her side because you, I am happy to say, are still not readable."

"Good, because my secrets will kill us all."

"I know. Let's go before Victoria notices we are talking without her, but remember, stay on alert and don't trust Peter or that Jeps kid."

"What about Aden? I don't trust him much."

"That is because Victoria thinks he is cute, not because he is on the wrong side. Be careful not to let your emotions impair your judgment! Aden is a good man, and he is loyal to the king and therefore to us."

Rupert finished talking and hurried out of the cave. Cornelius stood in the dark for a moment, thinking about what he had just been told. He sighed and took the small ring out of his pocket. Maybe he would ask Victoria to wear it on a string around her neck as a reminder of their betrothal.

By the nightfall the next day, all the troops were at the caves. Malachi arrived with fresh supplies. Dried meats and breads were in ample supply in case the hunting near the caves was unsuccessful.

CHAPTER 21

Life at the Caves

Soon they all settled into a routine. The boys stayed divided by groups. Every week, each group had a chore.

Bartholomew was growing stronger as a leader. By the end of the second week, his group, though they were the smallest, was able to do their chores very well and without complaint and sometimes even faster than the larger groups.

After two weeks of life in the caves, Cornelius and Rupert found Victoria sitting in the far back of the second cave watching the sunset through the hole in the cave's wall.

"Are you all right?" Cornelius asked, leaning in and hugging her frame. He kissed the top of her head.

"I was just thinking over a few things," she said quietly, looking up at him.

"What are you thinking about?" Cornelius said.

"About what would happen if we just went home. I am not sure I want to do this anymore. Can we quit if we want to, or is there some force that governs our actions?"

"I don't know if we could quit if we wanted to, but we are meant to do this."

"But why? Who says we three have to save the world!"

"No one said we *have* to, but we can. Or at least Rupert can. And you, Victoria, are the heir to the throne. I know in my heart that none of us will be happy unless we see this through."

"But can I choose to walk away?" Rupert asked. "What if I don't want this?"

"I am sure we can all walk away, but what kind of life would we have or our kids have with Kybon in charge? Especially knowing that we could have stopped him. We could have made things better," Cornelius argued but in a gentle manner.

"Maybe we should discuss this with Adrian. He talks about fate and a higher power," Victoria said quietly. The other two nodded.

Adrian had many tasks at the caves, but one of them and the most important was a religious service he held near the makeshift stables ones a week. Only a few of the boys attended, but it was important to those who did. Victoria knew there was a higher power governing them. But she had never been to any religious ceremony to honor a deity. She decided that she would make time to go and listen to Adrian speak about a god she wanted now more than ever to learn about. Aden and Peter both attended the service. It would be a few days until the next meeting, but she would go.

Before anyone could speak again, they heard footsteps behind them in the cave. Rupert broke the silence. He was not clairvoyant when he was awake, but he had learned to listen carefully to the world around him. He could tell by the sound of the footfalls that it was Malachi coming toward them.

"Malichi wants to discuss something with us. I am guessing Mark's hunting party," Rupert said.

Malichi came up to them carefully in the dimming light. "I wish to speak with you, Mark," he said.

"I know, Malachi. Everything is ready. Aden is an avid hunter."

"I am worried about the rains. It is beginning to rain earlier in the days. We have enough supplies to survive only a few days without fresh meat. Randolph's group met with little success.

"I think we will do all right. If we don't, we will think up something."

"All right, I will leave it in your hands, but tell your boys to stay clear of Corslan. I don't want the city alerted to our presence just yet."

"I know. I have heard bad things about that place."

"It is an evil city! It is Kybon's main stronghold," Rupert interjected.

"Yes, and if they decide to attack, we have nowhere to run except over the mountain," Malachi said.

"I am working on an escape plan should we need it," Rupert continued.

Victoria stood up with the help of Cornelius because she had been sitting for nearly an hour and her feet were asleep. Malachi nodded quickly and walked carefully back toward the front of the cave.

"Rupert, I am making Peter and Jeps stay here. I don't trust Jeps. And I am nearly positive that Peter is Colin's keeper," Victoria said.

"Yes, both boys have connections to Corslan. I will keep them occupied."

"Thank you!"

The next morning, Aden and Victoria awoke their boys before sunrise. Aden divided them into groups of four. He wasn't in any group. They were all put on strict orders to stay away from Corslan. The first four days of the hunt were good for the group. They met with really good success, but the fifth day dawned cold with dark rain clouds heavy in the sky. Victoria and Aden took a small group of seven boys out but left the others to help with protecting the camp against the weather.

Aden's group killed three elk before the storm hit. Victoria's party was only able to kill one. Aden and Victoria met up near the edge of the hills just as the rain began to fall. "I think we have enough for today. Let's head back before the storm soaks us," Victoria said quickly.

Aden agreed and gave the order to get back up the hill. So the sixteen of them began to climb up the muddy path. The four strongest boys carried the dead animals in what would now be known as the fireman's carry on their shoulders as they climbed.

Victoria was sixth in the line. She was about halfway up when she heard a scream behind her. She looked back and saw the last two boys in line had slipped back down the hill. Without thinking about it, she turned and hurried back down the hill as the rain began to fall in blinding sheets that stung when it collided with the skin. One of the boys, Kelvin, was hurt. The other boy, George, was getting to his feet as she reached them.

"Kelvin, are you all right?" she said as panic began to rise in her voice.

Kelvin responded with a groan and pointed to his leg. Victoria could tell as she looked at his left leg that is was broken. There was no way he would be able to climb the narrow muddy trail.

"George, Kelvin's leg is broken. Can you help me carry him up?"

"Should we get help?" George asked quickly.

Before she could respond, Rupert appeared from behind them. Aden and Malachi were with him. They were calling to Mark and the boys in the pelting rain, but the loudness of the storm drowned out their voices.

"Wait, let me splint his leg before we move him!" Malachi yelled finally in earshot from only a foot or so away. The others watched as he tied three sturdy pieces of wood tightly to Kelvin's leg. His hands were steady, and the string didn't slip once even though it was soaked through.

As soon as he was done with the splint, Malichi beckoned for help, and the five of them picked up the small boy and struggled up the hill. Rupert was in the lead, groping the hill with his hand and walking crouched down as they climbed. The cold rain soaked through their clothing to their skin.

When they got to the top, there were several others waiting to take Kelvin from them. They handed him off to the others, who brought him to the cave. The five of them hurried just behind the injured boy. Victoria dropped to the ground by the fire, shivering and exhausted.

"Quickly get your wet clothes off. You will warm up faster," Malachi said to everyone who was soaked through.

All of them began to strip but Victoria.

"Mark, you will catch your death if you stay wet," Malachi said in an exasperated tone.

"I...I p...prefer to st...st...stay in my cl...clothes," she said through chattering teeth while she waved off Cornelius as he came to help her pull off her wet clothes before he realized the conundrum.

Rupert was still half-dressed. Without saying a word, he grabbed her and her leather pack and pulled her back out into the rain. She caught on quickly and mustered her little remaining strength and ran quickly with him to the second cave. She stripped out of her wet clothes while he worked quickly to build a fire. In about five minutes, she was dressed again in dry clothes and lying by the very small fire. Rupert ran back to the other cave for dry wood because she only had kindling in her pack.

Cornelius helped by bringing over dry bedding. The other boys caught in the rain were brought over to the second cave in their underclothes. Then they changed into dry clothes. The rain was icy, and the boys were nearly hypothermic.

The rain continued all day and into the night. Victoria and the boys stayed in the second cave. She was warm and dry, but the damage was done. She began to cough less than an hour after she came into the caves. Cornelius stayed near her, but he was careful not to give away their relationship.

By morning Victoria, George, and Kelvin all had fever. Rupert had over the weeks used many of the herbs he had gotten from Raven. Malachi knew a few remedies for fever, but supplies were hard to come by.

"We have to barter for the service of a doctor in Corslan," said Malachi on the morning of the third day after the three got sick. Their conditions were not improving and others were starting to get sick.

"No, Corslan is an evil place. Their doctors will betray us," Rupert said.

"We may have already been betrayed!" Cornelius said quietly as he walked into the cave with Aden at his heels.

"What do you mean?" Malachi asked.

"Sirs, I just caught Jeps and Peter sneaking out of camp. I think they have left before. Jeps is from Corslan. He said he just wanted to see his family. He claims he said nothing about where we were. I am not sure I believe him," Aden said.

"Rupert, you should talk to him and see what you can tell," Cornelius said.

"I might, but Malachi is right. We need a doctor. It has been three days. George and Kelvin are getting better, but Mark is not improving.

"I think that we are not facing an epidemic, but we do not have the means to help Mark's condition. Does he get sick a lot?" Malichi asked.

Rupert and Cornelius looked at each other intently. Victoria was lying near them. They were not sure how much she could hear, but they both knew that she would not like being looked at as sickly. But before either of them could answer, she spoke quietly from her sick bed.

"Yes, sickliness runs in my family. My uncle knew the signs of me getting sick, but I don't think he could have helped with this one. But I would rather die than make a deal with Corslan." There was a great deal of brevity in her weakened voice.

"Well, the nearest city from here save Corslan is either Thornvalley or Pallen, depending on what road we take," Cornelius said.

"Mark should go to Pallen. It is where we need to end up, anyway," Aden said.

"Well, it is where he needs to end up," Rupert said.

"Yes, I am afraid that we need at least two of you here. If Corslan does attack, we need strong, trained men," said Malachi.

"Look, we have other business to attend to now. I say we check his condition and decide in the morning," Aden said.

"I agree. I want to talk with Jeps," Rupert said quickly.

Everyone left the cave except Cornelius. He sat next to Victoria and listened to her breathing. He took out the last of the herbs Rupert had ground up. He mixed them in three small cups next to the fire. He gave the sleeping herbs to Kelvin and George first. He waited until he could hear their steady rhythmic but labored breathing, and then he spoke quietly to Victoria.

"Are you awake?" he asked, running his figures through her short brown hair.

"Yes," she said in a raspy voice.

"Do you want to go to Pallen? Are you up for a trip?"

"Yes, I need sleep to get better, but I can't sleep well out here alone."

"The other two boys are asleep already. I can sleep next to you tonight, if you want."

"That would be nice, but someone might notice. Besides, the last thing we need is for you to get sick too." She finished with a coughing fit.

"Don't talk if it makes you cough."

"I am fine!"

"I know, but I worry about you. And it is not because I...well, I love you, and I just wish we could be done with all this."

She pulled herself up and leaned into his arms. "No, you were right before. We can make this world a better place, so we should."

"But at the cost of our lives?"

"Cornelius, I am not going to die from this sickness. It is not as bad as it has been in the past."

"I don't like watching you in pain."

"Honey, if you are going to marry me, you better get used to it." She finished in another coughing fit.

"Here, drink the sleeping herbs. We will spare someone to get you to Pallen. I am needed here for now."

"I know. Send Aden."

"Why, because he is good-looking?"

"Ha-ha! No! Because he should be in Pallen with his family."

"Family?"

"Yeah, he has a child he has not seen in several months. I would give anything to have known my father. Aden and his family are making a great sacrifice for us!"

"I know. Lie back down now and go to sleep. You need as much strength as you can to make the trip tomorrow."

"Aye, and, Cornelius, I love you too."

She was asleep in about two minutes. Her breathing was raspy and labored. Cornelius covered her with her cloak and the blanket from his bed role. He got up and slowly walked out of the cave to find Aden.

There was a small crowd of boys standing near the mouth of the first cave. Cornelius could hear yelling, but he could not tell whose voice it was. He quickened his pace to find out what was going on. He reached the crowd just as a Jeps came rushing out of the cave with a sword drawn on Randolph, who appeared to be unarmed. No one seemed willing to help; boys just stood by and watched.

"You know nothing of my life!" Jeps screamed.

"I know enough not to trust you!" Randolph said in a scathing voice. He moved his head slightly in both directions and then drew his own sword. But before he could swing it, Rupert came running from the cave. Cornelius didn't think. He ran forward and disarmed Jeps while pulling him out of the reach of Randolph's sword. Rupert did the same thing to Randolph except he pushed him to the ground. Then drew his own sword to keep him there.

"What is going on here?" Cornelius asked as he held Jeps in a tight hold around his shoulders.

"He says I went to Corslan and told them we are here!"

"Did you?" Cornelius asked.

"I told him no already!" Jeps yelled, pointing his head toward Rupert.

"Well, I was not there, and the story changes with every person who speaks, so tell me," Cornelius said.

Jeps breathed out. Cornelius loosened his grip but only enough for Jeps to breath fully.

"I went to Corslan to see my mother. I didn't tell her where we are staying, not that she would tell anyone. I haven't seen her in nearly a year," Jeps said. Cornelius felt a quiver run through Jeps. The boy was holding back tears.

Cornelius had acquired many secrets through his tenure as a messenger. He knew that Jeps was born and raised in Corslan to a mistress of Kybon, but his mother was not evil or interested in helping Kybon. Randolph, on the other hand, had been raised by a family that were suspected of being loyal to Kybon. He knew now that Randolph was the spy, not Jeps. Jeps was just a lonely fourteen-year-old boy who missed his mother. Though if he were actually Kybon's son, he would be a powerful sorcerer one day in the not-so-distant future.

He loosened his grip completely and stepped in front of Jeps with his back to Rupert, who was still keeping Randolph on the ground with the point of his sword.

"I believe you," Cornelius said.

"Thank you!" Jeps said meekly.

"Now go back to the cave and get some sleep." He turned toward the crowd of boys watching and listening. "That goes for all of you."

Jeps walked slowly past Cornelius and Rupert. The other boys all went back inside as Jeps stopped at the mouth of the cave and turned back and looked at Rupert.

"Yes, I believe you too!" Rupert said before Jeps could articulate his question.

Jeps didn't seem at all surprised that Rupert didn't have to ask. He simply smiled and shuffled his feet as he walked back into the cave.

Cornelius walked up and stood over Randolph, who was next to Rupert. "Should we let him up?" he asked, smirking at Rupert.

"No. We *should* kill him, but I suppose we can't!" Rupert replied.

"How much does he know?"

"Enough that we need to get her out of here tonight."

Cornelius realized that Rupert was not making an effort to hide Victoria's identity. He realized that Randolph knew a lot more than he thought. It was now apparent their situation was more precarious than he had originally thought. He was not sure what to do next. Should they let Randolph go? He decided to prolong the conversation.

"Why can't we kill him?" Cornelius asked.

"Because it is bad luck to kill an unarmed man," Rupert said.

Just as he finished speaking, Malachi walked up to them from somewhere below. Aden was not far behind him. "I will take care of Randolph. He is my responsibility anyway," Malachi said in a strong, dominant voice.

Malichi bent down as Rupert lifted his sword from its place a millimeter above Randolph's Adam's apple. Malachi forced the betrayer to his feet and led him by his neck off in the direction of one of the much smaller caves.

"Now what do we do?" Cornelius asked, angry with himself for missing it before now.

"We need to get Victoria out of here. Randolph knows, and I am willing to bet he has other spies with him who know too," Rupert said.

"You and I are needed here now more than ever. So that leaves you, Aden," Cornelius said, turning his head toward the taller man standing next to him. "She wants you to take her, anyway."

"Really? Why?"

"She thinks you are good-looking or something," Rupert said, laughing and pushing Cornelius's shoulder.

"She wants you to take her because you are familiar with Pallen, and she wants you home with your child," Cornelius said, shoving Rupert back who was caught off guard. Rupert fell to the ground.

"I would be very glad to see my family again. And you are right. You are needed here more than I am. I was sent to protect her. So I need to go where she goes," Aden answered as he gave Rupert a hand to pull himself up.

"Who sent you to protect her? She can protect herself. And if anyone else is needed, it should be me!" Cornelius said very heatedly.

Rupert put his hand on his friend's shoulder to steady him. "Calm down, Corn. You know Aden's family is the king's blacksmith. And you know that his mother was Victoria's mother's best friend. He was nearly five when she was sent to live with Thomas. I was only kidding about her thinking he is handsome. Fighting with him is not going to help any of us, least of all her."

There was silence for a moment. Cornelius did not want to answer, and Aden was not sure he should respond.

It was Aden that broke the silence by going back to the original topic. "So I will take her out of here, but where? She is sick and Pallen is four days away. She needs a doctor now."

"Shh! Don't speak for a second," Rupert said quickly.

Cornelius and Aden stood in awkward silence while Rupert closed his eyes and covered his ears. After nearly a minute passed, he opened his eyes and spoke. "Take her to Thornvalley first. It is a little closer. Kylan will be there. She knows a doctor that we can trust. She will accompany you and Victoria to Pallen when Victoria has recovered her strength."

Aden looked at Rupert in awe. "Did you just read her thoughts from very far away?"

"No, today is her birthday, so she has her full powers. One of them is speaking to those of us receptive to it from far away. I am still five months from my birthday, so it is her powers, not mine."

"Well, I guess we should get ready. I will draw you a map to Thornvalley, Aden. Did she say where in Thornvalley to meet her?" Cornelius asked.

"No, but you don't need to draw him a map. He is taking Thunderstorm," Rupert replied.

"What? I can't take your horse." Aden said. He knew that Thunderstorm was important to Rupert.

"You have to. He is the only one in the group big enough to ride two people and the gear for that far. Plus he knows the way. You will be safe with him," Rupert said in a slightly mysterious voice.

"I guess I cannot say no then," Aden said.

"No. Meet me down at the stable grounds in a few minutes. I will go and tell Thunder what is going on. And, Cornelius, don't feel bad about not knowing the spy was Randolph. I didn't see it either."

"How did you know that? You can't read my mind, can you?" Cornelius asked with a hint of panic in his voice.

"I can't *read* your mind, but we have been friends our whole lives. I can read your face," he said as he walked off into the darkness toward the trail to the stables just down the hill.

"If anything happens to her, I will kill you," Cornelius told Aden, but there was no real malice in his voice now.

"Fair enough, I guess," Aden replied. "If you kill me though, you will have to take care of my family."

"Maybe I won't kill you then! I will just maim you or something. I don't want to take care of a woman I don't know!"

"But you know my wife well. You used to dance with Joanna at the tavern when you were in Pallen delivering messages."

"Joanna is you wife?"

"Yes, two years now."

"She is very pretty, but I like Victoria more, even with her hair short, but I hope you disagree."

"I do! Joanna is very beautiful. She told me before I left to tell you hi for her. She wonders if you are still very handsome, like you were at fourteen."

"She said that?"

"Yes, she thinks you are handsome. Victoria thinks I am handsome. I say we are even. And women are very strange."

Cornelius laughed too hard to answer. But he shook Aden's hand and sent him toward the stable. Cornelius headed back to Victoria in the cave. He was not comfortable with her unconscious and unguarded. When he stepped inside the cave, Bartholomew was sitting next to her.

"Barth, you should be sleeping."

"I was guarding her. There are evil people around. And she is my sister. It is the least I can do."

"That is noble, but things will be very bad if you are both dead."

"I can protect myself, Cornelius."

"I know but you have the same father. I don't want you sick too. Whether either of you like it or not, you both have to protect yourselves against nature more than other people. Now go on to bed. Sleep helps fight sickness. I will watch until Aden comes for her."

"I wanted to tell her good-bye."

"Why? You will see her again. You only need to say good-bye to people when you will not see them again for a long time."

"But what if I don't see her again?"

"You will, Barth. Now go to sleep. If Corslan's soldiers attack, we will need you."

"Aye, have a good night, brother-in-law," he said as he walked quickly out of the cave.

Once he was alone, Cornelius took out his blank book and began writing down everything that happened. He did this mostly to keep his mind occupied until Aden was ready for Victoria.

Two hours later, Aden and Rupert came into the cave. Rupert was holding an unlit torch in one hand, and he had a large leather pack slung over his shoulder. In his other hand, he had Victoria's sword and two other beautifully crafted swords. Aden had a smaller pack and his bedroll.

"How much of the sleeping herbs did you give her?" Rupert asked quietly.

"A spoonful in that cup full of water," Cornelius said, pointing to the largest of the three cups by the fire.

"Aye, we need to wake her up to get her on the horse. She will refuse to be on a litter."

"She can ride even while she is sick. Thomas made sure of that," Cornelius said.

"Can she ride asleep?" Aden asked in jest.

"Probably," they both said at once.

"Don't you have wake-up herbs?" Aden asked.

"No, but she will wake up soon enough. But we may have to carry her down the hill to Thunderstorm. And we have to be very quiet. Malachi will not be able to keep Randolph detained for long."

"Let's get going then," Cornelius said. He leaned over and kissed Victoria's feverish forehead as he ran his fingers through her hair and smiled softly. "I will see you soon."

Rupert picked up the unlit torch in his belt and put down the swords. "Aden and I will carry her. You roll up the bedding and carry the swords. Meet us at the stable, and be careful on your way down. It is still slippery from the rains."

"Good to know," Cornelius said.

It took them twenty minutes to carefully get down the hillside. By the time Cornelius arrived two minutes later, Victoria was beginning to stir.

"Time to leave?" she asked quietly.

Cornelius answered her, "Yes, you are riding Thunderstorm with Aden to a doctor. I will meet you in Pallen when I know things are safe here."

"I know. Kiss me so we can leave."

He kissed her as she mounted the horse slowly. Rupert carefully attached the leather packs to a blanket on the horse. Thunderstorm didn't like it, but he was willing to put up with the discomfort to get Victoria safely away. Once the two extra swords were secured, Rupert handed Victoria hers. She attached it to her belt. Then Aden mounted the horse.

"Everything is ready. Don't light the torch until you are sure that no one will see what direction you have gone," Rupert told Aden, then he looked his horse in the eye. "Take care of them, boy!"

The horse gave a nod, made a low sound, and started forward slowly and smoothly. He walked in a direction toward Thornvalley but not on any path. It was faster and safer to stay off the roads.

Cornelius and Rupert watched them go. It was a moonless night, so it was not long before Thunderstorm was out of sight. They stood waiting quietly in the cold night air. The thick cloud cover made Cornelius worry that Aden and Victoria may encounter rain. Rain would not help her condition.

"They will be all right, Corn, but come on, we need go and see what is happening with Randolph," Rupert said.

Cornelius sighed. For the first time since this journey started, he felt truly scared that things might not work out the way he hoped. Their walk back to the caves in the dark was hard for both of them, not because they could not see the path, but because Rupert was just as scared as Cornelius.

"How did I not know? Maybe I am not clairvoyant at all. I should have dreamed it or felt it in him when I walked past him," Rupert said quietly.

"Rupe, he is a spy for Kybon. There is probably some special magic that protects him from being found out."

"It couldn't have been a good spell because it quit working there at the end. I should have seen it sooner."

"Don't be too hard on yourself. I know Randolph's family history, and I didn't suspect him either. I think we both just wanted to trust him. I guess I believed him when he said he changed."

"What exactly did he do in the past?"

"I am not sure exactly, but I believe he aided Colin and Kybon in the plot to kill your father," Cornelius said, realizing he should have told Rupert his suspicions sooner.

"Wait, that is the same Randolph?"

"Yes, I think so. I could be completely wrong. I was eleven the last time I saw him in an inn in Kelter talking about it. He looks a little different now, so I didn't trust my memory."

"Aye, so we both slipped up. I guess we need to trust ourselves more."

They both fell silent as they got within earshot of the caves. Randolph was detained in one of the much smaller caves. Malachi met them at the entrance to the first cave. He told them to sleep in the second cave with the sick boys. They would deal with Randolph in the morning.

CHAPTER 22

Those Still at the Caves

Neither of them slept well that night. It was one of the worst nights they both experienced since the adventure had stated.

Randolph was allowed to eat among the others at breakfast. "Where did she go? She left with Aden in the night. I bet that is a blow to your ego, Cornelius!" Randolph said as scathingly as possible.

Cornelius said nothing. He knew that Randolph was trying to get a rise out of him. But there were more important things to worry about. Jeps was being ostracized by the other boys now.

Cornelius found him sitting alone near the lookout post facing the road from Bale. "Jeps, are you all right?" he asked.

"I will be I think. I am sad, though. I was finally making friends, and now the other boys won't talk to me."

"Why not?"

"Because I am from Corslan."

"That is not a good reason."

"Cornelius, Corslan *is* an evil place. The people there steal from other cities and kill people who stand in their way. I grew up there because that is where my mother was born, but she is a good person. She doesn't agree with their ways, but she can't leave."

"Why not?"

"She had a child outside of marriage. It doesn't matter to anyone there that Kybon took her by force, then left her there to take care of me alone."

Cornelius made a sound but said nothing.

"I know there isn't much to say to that. I want to help you and Rupert. All I have ever really wanted is to find a place for my mother and me away from Corslan."

"Well go and get her then. She can come with us when we leave."

"Really?" Jeps said with great skepticism in his voice.

"Yes, look, I know it is hard to trust us when you have been betrayed your whole life, but you need to learn to trust some people."

"I don't trust you! But I can see that you are good men. A double cross by you is better than her fate if she stays in Corslan! I will go for her. How is Mark? I mean, what is his, I mean, her real name anyway?" Jeps finally looked up when he asked the final question.

"Victoria."

"Right! Is Victoria safely away? Randolph is going to go after her. But he won't find her. Pallen is a big city. I have been there once. I wanted to find my father, but I could never get to the palace. It is too well guarded."

"There are ways around the guards. And yes, she is away and not to Pallen."

"Good because Peter and I were put on watch last night by Malachi. We could tell that they didn't head for Pallen, but we decided to tell everyone that is where they went."

"How could you tell what direction they went? Last night was the darkest we have had in many weeks."

"I am going to be a sorcerer. I think one of my gifts is really good vision."

"Good to know. Well, you and Peter tell Randolph what you want, and I promise I will do everything I can to help your mother."

"I would hug you, but Randolph might see," Jeps said, holding back tears of joy.

"Aye."

Without another word, Cornelius walked away toward the caves to find Rupert. Jeps got up from the ground slowly and walked even more slowly to the caves to find Peter.

At midday, by Rupert's request, Malachi sent Jeps and Peter to guard Randolph in his small makeshift prison. Jeps and Peter found Rupert and Cornelius in the second cave before they went.

"Rupert, thank you for trusting me," Jeps said. "And, Cornelius, can you draw up a fake map from here to Pallen so I can tell Randolph that I stole it? He doesn't know the way from here, and if we are lucky, he will be on foot, but he might try to steal a horse."

"All of the horses are secured, and Adrian and Athine and his cousin Lucas from Kelter are guarding them," Rupert said as he watched Cornelius quickly but carefully draw a map leading to the thickest part of the mountains and avoiding all civilizations.

"There, that should have him wandering for quite a while." Cornelius smirked. "Oh yeah, here take some of the food for him too. I don't want him coming back to steal food from us when our guard is down."

The boys took the food and walked to the other two boys guarding Randolph.

"We are your relief. Malachi needs your help with some other things," Jeps said.

"What's in the pack, dirt face?" said the taller of the two guards.

"None of your business! Now get lost before Malichi comes looking for you," Jeps said in his toughest voice.

"What if you are lying?" the tall one asked again.

"Malichi would have me in here next if I were," Jeps answered.

"Yeah, both of us!" Peter said.

The other two boys shrugged and scampered off toward the camp.

"Randolph, here we brought you a map and some food. Last night, the girl left with Aden. They went toward Pallen," Jeps said.

"If you are lying—" Randolph's voice was harsh.

"Why would I lie?" Jeps showed no fear when he spoke.

"I saw you talking to Cornelius this morning!" Randolph said.

"Well, yeah, I had to get him to trust me. How else was I gonna steal you a map and some food?"

"How do I know that they didn't give you this?" Randolph's skepticism was clear.

"Randolph, after the boy hurt himself hunting, we haven't been back out. There is very little food left here. Do you really think they would just hand over food to a criminal so you can more easily escape? I mean, it doesn't matter what way we saw them go, anyway. They have to go to Pallen. The girl is sick."

"I know! Kybon wants her alive—" Randolph sounded horrified that she might die.

"The first place they are going is to a doctor. They won't let her die, so you're off the hook for that one, but you should go quickly before Malachi realizes we are on watch," Jeps said.

Randolph thought about what he had just been told and then grabbed the map and food quickly. He ran off toward the trail back to Bale just as Rupert and Malachi came running in their direction. They were screaming for Randolph to stop. Rupert even pretended to chase him down but tripped before he could catch him. The other three ran to Rupert to make sure he was okay.

"I am fine. I just pretended to trip. I take it he took the bait," Rupert said in a quiet voice."

"Yeah, but there are other spies about. We need to leave here," Jeps said.

"We have to leave, anyway. A messenger from the sorcerer's council just showed up. He says that Mathew and his army have declared war. We will be trapped if the war is fought here," Malachi said sadly.

"A messenger? Is his name Colin?" Peter asked.

"Yes! He also said that you are not allowed to fight, Peter."

"That is my choice."

"Maybe! But right now, we need both of you to come help pack. We will be on march by tomorrow, and this time, we will all be going together."

"Where are we going?" Jeps and Peter asked together.

"There is a place called the Outerlands, which are the lands between Thornvalley and Pallen. That has been the sight of many battles, and it looks like there will be another one," Rupert said with sadness in his voice.

"But a war is pointless! Whoever wins will find himself a second puppet to Kybon," Jeps said quickly.

"I agree, but I am not sure there is much we can do to stop it yet," Rupert said.

"We will find a way to stop Kybon. My mother knows things that might help us."

"I know. Cornelius just left to go and get her from Corslan."

"What? Really? I was going to go."

"There is not time for you to go. He promised to help her, and he will."

Rupert clapped Jeps on the shoulder and walked away back to the caves.

Jeps stood in silence for a moment. He had never known anyone who made sure to keep promises. He smiled for the first time in days. "Maybe," he said, "I have finally met people I can call friends?"

Rupert turned around and came back. "Yeah, Jeps, we are your friends. I promise!"

Jeps's smile broadened.

"And that eyesight of yours is going to be very useful to us, so don't think for one minute that you aren't as good as us. Younger, yes! But one day, when you are eighteen, we will be equals!"

"Thank you!" Jeps said. He wasn't sure what else to say, but he was happy to have a place with them.

"I will keep you informed on what is happening!" Rupert said.

The rest of the day was spent packing up.

CHAPTER 23

Thornvalley

By nightfall, Thunderstorm and his riders reached the edge of Thornvalley. They had been traveling through rough hilly landscape most of the day. Just as the sun was going down, the horse stopped and whinnied loudly, waking Victoria out of her broken sleep.

"What?' she groaned.

"I think we are there!" Aden said softly.

Just then a dark hooded figure on a horse appeared from behind a tree. Aden could not tell if the person was male or female. He reached down and put his left hand on one of the swords in the side pack. But before he could draw it, he heard jovial laughter from behind the hood of the stranger.

"It would take more than a sword to kill a sorceress, even if you are the best swordsman in the kingdom," Kylan said happily as she pushed her hood back to reveal her smiling her face.

"Kylan, wow, I am so embarrassed! Rupert said that you would meet us here, but I guess I didn't realize I knew you."

"I guess I am going to have to tell your mother the next time I see her that you didn't remember your own cousin! But we can catch up later. We have to get Victoria to a doctor."

"Yes, she will be all right, though, won't she?"

"I don't know! I assume so."

"But you are a powerful sorceress!"

"I can read minds! Not the future. There are few who can read the future, and those who can are never certain to be right!" She reached out and took Thunderstorm's reins. Aden had not been using them because the horse had decided the way.

"I brought you a carrot, Thunderstorm," Kylan said as she leaned in from her horse to rub Thunderstorm's nose. He whinnied happily and allowed her to lead him to a small path that lead to Thornvalley.

They had not gone far on the path when a small house came into view. There was a fence made of jagged, uneven pieces of wood all the way around the house with a gate in front by the road, but it was closed and locked.

Kylan dismounted off her horse and walked quickly to the gate. She knocked twice. Within a few seconds, Aden heard the door to the house open. Thunderstorm was a tall horse, so from his seat on the horse's back, Aden could see over the fence. The man was wearing a cloak similar to Kylan's, but the hood was not over his head as Kylan's had been. In the dark, Aden could not tell any of the man's features other than he was very tall and thin. The man quickly opened the gate and beckoned them in.

Kylan took her horse's reins and led him in. Thunderstorm walked in behind her without being led. She tied her horse to a post on the side of the house. There was a cover on the post to protect against rain or snow. A small pile of hay flanked the poll under the awning. Thunderstorm stopped right in front of the steps that led to the door.

Aden carefully dismounted. He kept his hand on Victoria's side to keep her from falling off. Kylan and the tall man walked up and stood next to Aden on the first step. The three of them carefully lifted Victoria off the horse. She was drifting in an out of consciousness, but she knew what was happening, so she tried in her sick stupor to do what they told her. Once she was off the horse, the two men carried her inside.

Kylan took out the carrot from a pocket in her cloak and fed it to Thunderstorm. The horse nudged her face. Kylan then removed the blanket and packs from his back. When she was done, he walked to the hay by the other horse and began to eat. She went in the house without tying him up.

Aden and his new friend laid Victoria in a bed by the fire. There was a pot hanging over the flames. Victoria was still half-awake, and she could smell what was cooking in the fireplace. It was a kind of soup that was made from different herbs. Thomas cooked the same thing when she got sick as a child. She felt better already. She knew now that she would be back to her old self in only a few days. She relaxed in the soft bed and fell into a deep sleep.

Kylan removed the long black cloak as soon as the door closed. It was starting to warm up into spring, and the fire made the house comfortable. She walked quickly to Aden and pulled him to the table in the center of the room.

"Here is food ready for you. Garvan and I have already eaten."

"Thank you."

Aden was very hungry from the long ride. He was very grateful for the hot food. When he was finished eating, he helped Garvan and Kylan rouse Victoria enough to get some of the soup in her. Then Garvan gave Aden a warm drink and gestured for him to lie down in a bed on the other side of the room. Aden was asleep as soon as his head hit the pillow.

The next morning, Victoria awoke feeling better. She was still very sick, but her breathing was better and she was not as tired. She sat up and surveyed the small house.

She was by the fireplace, which was in the center of the back wall. The house was made up of only one large room. Above the fireplace was a mantle with many small figurines like the ones Thomas had. Some of them were the same! On the wall above the mantle was a large mirror with a very ornate framework. She could not make out what the exact design was, but it looked to be some sort of plant.

Directly across from her was Aden's bed. There was a small table in the back corner with only one chair. The table was covered with open books and loose pieces of parchment. Next to that was a back door. On the other side of the door was a pole where several colored cloaks were hanging. The rest of the house was bare with unadorned walls. Victoria wondered how much time Garvan actually spent here.

Just then Garvan came in the front door. He saw her sitting up and smiled. Aden was beginning to stir, and Kylan came in the back door carrying sprigs of a strange-looking plant.

"Ah, you are feeling better, I see," she said to Victoria.

"Yes, a little," she responded, her voice was hoarse and raspy.

"Breakfast will be done soon. Garvan, how are the horses?"

Garvan nodded his head and walked to a cupboard, where he began removing dishes for breakfast. Aden sat up and rubbed his eyes. He was still wearing his clothes from the night before except for his boots. He groggily put on his boots then offered to help with breakfast. Kylan asked him to help pull the table over to Victoria's bedside.

"You really need to stay in bed, Victoria, and I will not argue with you about it," Kylan said. Victoria knew it wasn't worth the effort, so she said nothing.

After breakfast, Garvan went back outside without warning. Aden watched him go.

"Does he talk at all?" he asked in a low voice to Kylan.

"Yes, but not often. He has lived alone for many years, so he only needs to talk when he is saying spells."

"I thought he was a doctor?"

"Well, actually, he is a shoemaker, but he is also a wizard."

"Why is a powerful sorceress in the company of a wizard? And how does that make him a doctor?"

"My powers are inherent and his are learned, but he has been learning magic for nearly forty years. I have been a sorceress for three days! He is a powerful friend to have in these tumultuous times. In addition, he has learned a great deal of remedies both magical and nonmagical."

"You are clairvoyant, right?"

"Yes. Rupert and Cornelius are all right. They are marching this way, though. War has been declared."

"What?"

"Nothing has started yet. I will keep you updated."

"Keep me updated too! After all they are my two best friends!" Victoria said from the bed.

The next few days were very interesting to Victoria. Garvan was completely silent while Kylan communicated for him. Victoria herself didn't even need to speak. Kylan would answer her questions or respond to her thoughts before she could speak. Aden had retreated to a corner of the room and rarely interacted with anyone.

The rain had become nearly constant. Victoria slept on and off. She drifted in and out of sleep while listening to the rain thud quietly on the thatched roof.

By dusk on the third day, Victoria's strength had returned. She helped Kylan cook dinner, and for the first time, she had a conversation with Kylan using words.

"Thank you for your help, Victoria. I have been a little overwhelmed this week."

"Really, I figured you were used to this sort of thing. You know, helping to take care of people like you did when we were in the clearing for the festival."

"Well, yeah, but my parents were there for one thing. I really miss them."

"Yeah, I know what you mean. I miss Uncle Thomas."

"I miss Dad's stories and Mom's advice."

"Well, can't you speak to them with your mind from here?"

"I can, but it isn't the same as talking. I mean I miss playing games with them. I miss being in their company. This is really my first time away from home," Kylan said sheepishly, looking at the ground. She sighed and continued. "And well, now things are different, and they will never be the same."

"Yes, things are changing, but, Kylan, we have to accept the changes, or we will be miserable for the rest of our lives, and for you, that is a very long time."

"I know, Victoria. I am glad we are friends. In all that has happened, I never told you that I am glad that you and Rupert and Cornelius are part of my life now. We can all accept the changes together."

"Thank you, I am glad to have met you too, but I guess you already knew that."

"Yes, I know a lot more than I want to right now. I am glad you got sick and I was sent here. When I am around more than five people, I hear too much at once, and I feel like I am going mad."

Victoria frowned and then hugged Kylan as she stirred the pot on the fire. "I am so sorry. I was so absorbed in my own thoughts that I guess I didn't really think about what you are going through. I mean, I figured it would be wonderful to be able to read minds and know what other people think, but I bet it takes some getting used to."

"Yes, I need a great deal more practice at not going crazy!" Kylan said in a voice that didn't hide her laughter.

"Well, we are all in this together."

Just then Aden came inside. He had been out in the rain helping Garvan fix the gate that had been broken by a strong gust of wind carrying a large tree limb. He had borrowed Kylan's cloak. The hood was pulled tightly over his head. The cloak dripped from the bottom and from the hood. He quickly pulled back the hood, but water still dripped from his soaked hair and streaked on his face as he walked over to them.

"The gate is fixed! It only took all day. What are you cooking? It smells really good," Aden exclaimed.

"Rabbit stew! There isn't much meat, though, or much vegetables, so I am afraid there will be meager rations tonight because Victoria has gotten her appetite back." Kylan laughed.

"Good thing Rupert packed some bread for us. I don't know how he managed it, but he wrapped it in some strange cloth that kept it fresh."

"Great! Now take off my cloak and hang it by the fire. We are leaving tomorrow, and I don't want to wear it wet."

"We are leaving tomorrow?" Victoria asked.

"Yeah, I think so, anyway. Bartholomew's troops reached the battlefield about five minutes ago. Rupert says that Cornelius is coming to get us. He wants to come too, but it looks like they can't spare him. And since I can't read Cornelius's mind, we won't know exactly when he will get here."

"How far away are they?"

"Not far actually, maybe half a day's ride in good weather."

"Then Cornelius will be here by morning if he leaves now," Victoria said.

"Probably sooner. He is riding on Thunderstorm, who knows the shortest way here.

"I thought Thunderstorm was here with us?" Victoria said.

"No, he went back to Rupert soon after we got here," Kylan said. "He was needed there, so he went. Now he is needed again, so he will be coming back. I can read his mind too. He thinks a bit differently, but he is quite remarkable. He may let me know when they approach, but he may not."

"So even now, with your full powers, you can't read Cornelius's mind?" Aden asked.

"No, there is very difficult magic on him to keep his secrets a secret. It is very important that messengers to the king be unreadable."

"That is too bad! It would be nice to know how he really feels about me," Victoria said sadly.

"What are you talking about?" Aden and Kylan said at once. Kylan was practicing blocking people's thoughts, so she wasn't sure what Victoria meant.

"I sometimes wonder if he wants to marry me just so he can be king!"

"No, Victoria, he loves you. I can tell that without reading his mind! It is written all over his face every time he looks at you," Kylan said.

"Really?"

"Yeah, Victoria, I see it too," said Aden. "Besides, he and Rupert and I were planning to make him king since we were kids. When he fell in love with you, I started to worry that he wouldn't want to be king anymore, and I would have to do it."

"Wait, explain that to me! How long have you had this planned?" Victoria asked half-laughingly.

"Well, we didn't exactly have it planned this way."

"I didn't know you two even knew each other before this!"

"Victoria, Corn is a messenger, so I have known him for many years. My father was the king's blacksmith, so we lived on the palace grounds. Cornelius used to come to my house to sleep before he would head home. It was always fun for me. He told me about all the places he had seen on the way to the palace. I didn't leave the palace much because we were busy keeping the weapons made. All I have are sisters. It was great to have a boy my own age to talk to.

"After a few visits, I learned that he was a friend of Oberon's son, so we started planning to overthrow Kybon and make Cornelius king. It was a fun plan as boys, and then we grew up. And he started staying other places in Pallen to stay safe. I got married, and he fell in love with you. I didn't know who you were, so I gave up hope on him. It looks like other people made plans too. So here we are now years later on a plot to overthrow Kybon and make you and him queen and king. We never really thought it would ever happen, especially not this way."

"I didn't realize you guys knew each other. I guess there is a lot he hasn't told me yet."

"Don't be upset. There hasn't been a lot of time. He truly loves you, and I know that as soon as we are done with this mess we are in, he will share more of his life with you."

"Thank you, Aden. I feel better now. I don't know why I am so insecure about him."

"Because you are human, Victoria. We are all insecure. I can read minds, and I still wonder if people are lying to me without knowing it. I guess we just have to trust ourselves and the people we love," Kylan cut in.

"Yeah, or the people you almost love!" Victoria said with a grin.

"I am going to pretend that you didn't say that," Kylan said, unable to hide her blushing.

"What are you two giggling about?" Aden asked, confused.

"Nothing," Kylan said quickly.

"Oh, I am teasing her about liking someone!"

"Oh, Rupert right?"

"Maybe!" Kylan said, blushing severely.

"You two would make a powerful couple. And it fits. You and I have known each other for years. You always wanted to help overthrow Kybon, but you wanted someone else to actually do it. I wonder if this was all planned for us or if it just worked out this way," Aden said in a serious tone.

Kylan was no longer laughing or blushing. "There are forces at work in our lives we as humans can't understand. I am afraid to think about it. I am on the edge of sanity right now, anyway. Let's talk about it in ten years when we have our lives under control."

As Kylan finished speaking, Garvan came in the door. The sound of the pouring rain outside brought them back to the task at hand. Garvan carefully closed the door behind him but then rushed to the back of the room and went behind a curtain that had been hung for changing clothes. He came back stone dry in a matter of seconds.

"Garvan says it is time for dinner," Kylan said.

The four of them quickly set the table. Aden went to his pack in the corner and got the bread. Their meal was good, and surprisingly, they all got their fill.

Victoria lay awake, watching the fire that night. She wasn't sleepy after having slept for nearly three days. She listened to Aden snoring in his bed. Kylan was sleeping soundlessly in a chair, and Garvan was sitting at the table next to a tiny lamp, writing slowly and thoughtfully on a piece of paper. The scratching of the feather pen was beginning to lull Victoria to sleep.

Just as she was about to drift off into sleep, the scratching stopped. She opened her eyes and saw Garvan was standing over her. She sat up and looked at him intently.

"Yes?"

"Give this to Cornelius when he arrives...please," Garvan said in a very scratchy and low voice. Victoria could tell he was not used to normal speech. He spoke slowly because he had to think about each word as he said it. He handed her a thick envelope, but it was not sealed.

"Uh, sure. Are you going somewhere?"

"Yes, I am leaving now. You heard about the coming war. I must go and see if I can help your friends."

"Um, thank you for everything."

"You are welcome. We will see each other again. Take care of yourself until then!"

"I will! You take care too, Garvan."

He did not answer. He only smiled at her. Then he turned to leave. He stopped at the door and looked back at her. "Take care of Kylan too! She is in a precarious time right now." Then he opened the door quietly and left the house.

Victoria lay back down and closed her eyes. Cornelius would be there soon. The thought brought her more joy than she expected.

It seemed like only a few minutes had passed when she felt a soft kiss on her forehead. She opened her eyes quickly and grabbed Cornelius by the arm as he walked away from her toward the fire. He turned and leaned toward her. She sat up. Their eyes met. She pulled him closer to her and kissed him with more affection than he had felt from her before.

"Whoa," was all he could say when she loosened her embrace on him.

"I missed you."

"Yeah, I can tell. I missed you too, and I was worried."

"Aden and Kylan took good care of me. And Garvan too."

"Yeah, I felt better when I found out they brought you here. Garvan and I go back a long way."

"I figured you at least knew him. He asked me to give you this." She handed him the envelope Garvan left her.

Cornelius took it from her slowly. He took the thick parchment out and unfolded it. He took a step closer to the fire so he could see it better.

There were several maps and diagrams. The first page was a letter addressed to him. He read through it quickly and then asked Victoria to come sit by the fire with him so he could read it to her.

Dear Cornelius,

It has truly been a pleasure to host your friends here. As you know, I don't get a lot of company way out here. I am sad that I had to leave before your arrival. I look on you as a dear friend! But alas, I am needed at the battleground with Rupert and Prince Bartholomew. I have been looking to the future in the pond outside behind the house. Nothing is decided yet. Colin has not made up his mind about which side he is on. His decision makes all the difference in the future.

I do know that we will succeed, but I do not see that in the water. That I know in my heart. Speaking of hearts, I do hope that you let me perform the rites of marriage for you and Victoria.

I have gotten word that you and your bride need to go with Aden to Pallen. You are to stay as far away from the battlefield as possible. Aden misses his family, so he will be leaving in the morning. Go with him. Kylan will be heading to the battlefield. Rupert needs her now. I made a pair of boots just like yours for Victoria.

They are by the door. Her hair is getting longer. You should cut it again before you leave. Also there is food on the fire for you. Get some sleep tonight if you can. Your judgment will be better with sleep.

This is all the advice I can give you now. I will see you soon in Pallen.

Garvan

"I like your hair long," Cornelius said when he finished reading.

"I do too! But that is a lot to take in. Right, let me get this straight. You and I and Aden are going to Pallen, Kylan is going to the battlefield to help Rupert, I need to cut my hair, and he made me boots like yours. What does that mean?"

"Well, I keep a knife in each boot, but you can't just drop a knife in a boot and expect it to be comfortable. So he made me boots with a pocket in it to hold the knife."

"So he wants me to have a knife in my boot?"

"Yes, I guess he figures that I taught you to use a knife for protection."

"Well, you did a little. How did he make the boots so quickly?"

"A long time ago, he worked as a shoemaker. That was his trade. When he was in his twenties, he began to learn magic, but he continued to make shoes to buy his bread. He was one of the best. He could make shoes and cast spells on them! People loved it in the old days."

"Aye, he also said you should get some sleep so take off your boots and lay with me until morning."

She kissed him again as he leaned over her to take off his boots. He took off his shirt and boots and slid into the small cot. She lied down in his arms and pulled the blanket around them.

Cornelius was asleep as soon as his head hit the pillow. Victoria lay quietly in the dim light from the dying fire. It wasn't as cold as it had been, so she let it die.

It had been after midnight when Cornelius arrived. She got up after a few hours of dozing. She went to the door and tried on her new boots. Garvan had left a small knife in the pocket of the right boot. She could not see it well in the dark, but she felt the smooth gilding on the sheath. She wondered if it was Aden's work.

"It is!" Kylan's voice said in a low voice behind her.

Victoria jumped from the surprise. "Sorry I didn't mean to scare you."

"I thought you were asleep."

"Well, I was, but I got up a few minutes ago. I figure we can cut your hair before Cornelius wakes up. I doubt he will want to do it."

"No, he won't. So Aden did make this knife?"

"Yes. He is very talented. He has spent the last few weeks working on designs for new swords for you and Rupert and me! And a new set of knives for Cornelius as a present after your coronation!"

"I am glad he has faith in us."

"I am too! Come on, the sun is starting to come up. Let its first use be to cut your hair."

Victoria walked over to the hearth and picked up the pants and her cloak that Garvan had washed and left to dry. She changed out of her nightgown and into the clean clothes. She walked quickly back to the door and put on her new boots.

Kylan was already fully dressed when Victoria stood up. She went to open the door and then turned quickly. She reached out and grabbed her sword and scabbard that were leaning against the door.

"I feel funny without the sword now!" she said to Kylan.

"Yes, that is good. You should never be caught without your defense! Especially now in such dangerous times."

It was nearly thirty minutes when Cornelius came outside to find them. He nearly screamed when he saw Victoria.

"You cut off all of your hair," he said as she walked up to him with less than a centimeter of hair on her head.

"Yes, but hair grows, and Kylan and I talked about it. It is getting warmer. So if we cut it all off now, then we won't have to worry about it again," she said in a pleading voice.

"Yes, hopefully, this will all be over in only a few months. I will tolerate it, but I hope that you never have to cut your hair again. But I will still love you if you do!" He pulled her by the hand to him and kissed her. She put her arms around him as he put his around her.

Kylan walked up and cleared her throat. "All right, you two! I see the haircut hasn't affected much. When you are done, Victoria, can you help me pack the horses? And, Cornelius, you need to go wake up Aden. We need to be getting on our way soon."

CHAPTER 24

Another Departure

It only took them an hour to eat breakfast and get back upon the horses. There were three horses. Garvin had taken one of his two horses, so he had arranged for Aden to take his other horse, Raush. Victoria and Cornelius rode together on Thunderstorm.

They traveled together nearly all day. They were very quiet. All four of them were lost in thought. Every once in a while, Kylan announced the goings-on at the battlefield.

"There is no action yet. The boys are training hard. Rupert and Bartholomew are going to talk with Mathew and one of his men at sundown. I hope to be there soon after that. The battle is set to start at sunup."

"You will, and we will be in Pallen by midday," Cornelius said.

They were silent for the rest of the trip until they got to a crossroad a few hours later.

"Aye, this is where we part. I will see the three of you in Pallen. Hopefully sooner rather than later," Kylan said.

Thunderstorm let out a low whinny as Kylan turned to head down the other path. She turned around and looked the horse in his eyes. "I will take care of him! I promise," Kylan said in a steady voice to the horse. Thunderstorm bobbed his head as if he were nodding. Kylan rubbed his nose. Then she turned and rode off without looking back again.

The other three continued down the darkening road. Thunderstorm knew the way even in the dark and showed no fear. He decided to ride on through the night.

"We can rest in Pallen," Aden said cheerfully to Raush, who reluctantly kept going. Cornelius and Victoria both noticed that the closer they got to Pallen, the happier Aden became.

They made good time through the night. By sunrise, they could see Pallen in the distance. They were still on the hills so they were looking down on the large walled city—a view that Cornelius never grew tired of.

"There it is, Vic, the capital city." Cornelius pointed to the bright city.

It was a clear day. Victoria looked down at the city. A flash of recognition ran through her mind. She had been in this spot before, but it was dark, and she had looked down at the city with tears in her eyes. Now she looked at it with clear vision. The sunshine made all the details of the city clear and vibrant in her eyes.

There was one broad road that led to a large wrought-iron gate that stood between a large stone wall that went all the way around. On the other side of the gate, the road almost immediately divided into many different directions. The streets wound through the city, past shops and homes. They all led to the middle of the city. There stood a large castle with three turrets, each donning a flag. They were too far way to see what was on the flag, but Victoria knew that it was the same crest housed in the middle of the hilt of her sword.

She could see a few people walking along the streets, but there was not a bustle like she had read about in her history books or heard in stories about what life was like in a city. Something was wrong— too many people were missing from the capital city.

"There is the castle," Cornelius said with childlike enthusiasm. "Aden, you live pretty close to it. Can you see the tavern were Joanna works? I think I can see my grandfather's inn."

"I can't actually see the tavern, but I know where it is, so I can imagine it. Come on, let's go. I can't wait to get home."

"Wait, I want to take a break and eat something. Guys, I am very hungry," Victoria said.

"Oh yeah, I am too. I guess we can eat quickly," Aden said.

Victoria took in the sight of what she knew would soon be her home. She wanted to stay longer, but there was no way to contain Aden's impatience anymore. He was so close to his home now.

They did eat very quickly. There wasn't much food left, so they ate the rest of it, and as soon as it was gone, they got back on the horses. Victoria gave Thunderstorm and Raush the last two carrots. Thunderstorm nodded his approval and began to trot. Raush was a much smaller horse and had a bit of trouble keeping up with Thunderstorm's large strides.

They rode on for three hours. Aden chattered on about his family, and Cornelius told Victoria all about the city. She could tell that he loved the time he spent there. It would be harder for her to adjust to living in the city. But Victoria knew Cornelius and Aden would help her adjust.

They got to the gates of the city just before midday.

"Victoria, put this belt over your cloak at a diagonal to cover the crest," Cornelius said, handing her a thick leather sash.

"Thank you. Why?"

"Well, that is a soldier's rank. It means you are an officer in one of the armies. It is designed so that you don't give away whose side you are on, but no one will mess with you. And we need to cover the crest. Thomas is well known here, and everyone knows he only has one living relative."

Victoria finished clasping the sash just as they got to the gate guard, who stood several feet in front of the gate blocking the way into the city. There were two other men stationed on either side of the gate itself.

"Welcome to Pallen, men. What are your names?" the guard asked.

"I am Aden, the king's swordsmith."

"Cornelius of Bale, son of Malcolm the Merchant."

"Mark of Bale," Victoria said, trying the best she could to disguise her voice.

"You are a bit young to have a ranking," the guard said.

"He is my guard. I have very important business here," Cornelius said.

"Yes, sir," the guard said. "I will allow you in, but be careful. Things are getting dangerous in the city. I am not supposed to let in strangers."

"I am not a stranger, and neither is Cornelius. Our friends are not strangers, Ben," said Aden. There was a hint of authority in Aden's voice.

"Yes, and we are aware of the goings-on here," Cornelius said in his toughest voice.

"How long will you three be staying?" the guard asked.

"We do not know yet. I will be back in a few days and let you know. You have my word on that, Ben," Cornelius said.

"Fine," the guard said and extended his hand to Cornelius. He turned and signaled to the men at the gate. One screamed "Heave!" and three other men began pulling the large ropes to raise the portcullis.

Victoria had been holding the hilt of her sword, covering her father's crest. As the gate lifted, she put her arms carefully on Cornelius's shoulders. Thunderstorm walked through the gates slowly and smoothly, knowing that Victoria was not holding on as tightly as she should.

Cornelius looked at Aden and said in a low voice, "We have to be careful. There are spies all over the city. Many are on the lookout for us."

"I think we should split up. I will go home. Meet me at the tavern in two hours," Aden responded.

"Good idea. I am going to bring Thunderstorm to my grandfather's stable. He will be happy there, won't you, boy?" he said, patting the side of Thunderstorm's head.

Thunderstorm reared up.

"What is the matter?" Cornelius asked.

"We can't stable him. We have to let him go. He has gotten us safely to Pallen. Now it is time we let him go back to Rupert. Aden, I have a different idea," said Victoria.

She dismounted Thunderstorm. Cornelius followed her. They had very little cargo with them, so she untied the small leather pack Thunderstorm had allowed them to carry on his side and slung it over her shoulder. Then she removed the reins. Thunderstorm stood still for a moment and looked at her carefully.

She hugged the horse with a tear in each eye. "Take care of Rupert for us," she said, trying not to let the boys see she was crying. Thunderstorm nudged her face gently, then turned and trotted off in the direction of the city gate. Aden rode back and convinced the gate guards to up the gate to let the horse out.

Cornelius took Victoria's hand and sighed. They waited a couple minutes until Aden came back.

"I guess we are on foot now. Don't worry, Victoria. Rupert will be all right, and Thunder, well, he is not your average horse. Come on, it will take us nearly an hour to walk to the tavern from here," Cornelius said.

"It will take us longer. We shouldn't split up yet. But since they are looking for us, we will have to fool them," Victoria said.

"Why can't we split up?"

"Because there is safety in numbers. And I am not worried about spies. If there are spies, they already know we are here. I am worried about the men out to kill me. If I die, Kybon's reign dies with me. Those who want me dead are growing in number."

"You are right. So what is your plan to hide from the assassins?"

"A lot of people know what you both look like. And the guard Ben said I am too young to be of rank. So let's see. Cornelius, here, put on my cloak, and take the sash and put it diagonally across your chest the opposite direction as I have it. That way, my uncle's crest will show. He is well known but also well feared. Pull the hood over your head to cover your face. Then I will be your servant boy. He usually hires a helper when he is here on business for Bale. Aden is the swordsmith, so Uncle Thomas would have business with him, anyway." She was handing Cornelius her cloak and rank sash as she finished speaking. She also switched swords with Aden and him to carry it. It would be less conspicuous if the sword-maker were carrying a sword with the king's crest on it.

Cornelius stared at her in awe for a moment. "How do you know about the direction of the rank sash?" he asked slowly. He was nearly speechless.

"I learned about it in school."

"Oh yeah, you and Rupert both went to school. I was educated differently as the town's messenger," he said, frowning, wondering what else he had missed by not going to school. He pulled the cloak over his head with a scoff.

She saw the look on his face and smiled softly at him. "We are the ones that missed out. Until a few months ago, I had never been out of Bale. You got to see so much of the kingdom! I am the one that should be jealous. But there isn't time for that now." She reached out and helped him clasp the rank sash. She smiled at how handsome and strong he looked. Then Aden dismounted his horse and handed the reins to Cornelius.

They began to walk. They walked along the smooth cobblestone street for over an hour before they reached the tavern. It was a small stone building like all the others in the city.

Victoria realized that very few of the buildings had signs on them. She leaned into Cornelius to ask him the question as soon as no one else would hear. "Why are there no signs on the buildings? Do you have to just know where you are going here?" she asked.

He answered quietly as they reached the door of what she assumed to be the tavern. "Yes, it is harder for spies to find you if they are unsure of where they are. It has been this way as long as I can remember. If you are not known at a place, you are not welcome. But my father and my grandfather both told me it was different years ago before Kybon. Everyone used to be welcome everywhere."

"So they know you and Aden here?" she asked as Aden tied up the horse with a clover hitch knot to the railing on the wall.

A large man sat on a stool by the door. He looked pleasant enough, but Victoria could tell he was a man you didn't want to cross. She quietly fell in line behind Aden but in front of Cornelius. They had not really discussed it, but she knew that he did not want her out of his line of vision. Under the circumstances, she agreed. The custom of the city dictated that servants remain behind their masters in case someone tried to ambush, but customs were not always followed.

When Aden stepped on to the wooden planks that led to the tavern door, the doorman looked up. He gave out a low gasp and jumped to his feet. Victoria thought they might be in trouble. She began to wonder how hard it would be to get to the knife in her boot.

Aden, however, did not put up his defense. He began to laugh instead and then cried out in joy, "Yes, it is really me. Your brother-in-law is finally home."

"Is it for good this time?" the doorman asked in a deep voice.

"I don't know yet," Aden said.

Cornelius nudged Victoria up the step onto the planks and spoke from behind her. "He is going to be here for a while, and so will I, Dors, but we have been travelling a long time. So we are going to go inside for refreshments. When our hunger is satiated, we will come back out and tell you all about our adventures. Or at least I will. Aden will probably run off to visit Joanna, as they have not seen each other in almost a year."

"Who's the boy?" Dors asked.

"He is a kid from Bale. His family was indebted to my father, so Mark here offered to work off his family's debt as my servant. He has been quite useful, but he doesn't speak except to me."

"Is that your rule?"

"No! He has never been out of Bale before or away from his family. I think he is a bit overwhelmed. He is a good servant, and I like having the extra set of hands, so I am willing to overlook his not wanting to speak."

"Aye, I will take your word that he is trustworthy. If he causes trouble, it is on your head, not mine.

"Agreed." Cornelius reached out and shook Dors's hand.

"Come now, Mark. It is time for food. Aden, you lead the way.

I will enjoy the look on Joanna's face when she sees you."

The three of them walked in. Victoria was about to walk to a table, but Cornelius grabbed her shoulder. "Wait, we have to wait for them to give us a table. Dors is only the first bit of security," he warned.

Just then a tall woman walked up to them. She had long curly dark-brown hair. She was wearing a flowing skirt with a beautifully crafted sword at her side. "Aden," she said under her breath. "Ah, table for three," she said in her everyday voice.

"Yes, ma'am, preferably one in the back. We have been traveling for two days, and we would like to sit a while," Cornelius said.

The young women's eyes left Aden's face, and she looked at Cornelius. Her expression changed. "Cornelius, how have you been?" she asked as they followed her to a table in the very back corner of the room. "It has been nearly four years since I last saw you."

There was only a handful of people in the tavern at this time of day. And between Aden and Cornelius, they knew everyone in there, so Cornelius spoke more freely than he originally planned to. "I have been doing well. I planned to be married already, but the war changed my plans."

"The war changed everyone's plans. How long are you staying this time?" she asked with a sad tinge in her voice she could not hide. She didn't look at Aden when she asked.

"We aren't planning to leave. Aden is needed here, and I am on a mission that requires me to stay here, not the battlefield."

Joanna's face lit up when she realized her husband would be staying longer than the night. She turned to him and smiled broadly, trying to hide her tears of joy. "Welcome home," she said as she hurried off to bring them food.

"Aden, you should go and help your wife, then head home to your child. Mark and I will stay here awhile."

"Where are you going to live since we are here indefinitely?"

"I was thinking about my grandfather's inn."

"No, you are staying with some of my kin. Those who are after her will be watching the inn. She stays with us out of sight," Aden said in a very low voice.

"I agree with Aden. I overheard too much at the camp. I am sure now that Colin wants me dead, and he has men who agree with him. Kybon, of course, will be sure to keep me alive, but I doubt he will give me a nice room in the palace. So even in this 'disguise,' I need to be out of sight from Colin's spies."

"Aye, but, Aden, many of Joanna's family and yours are struggling to make ends meet. Can they afford to house us? We cannot pay them, not yet."

"I have thought about that. We will find a way to afford the extra mouths. I can't guarantee that you will get your fill to eat, but there will be enough food to live."

The three of them got their fill that day, however. Joanna saw to it that her husband and her friends were well fed. Victoria was glad for the fresh, hot meal. Aden took his leave soon after he got his fill. Victoria and Cornelius spent the rest of the afternoon making plans and discussing who they would stay with and where.

CHAPTER 25

The Battlefield

Earlier that morning before sunrise, Kylan reached the battlefield. Rupert was waiting for her at the edge of the road.

"Hi, um, how are you?" he asked sheepishly.

"Cut with the small talk, Rupert. I am hungry, and there is a lot to discuss." She dismounted her horse and held the reins with one hand, took Rupert's hand with her other, and led him and her horse to the camp, where the boys were all sitting around fires. Many of them looked very scared.

When Kylan found a seat in the back of the group, she closed her eyes and rubbed her head.

"Are you okay?" Rupert asked.

"I am trying to turn off their voices. I can hear them all. Your men are horrified. I think I am going to go crazy!" she said in a weak voice.

"I know the condition of my troops. They are horrified! But few of them are men. Most of them can't grow hair on their faces! Why are you going crazy?" he asked as he looked into her barely focused eyes.

"Because..." She strained to get the words out. "I have my full powers! I can read minds, hear people's thoughts! Well, right now, I hear a thousand voices at once…" Kylan paused and closed her eyes. "I can't shut them out long enough to… think… clearly for my… self." She fell to her knees and buried her face in her hands. Rupert looked around in despair; he did not know how to help her.

Garvin was sitting near them with Jeps and Peter. He had arrived several hours earlier. He motioned to the boys to follow him. He walked briskly to Kylan with the two boys just behind him. He didn't say a word to her but simply put his hand on her head and whispered several words in the old language. Rupert recognized a few of the words from his studies, but he didn't know what Garvan said.

Kylan looked up when he removed his hand. "Thank you, Garvan," she said.

"You are welcome, child," he said in the same slow, quiet voice he used with Victoria. "Now we must talk quickly. That spell only lasts for three or four hours. But I promise you will learn to control it. I didn't know you were coming here. Why didn't you stay with the others?"

"Rupert needs me here, Garvan. By the way, Rupert," she said, talking quickly, "have you two met already?"

"Yes, we actually met years ago. He was in Bale once. I was seven or eight, so I don't remember why, but he stayed with us. My mother has a lot of respect for him. But we will talk about the past later. We need to talk about the future now."

"Where is Bartholomew?"

"He and Malachi have a meeting with Prince Mathew. The bloodshed is set to start at dawn. So really we have less than two hours to finish this discussion."

"Aye, first things first. Jeps and Peter are to go to Pallen before the fighting starts. Garvan, you will go with them. I will stay here with Rupert for a few days more, then we will head to Pallen too."

"But I need to leave to go to see the sorcerer's council. I will be eighteen in two months," said Rupert.

"You can't go yet. We need you here. I have these orders from the high sorceress herself. You don't have to go before you get your powers," Kylan said in one breath.

"Rupert, I will teach you things you need to know when we are all in Pallen. I will admit I am not a sorcerer, but I have been around magic for many years now. The rules change in time of war," Garvan said in his slow, thoughtful way.

"I don't want to leave Bartholomew either," Rupert said.

"Rupert, he has to fight this war on his own. This is his army. Our mission is elsewhere," Kylan said with a bit of desperation in her voice.

Rupert got up quickly and walked to the fire in the middle of the camp. He spoke quickly to one of the older boys, who came back with him.

The boy handed Kylan a bowl of stew. "Here you are, miss. There is more if you need it. I cooked enough to feed an army!" He winked at her and hurried off back to his cooking.

Kylan began to eat as Rupert sat back down to finish the conversation. She mumbled "Thank you" as Rupert casually said "You're welcome."

Bartholomew returned just before dawn. He waved to Kylan. She could see the tired and worried look in his eyes. She walked to him with her black traveling cloak and long skirt blowing in the strong wind. A few of the older boys whistled at her. She decided not to show her powers just yet.

"I take it you could not talk him out of fighting," Kylan said, ignoring the rest of the gathering crowd.

"No, we march to battle at first light. So I need to get them lined up."

"Aye, Barth, take care of yourself. I have big plans for you."

"I am marching in with my men. Unlike my coward of a brother, I am willing to die with them. Though I still think there is no reason for the war. Kybon will win either way."

"No, he won't. This war is more important than you think. Kybon's days are coming to an end sooner than we know. Win this battle. Sadly, Rupert will have to leave you to fight on your own, and I can't help you either," Kylan said.

"I know magic law forbids your help. I have been learning about magic. Maybe after the war, I can go with Rupert to the council and learn even more. I won't be ruler—that is Victoria's job, so I want to be a magician and help her and my bloodline rule this kingdom justly for many years."

"That is a good plan," she said to him, and then she turned and called Rupert to him. "Tell him your plan for after the war."

"I want to go with you to see the council after this war is through," Bartholomew said.

Rupert hesitated. He could not read Kylan's thoughts because of the spell Garvan cast, but he looked carefully at the expression on her face. He knew that if he agreed to wait for Bartholomew it could be well after his birthday before the war ended. (A sorcerer's promises were binding! If he agreed, he could not go back on his word.) Kylan seemed to think it was a good idea. So he begrudgingly agreed. He had been looking forward to his meeting with the sorcerers for a several years now, especially his grandfather.

They made the pact, to then lining up his men for battle, and Bartholomew left happy. Garvan went with him. Kylan and Rupert stood together alone by the fire.

"Now I have to wait longer to go to the council. Why?" Rupert knew there must be a deeper reason.

"Look. There are reasons. You have to be happy with that answer," Kylan said.

"Fine, don't tell me. I will find out in due time, right?" he said in irritation as he walked away toward Bartholomew.

"Wait, you can't help him. We already covered that."

Rupert turned around quickly. There was anger in his eyes. "Don't you think I know that? I know what has to happen, but I don't have to be happy about it! Just let me be for a few minutes. I want to bask in the peace we have until sunrise!" With that, he stormed off to sit by himself as far away from the group as he could. He didn't notice the wind was growing stronger and the stars were no longer visible in the sky.

At sunrise, the armies assembled in rows. There was about one hundred yards between the two groups. Rupert watched from his seat and waited for the boys to run toward each other and fight with swords and knives in hand-to-hand combat. Jeps and Peter walked up and sat down near him. They didn't say a word. Garvan walked up too, with Kylan at his heels.

They each sat quietly, trying not to watch as the yells from the lines began. Then Kylan gasped and pointed toward the field. They all looked down. The winds were so strong many of the boys could barely stand. Bartholomew's side would be running into the wind. He yelled charge, but only the largest boys could move at all. Mathew's biggest were sent out, and the boys were forced to be in a grappling match instead of a war. Each side was yelling for his own man to win.

Rupert turned around and saw the beautiful tall woman from Thomas's woodshed standing a few feet from them. She put her finger up to her mouth. He said nothing. She pointed to a far cliff that was barely visible in the distance. He could see a human-shaped figure standing at the edge with arms in the air. Rupert knew it was his grandfather, who could manipulate weather! Ashel handed Rupert two letters. The others noticed her presence then. But before Jeps or Peter could ask who this strange woman was, she disappeared. Kylan explained quickly who she was to them.

Rupert opened the first letter.

Young Rupert,

Do not worry about or dwell on things you cannot control. There are things in motion that will protect you and your friends. None of you are alone in your quest! Since Cornelius is busy at the moment, I told your grandfather I would deliver to you his letter.

Until we meet again,

Ashel
High Sorceress of the Council of Sorcerers

Rupert took a deep breath. He squeezed his grandfather's letter through the parchment envelop. It was thick. He knew it had no bearing on the situation at hand. So he decided to wait to read the second letter that was easily ten pages long until he had more time. Kylan looked at him curiously. He handed her Ashel's letter and tucked his grandfather's letter into the pocket inside his shirt.

"She is watching over us. We are in good hands," Kylan said quietly.

"Yes, I know. And this wind is my grandfather's doing. You see him there on that distant cliff making winds blow too hard to fight the war."

Jeps looked out at where Rupert was pointing. "Good Lord! That is your grandfather! I saw him there earlier, but I was afraid to say anything I thought he might have been on Kybon's side.

"He is on our side. Just about everyone but Colin and a handful of his friends is on our side!" Kylan said.

Garvan nodded in agreement and then pointed to the battlefield again. There were now four separate grappling matches going on, but neither side was winning. Most of the boys were forced to watch from the ground because they could not stand. The winds were so strong that Rupert had to sit back down himself to keep from falling over. They sat and watched when they could keep their eyes open.

It was still a few hours before noon when they all heard a sound of galloping coming down the road. Kylan stood quickly. Jeps got up too and looked down the road.

"It is a large horse coming toward us. But there is no rider, not even a saddle," Jeps said.

Rupert jumped to his feet and looked down the road himself. He knew before looking that is was Thunderstorm. "Thunderstorm!" he said to Kylan.

Peter had gotten up and walked to see what was happening. "Thunderstorm? That is not the sound of thunder!" he said from behind them.

"No, Thunderstorm is the name of my horse. Aden took him to Pallen."

"Yes, but I am willing to bet Victoria sent him back to you," Kylan said.

"Speaking of thunderstorms, it looks like there will be a real thunderstorm soon!" Peter said, looking at the thick dark clouds rolling in over the battlefield.

Rupert only smiled. He was glad to have his horse back, but he began to wonder about Victoria and Cornelius. He began to miss them as he listened to the sounds of the wind and muffled shouts from the battlefield.

As noon approached, the weather did change. The winds stopped, and sheets of rain began to fall from the sky. The grappling began to look like a sloppy mud fight. Within an hour, it was raining so hard that both sides were forced to retreat to try to find shelter from the blinding rain.

Rupert and Kylan sat together under a small blanket. Kylan held her hand in the air and concentrated very hard for a few seconds. The blanket became rigid, and the rain did not come through. She held her other hand out palm up and snapped her fingers. A small ball of fire ignited in her hand.

Rupert looked mildly impressed. "You are powerful indeed if you can work two spells at once after only a week."

"I can, but I think it will make me very tired, so I won't be able to hold out the rains for long."

"I know. So I have decided that we should leave for Pallen today while it is raining. The battle will have to be stopped for a least two days because the rain won't stop before then."

"How do you know that?"

Rupert shrugged and said quietly, "I don't know. I have always known the weather. I get it from grandfather."

Kylan was one of the only people he knew that would understand that. "I wonder if the weather would be your gift. I guess I should have thought. Your grandfather is famous for it."

"I never thought about it. My father could not do a thing about the weather. I will figure out my powers when I get them, but right now, we have to figure out how to not die until then."

"I know."

"There is now two months and a day until my birthday. But I have a feeling that we are needed there now. Bartholomew and Malachi have things under control at least until the rain stops. My grandfather can only manipulate the weather. He can't really change it. He made the winds get here sooner that is all. I just want—"

"Rupert, I can't interfere in the war. I wish I could too, but I can't help them, not yet anyway."

"I know! But I don't know what good will come from some of those boys dying."

"Well, we will have to come to terms with losing friends! Sorcerers live longer than normal people."

They fell silent for a few minutes. Then Rupert felt a drop of water come through the blanket. He looked at Kylan. The fire in her hand was getting smaller. He reached over and put his hand in hers putting out the light. Then he pulled her close to him. She was very weak.

"Let in the rain and save your strength. We need it for our trip."

She leaned into his embrace as the rain poured through the blanket. She reached up to his wet face. "Rupert, kiss me already, so we can get on with things."

"What makes you think I want to kiss you?" he asked in a sarcastic tone.

"I can read minds!"

"Maybe you want to kiss me, and you are pretending that it is my thought!" he said as stubbornly as possible.

Kylan decided that she didn't want to play this game anymore. She turned her head and found the last of her strength. She kissed Rupert as the rain streamed down both of their faces. Then she got up and walked away slowly and carefully on unsteady legs.

Rupert lay on the ground for a minute. He took a deep breath of wet air and then got up himself.

CHAPTER 26

Meeting Up in Pallen

The rain made their trip to Pallen long and difficult. Though they still made it in a day. Kylan had tried to keep the rain off with magic, but her strength ran out halfway there. They had ridden together on Thunderstorm, who took them the shortest way possible. It was nearly nightfall when they arrived, but they could not tell because the sun had not been out all day.

Kylan fought through the voices around her and found Aden, and he led them to the others. Aden walked quickly in front of them with a large pack. He was wearing boots to his knees with a cloak over him. Rupert wondered if Aden's cloak was any better than his own, which seemed useless.

Victoria (dressed as Mark) and Cornelius were at the tavern when Kylan and Rupert arrived, soaked to the bone. Aden had to yell over the pounding of the rain. "They are in there! I need to speak to the doorman. I will be in just behind you."

When Kylan and Rupert stepped inside the tavern, Joanna met them at the door. Cornelius and Victoria were sitting at the same table in the back, but they were now the only people in the room besides the hostess. Aden came carrying his pack. All three of them were dripping with water.

Cornelius and Victoria had spent the night before at the inn. Victoria was tired of her game of pretend, so she went straight to bed. Cornelius stayed up most of the night, catching up with his grandfather. He also checked on Jep's mother, who was now happily working there. They went back to the tavern in the rain in midafternoon.

Joanna led Kylan, Rupert, and Aden to the table next to Cornelius and Victoria. Aden and Joanna both ran off in opposite directions. Aden came back quickly in a dry shirt. Joanna came back quickly with hot soups in one hand and a clean rag in another. She dropped the rag on Aden's dripping head and handed the soup to Kylan and Rupert.

Kylan ate the soup quickly. She asked if there was a closet nearby. Aden showed her to a small pantry and handed her dry clothes from his pack.

"No, thank you, Aden. I don't need dry clothes." She closed the door and opened it again in about three seconds. Her clothes were completely dry and clean. Her hair that came to the middle of her back was neatly braided.

"Grand," was all Aden could say.

When she returned, Rupert took the dry clothes Aden had given him and walked to the same pantry. He walked out nearly five minutes later. Joanna took his wet clothes from him. He thanked her. Then she dropped a dry rag on his head too. He took it and walked back to the table as he rubbed the towel over his hair to dry it.

As Rupert finished his soup, Kylan talked quietly to Cornelius and Mark. Aden was in and out of the conversation. When Rupert finished, he joined them.

Joanna came up and began cleaning the table. "So, Aden honey, if I am here and you are here, where is our child?"

"He is with your brother. Jo is teaching him to read. I didn't want him out in this rain."

"He is two years old. How is he teaching him to read?"

"He is teaching the older children to read, but Aquin is learning in some way."

"When it stops raining, he is coming here to stay with me. Kybon's army has begun to search the city."

"Aquin will be fine for today," Aden assured her.

"I suppose. I don't think the soldiers will be out in this rain, anyway. The only thing they will accomplish is getting pneumonia!" Joanna said.

Rupert broke in. "Wait a minute. Kybon's army is searching for whom?"

"The Princess Victoria. It seems he can't kill her. His soldiers are not allowed to kill teenage girls. No one else is safe, though," said Joanna.

"How do you know that?" Aden asked.

"Well, while you were out gallivanting around the country, I have been here serving dinner to soldiers. I pay attention. Kybon's soldiers are the worst for thinking that I am unable to understand them. And they like to talk, especially when they are full of whiskey!"

"I think I will be spending some time here. I would like to know what they aren't saying," Rupert said.

"Speaking of spending time here, Aden, do you know of a place to stay? I don't think the inn is safe for us. I am almost certain Kybon is looking for me too. If he finds me, he will have me killed," Kylan said.

Joanna stepped in and put her hand on her husband's shoulder. "There is very little room for us in meager hovel were Aquin and I have been staying, but the safest place is with us or my family among the poor. There will be little comforts, but I figure you would rather be a little uncomfortable than dead."

"Yes, I would rather be alive, and I agree that we are safest among poor, but some of them can be bought," Cornelius said, thinking of his uncles.

"Not my family. Aden will take care of them all when these difficult times are over. They know better than to trust Kybon. He has double-crossed us in the past," Joanna said.

Just then, another group came inside from the rain. Kylan had already walked over to the door to let them in. Victoria and Rupert both recognized Garvan's tall, lanky figure in the doorway, with Jeps and Peter standing in front of him. They stripped off their cloaks and revealed their bone-dry clothes underneath. At second glance, Victoria realized the cloaks were dry too. Normally, Victoria would have thought that very odd. But she we beginning to understand that she was surrounded by magic and would be for the rest of her life.

"Glad you three could join us. Garvan, I trust you had a good trip?" Kylan said.

"Yes, the rain made it hard to navigate, but we found our way."

"Excuse me, miss," Jeps said to Joanna as she walked by them toward the kitchen.

"Yes, I will bring you out some hot food. You two boys go and sit by the others."

"Can you read minds too?" Jeps asked in amazement that she knew what he was going to ask.

"No, but I know the I-am-hungry look on a person's face. I have worked here four years now. Plus I have a child of my own," she said with a caring smile.

The two boys did as they were told. Joanna returned quickly with two steaming bowls of soup and toast and two small cups of juice. She sat down with them as they ate very quickly.

Jeps finished first and got up quickly to talk to Cornelius. "Cornelius, sir, umm, you brought my mom here, right? And got her a job?"

"Yes, she is working for my grandfather at his inn. I will bring you over there if you like."

"Now?"

"Sure. Maybe Garvan can come with us to keep us dry?" Cornelius said.

"Yes, Mark and Rupert and Kylan should come too."

"What about me?" Peter asked.

Joanna looked at Aden and knew by the look on his face that Peter should not go with his friends. So she took his hand and said quickly, "Aden and I need you to come and stay with us tonight. We have to get our place ready for everyone else, and we have our little boy to take care of so we could use an extra set of hands."

Peter smiled and went back to eating his soup. He wanted very much to be useful to his friends. Joanna was truly glad for the extra set of hands. She knew that she would have to house extra people sooner or later, but she was far from ready.

Jeps grabbed his cloak and ran to the door. "See you tomorrow, Peter! Come on let's go."

"Jeps, I know you want to see your mom, but hold on a moment. We have to get ready to go out. The rain is falling pretty hard out there," Rupert said as he walked up to the door, putting a steadying hand on Jeps's shoulder.

"Everyone line up and put on your cloaks," Garvan said in a low voice.

Cornelius didn't have a hooded cloak; all he had was his messenger coat. He was about to say something when Aden handed him the cloak he had been wearing. "Thank you but what are you going to wear to get home in this rain?" he asked.

"I will be fine without it," Aden said with a wink.

Five minutes later, the five of them were lined up. Garvan put his hand on each of their heads while saying barely audible words in the old language. He said it a little louder and more slowly when he got to Kylan who was last. She repeated the words to herself.

On a regular day, it would have taken them about twenty minutes to walk up the stone street from the tavern to the inn, but that evening was very irregular. The five of them trudged through the flooded street in a single file line. At first they bowed their heads out of habit in the blinding rain to protect their faces from the imposing water, but after a minute or two, they all realized they were not getting wet at all. The rain fell around them and even on their cloaks, but it beaded up and rolled off. The wind made a strange hissing sound in their ears.

Jeps was second in the line behind Cornelius, who was leading the way. Kylan walked behind him. Jeps kept an eye on his feet as they walked. He was not sure that the spell keeping them dry would work all the way to his boots. He had been poor in Corslan, so he had been wearing the same pair of shoes for three years now, and they were not new when he got them. His feet had just grown to fit them, but the holes were beginning to be a nuisance in the rain. He decided after about ten minutes that the spell did work to his shoes, and he walked happily, glad to have dry feet for once. Kylan made a mental note to ask Garvan to make Jeps a new pair of shoes as soon as possible.

The rain was so thick around them that Jeps and the others behind him didn't see the old, graying building until they were right in front of it. Cornelius stopped just in front of the steps that lead to the entrance.

"The third step is broken, so be careful on your way up!" he yelled over the sound of the rain pounding the wood in front of them.

They all carefully ascended the rickety stairs, while Cornelius stood next to the bottom step to help his friends up the slippery old wood. Victoria was the last of the group. Cornelius took her by the hand and walked with her up the stairs. Then they walked in the door to a dim room. There was a boy standing by a small table against the far wall next to another door. Victoria knew at once that the boy, who looked about twelve or thirteen, was related to Cornelius. The boy smiled genuinely as the group walked in.

Cornelius greeted him brightly. "Hello, Cousin." This was not the boys given name, but nearly everyone called him Cousin, whether he was their cousin or not. Cornelius knew Cousin's given name, but he liked calling his favorite cousin by that nickname.

"Hello, Cornelius." The boy's eyes wandered to the others in the group. He surveyed them all, and then his eyes fell on Jeps for a second time. He pointed. "You must be Jeps. You look a lot like your mother."

"Yes, is she here?"

"Yeah, she is upstairs cleaning some of the vacant rooms. She is very nice. Grandfather has trouble finding good help, and when he does, they act as if I am too young to run this place, but your mother has never once second-guessed my decisions. I will own this place one day, you know! Right, Cornelius?"

"Yes, Cousin, you will."

"Can I go up to see my mom, or do I need to wait until she is done?" Jeps was quite anxious to see his mother, but Cousin was in charge; his mother taught her to respect that.

"Go on up and find her. We are short-handed these days, so I am sure she would be glad for help,"

Jeps started for the door, but just before he opened it, Cousin stopped him. "Oh yeah, keep track of the work you do. I will see to it that your mother is paid for your labors as well as hers." Cousin winked at Jeps and opened the door for him. There was a muffled "Thank you" that came back to their ears as everyone watched Jeps disappear up the stairs.

When the door closed, Cousin turned back and looked at the remaining crowd in the room. "So Garvan and Cornelius, what can I do for you? Grandfather said it would not be safe for you here."

"It will be for one night," said Garvan. "We only need one room."

"Just one, sir?" the boy said, slightly puzzled.

"Yes," said Garvan, offering no explanation to any of them.

"Aye," he said, taking a small key from the drawer in the table. "Room 5 is ready. Will you be going up right away?"

"Yes, we have pressing business, but I promise you, young man, your cousin will be able to visit with you soon," Garvan said quietly.

"Yes, Cousin, we will be in town for some time. I haven't forgotten my promise to tell you the stories of my travels," Cornelius said.

His young cousin smiled happily and opened the door for them. "It is the third door on the left."

CHAPTER 27

Garvan's Surprise

They walked quickly up the narrow staircase. Garvan unlocked the door without using the key and ushered the four of them in. He came in last and barred the door. As he did so, he held up his hand and mumbled more words. Then he turned to them.

"Now I have a promise to keep. Cornelius and Victoria, please come and stand by me, so I can perform the rites of marriage."

"Rites of marriage? Now! Today?" Victoria asked.

"Yes, today. You have put it off long enough," Garvan said.

"But I.. .well, this isn't how I pictured it!" Victoria said quietly, but the excitement was growing in her as she spoke.

"This isn't how I pictured it either, but Garvan is right. We should have been married months ago. Let's do it now, and we can have a big celebration after you are queen," Cornelius said as he took both of Victoria's hands.

"Besides, you have your two best friends here to annoy you!" Rupert said with a laugh.

"Don't make me hurt you because I can!" Victoria said.

"Only for two more months!" Rupert said in his best little kid voice.

Victoria didn't say a word. She only stuck her tongue out at him with a smile. Everyone laughed, mostly at the confused expression on Garvan's face.

"Aye, you two come and stand by the fireplace," Garvan said.

"Can we start a fire?" Victoria asked as she led Cornelius to the front of the room.

"There is no wood, and it would be soaked through, anyway," Rupert said.

Kylan giggled and left the room. "Wait here for a minute," she said as she left. She returned five minutes later, carrying a load of wood. She placed it carefully in the fireplace.

"Kylan, the wood is soaked. It will never light!"

"Rupert, you are silly!" Kylan said in a fit of laughter. She reached up her hand, and a ball of fire ignited in her hand. She held her hand in front of the soaked wood and blew the flame slowly in a line. The fire slowly spread down the wood. There was a loud crackling, and then there was a roaring fire.

"Oh, right, you are a sorceress! I forgot," Rupert said sheepishly.

"I know you forgot. I am clairvoyant too!" Kylan said with more laughter.

Victoria and Cornelius laughed very hard. Even Garvan chuckled. When they collected themselves, Victoria thanked Kylan. Then she and Cornelius took their places in front of the fireplace. Kylan pulled Rupert by his sleeve to the other side of the room. He went willingly. Then he pulled Kylan gently to a seat on the floor. They sat cross-legged on the floor as Garvan preformed the rites of marriage.

He asked Victoria and Cornelius to stand in front of him with their backs to the fire. He took a small leather pouch from the inside of his cloak and removed a thin rope and two flower garlands. Victoria and Cornelius reached out with their right hands as he handed the garland to them. They each curled the garland into a wreath and placed it on the other's head. Then they reached out their hands.

Cornelius's right hand was down, and Victoria's hand was up. They clasped their hands together as Garvan tied the rope around their wrists. Cornelius handed him two rings from his pocket with his left hand.

Garvan took the rings. "The garlands on your heads are a symbol of purity and fertility. The rope binds your hearts together as one, and these rings are a sign of your unending love for each other. Place the rings on each other's fingers."

Cornelius placed the ring on Victoria's left hand. Then Victoria placed the ring on his left hand.

Kylan and Rupert stood up and walked to their friends. They each took a side of the rope between the wrist and cut their friends free with small knives from Garvan's pouch.

Garvan took the garland and wreaths from their heads and switched them. He put his right hand on Cornelius's head and the left on Victoria's. "With flowers to guide and rope to bind and rings to prove, as these friends and the Almighty God are witnesses, let this love last forever."

He released them. They turned and faced each other.

"You are now married!" Garvan said with excitement in his mild voice. "When this war has settled, we shall have the ceremony you have dreamed of, but this is all you need for now. We shall now leave you two until tomorrow."

Rupert, Kylan, and Garvan left the room.

Garvan stopped Kylan just as the door closed. "Help me." "With what?"

"A spell—your magic is more powerful than mine. We have to protect them for the night. Hold up one hand and repeat the words I say carefully. *Erate eps tonus!*"

CHAPTER 28

The Married Couple

Garvan, Rupert, and Kylan left the inn with the rain still falling. Garvan said the same spell as before on their cloaks and then lead them to Aden and Joanna's small home they have lived in since they got married. Aden was still dreaming about the day he could return to the large home on the castle grounds his family had lived in for more than three generations.

The storm grew more violent around them as they walked. Rupert had a respectful fear of the storm. He knew that not even the most powerful of sorcerers could ever completely control the weather. That was up to an even high power. Kylan felt his fear. She had it too. She took his hand as they walked. They both felt a little more comfortable.

Meanwhile, Victoria and Cornelius sat by the small window in their room in each other's arms. Victoria loved to watch the rain. She wasn't sure why. Cornelius had always found rain to be an inconvenience in his travels so he had never watched it fall. So for the first time in his life, he sat still and watched through the tiny window designed to let air flow through the room to keep them from being stuffy on hot days and to let out smoke from the fireplace on cold nights.

On this night, the rain started to pool on the little ledge. The window let them enjoy the calming sound of the rain. As he sat, he began to run his fingers through her short hair. It was getting longer by the day, which pleased Cornelius.

A lightning flash illuminated the room, and a second later, there was aloud clap of thunder that shook the building. Cornelius smiled in spite of himself. He was mesmerized. Before he came back to reality, he realized that Victoria was kissing him. He took her fully into his arms, and they stood up. There was another flash of lightning, followed by more rattling thunder as they led each other to the bed.

The next morning dawned gray and drab. The worst of the storm passed in the night. By midday, the weather had cleared up completely. The sun had come out and glistened in the large pools of water that had not evaporated yet. Victoria breathed in the fresh damp air as she and her new husband walked back to the tavern to meet up with the others. She could feel the ring on the chain around her neck. She wondered when she would be able to wear it freely.

Victoria was again dressed in her disguise. Victoria decided it would be better to sit across from Cornelius rather than next to him. She was afraid she would lean in to his shoulder if she were next to him. It was going to be harder now more than ever before to hide the fact that she was a girl.

They ate quietly and discussed very little. Now that the rain had stopped, the room was full of people. Joanna waited on all of them cheerfully while she kept an eye on her son and his cousin playing in the corner. Three or four other children had joined their game.

Kylan broke the silence when everyone was done eating. She concentrated for a moment on each person in the room. *I am sure that there are two spies in this room, one for Kybon and for one Colin*, she thought. From what she could tell, neither of them had figured it out that Mark was actually Victoria, but there was some suspicion that she was in Pallen.

Kylan wondered for a moment if they would need a decoy, not that she knew anyone. Then suddenly it came to here. She would be the decoy. She was the only one of them who could defend herself against a sorcerer. And now it appeared they were up against two with very different purposes. She concentrated extra hard so that Rupert would understand her plan fully without having to speak. He nodded, understanding the plan. He got up and left without speaking.

Kylan spoke to Jeps and the others. "Hey, you and I are going back to the inn to visit your mother. I think Peter should come too. Cornelius, you and your servant should go and meet Rupert in the market soon," she said in as casual a voice as she could muster.

Kylan whispered something to Aden. He looked around then left the group. He returned a moment later. He slipped a note and a key in Victoria's hand as she stood to leave for the market. She tucked it away quickly.

Aden stayed at the tavern and played games with his son and the other children for most of the day while Victoria, Rupert, and Cornelius spent much of the day in the marketplace. Kylan took Jeps and Peter to the inn. Jeps helped his mother all day. So Kylan and Peter spent the day playing card games with some of the guests. Garvan went to the market and bought leather, and then he went to the shoemaker that had once been his apprentice. Together they made Jeps the finest pair of boots.

That night, they all gathered in the small room adjacent to Aden's small smith shop he was using until he could return to the palace. It was just after dark when they were all seated on the dirt floor. There were no windows and only one way in or out. The shop was in the center of town, not far from the palace gate. Victoria worried that they may be too close to Kybon.

"I just think we are sitting right under his nose," Victoria said in protest of the decision to stay there indefinitely.

"Sometimes, that is the best place to hide," Rupert responded.

"Yes, there are a lot of us here. Including the children, there are eleven of us. And also, Victoria, there are ways of getting in and out of places without being seen by unwanted eyes," Joanna said in a pretend mystical voice.

It didn't take long for Victoria to find out what she meant because just as Joanna finished speaking, there was a knock from the wall that Victoria thought was coming from the shop that shared a wall with the smith shop. But the stone was much too thick to make the hollow echo that accompanied the knocking.

"Ah, that would be Justin. He is right on time," Joanna said. She walked over to the side wall. She slid down a piece of the brick. It revealed a metal circle with a thin crossbar of metal that she turned and slid open part of the wall.

A young man in his early twenties walked in. Victoria realized that the man was standing in a very narrow passageway. She smiled as she realized her naivety of the world.

"Everyone, this is my brother, Justin. Justin, this is everyone. Now spill it," Joanna said.

"There are two groups looking for the princess," Justin replied. "One group wants her dead, but Kybon's goons and the royal guard have been ordered to detain her. We are under strict orders not to kill or harm any young woman that look to be about sixteen."

"We?" Rupert asked in an a questioning voice.

"Yes, *we*. I am in the royal guard, but I work for the true king, not the usurper Kybon."

Victoria looked closely at the crest on Justin's black cloak. It was her father's crest!

"Wait, I thought that Kybon can't knowingly lock Victoria up?" Cornelius said, looking at Kylan.

Before she could answer, Justin spoke again. "Well, the orders come from the king! The actual decree is cited as, 'Due to the war, all the young women are to be gathered and protected, because war is dangerous time.' It is a load of horse dung, but somehow Kybon convinced the king that the decree needed to be made. But look, I have to get back. I am on guard tonight at the palace. Beware of a sorcerer named Colin, and to those of you who have just discovered the passages, be careful. You will get lost if you don't know where you are going. I hope to see all of you again soon."

Justin reopened the secret door, walked out, and closed it behind him. Everyone sat quietly for a moment. Victoria was trying to take in what had just been said.

Then Peter broke the silence. "Don't worry. Colin won't kill you, Victoria. I won't let him."

"How are *you* gonna stop him?" Cornelius asked with fear and frustration.

"Don't worry about how. I can and I will stop him from hurting her."

"Thank you, Peter, and besides that, Colin is a coward and a wanted man in these parts. He will not kill her himself, but he is the only one who actually knows what she looks like," Kylan said.

"Why won't he do it himself?" Rupert asked.

"Because for one thing, he cannot enter the city. Kybon has a price on his head that is much too high for his comfort," Kylan said.

"I still think that to be safe, we should stay within the confines of the shop and the passageway. If you know where you are going, you can get anywhere in the city," Cornelius said.

"Fine, but you had better know your way around because I want to see the city, and I will go mad if I am to stay inside for more than a day," Victoria said indignantly.

Cornelius took her hand. He sighed and spoke softly. "Please don't fight us on this. I know you don't want to hear it, but it's for your own good."

Victoria remembered a day in school when her tutor had warned her that stubbornness would one day get her killed. So she acquiesced to Cornelius's wishes.

CHAPTER 29

Hiding Out

They spent the next week in hiding. Victoria followed Cornelius all over the passages between the buildings. They were very narrow hallways, only about three and a half feet in width. They were lit with torches along the walls. Cornelius explained that from the outside on the streets, the walls looked solid. The only way you could see the thin cracks of the sliding doors that lead outside was if you knew they were there. Most of the doors that led to different buildings could only be unlocked from the inside of the building.

Once in a while, they would meet someone else using the passages. It was difficult to pass if someone came from the other direction. One person would have to stand with their back against the wall while the other person did the same and walked sideways very slowly.

While Victoria and Cornelius explored, Kylan walked around the city unguarded. She bought food and supplies. She never told anyone her name. Rupert would sometimes help her, but he never called her by her name either. Peter tagged along with Rupert while Jeps spent his days with his mother. Aden was hard at work, making new swords and knives for Victoria and Cornelius. Now that they were married, it was tradition for them to have swords with their crests together.

On their third day of exploring the city, Kylan convinced Jeps to have lunch with her, Rupert, and Peter. When their picnic in a small park was done, she brought them over to Garvan's Shoe Store. The shop was still named for him, even though he had not worked there in nearly thirty years. Garvan was waiting for them at the shop. He beckoned them to a table he had set up in the back of the shop. When they were all seated, Garvan got a box from behind the counter and placed it on the table.

Then Kylan stood and cleared her throat. "Jeps, we would like to welcome you into our group of friends! I noticed that your boots are a bit tattered from years of wearing them, so since Garvan here is also a shoemaker, we thought you deserved a new pair of boots." She handed Jeps the box.

Jeps began to open it in a stunned silence. As he pulled them from the box, his eyes filled with tears. "I have never had a new pair of shoes," he said quickly before sobs overcame his ability to talk.

"Go ahead and try them on!" Rupert said with a kind smile.

Jeps pulled off his old, broken shoes. He pulled the shiny new boots on to his feet. He stood up and walked to the other end of the shop. He smiled through his tears and hugged everyone in the group and sobbed a "Thank you" to each of them.

On the first day of the next week, Cornelius told Victoria he had a special day planned for her. She was tired now after walking around the secret passage, but there was one hall they had not traveled yet. And somehow it struck some deep memory of hers.

Cornelius took her hands. "I am not sure how you will react to this, but I feel we must do it," he said in a low voice as he led her to the dark unlit passage.

"There is an inkling to me that I have been here before, but I was being carried, and there is a strange screaming."

"I was not there, so I don't know about the screaming, but this is the passage Thomas used to get you out of the palace. If the stories are true, then he kidnapped you in the night and made it look as if you had been murdered."

Victoria could only gasp.

"Tonight, Justin is on duty to guard the king's chambers. He will let us in to see your father."

"Well, come on then. It is going to be a long night if that is the case." She pulled him along the dark corridor.

Cornelius pulled her gently to him and whispered in her ear, "Let me lead. This passage is tricky, and you have not been inside it for fourteen years."

"I suppose that is wise," she said sheepishly. "Why is there no light in this passage?"

"Because it leads to the palace. They don't want to make it easy on outsiders to get in. I have been using this passage for years to bring messages to your father."

Victoria stopped dead in her tracks. "Wait a minute! How long have you known my father?" she demanded in a low but harsh voice. She somehow knew not to raise her voice in the tunnel.

Cornelius spun around. He could not see the anger in her eyes, but he knew it was there. "Victoria, you know I am messenger to the king. Of course, I know him."

"I didn't think you gave the messages directly to my father. I figured there was a guard or someone that would take them from you."

"Well, with normal correspondence, that is what would happen, but sometimes I need to get messages to the king without anyone, especially the queen and Kybon knowing about them."

Cornelius decided then to tell her as much as was safe about his job as a messenger. She deserved to know. "Victoria, let's sit down for a second," he suggested. He took a short lard candle from his shirt pocket and lit it in the dark on the first try. They sat in the dim light facing each other nearly face-to-face because of the thinness of the hall.

"I was a messenger from Bale for many years, that you know. I brought many messages to the king, but I never read any of them.

I had no idea what the correspondence between your uncle and the king meant. To tell you the truth, for many years, I didn't really care. The king paid me well. Then I started to get to know you more and more through my friendship with Rupert. I realized how much you resemble the king. I began to put things together, so I started listening more and more to idle banter. Now I carry a wealth of secret knowledge. Some of which I acquired from the oral messages I was sworn to death to reveal only to the intended receiver. Some I figured out, but I cannot tell you any of it! Ashel has gone to great trouble to keep what I know a secret."

"Promise me that you did not plan to marry me to gain access to the throne!" she said in a helpless sob.

"I promise you!" he said and kissed her gently. "Come, let's go and meet your father. He is very ill, but he wants to meet you."

"What do I say to him?"

"I don't know. I assume he will do most of the talking."

Then Cornelius blew out the candle and helped Victoria to her feet. He walked in the lead, holding her hand as she followed closely behind him. He warned her that there were very steep steps and helped her up them. There was a steep downward slope that went deep under the ground. He explained that they were passing under the palace grounds. There was another set of narrow steps that lead straight up to a door in the roof of the passageway.

"This door leads into the hallway to the king's chambers. There is a guard on both ends, but it is a very long hall, and this trapdoor is directly in the center. There is a small closet directly across from where you come up through the door. So we need to get the door opened silently, then slip into that closet without being seen by the guards," Cornelius whispered.

"Sure, that sounds quite easy!" Victoria whispered back with a sarcastic tone.

"Well, the guards are facing the other way. Very few people know about this passage and trapdoor, and those of us who do don't tell the guards about it. I don't think even Justin knows how we are getting in."

"Aye, so as long as they don't hear us, we are fine."

"Right, but that is not an easy task. Two feet doesn't seem far, but this is a silent hall, and the guards are good at what they do. And getting up through the door takes a great deal of upper-body strength," he whispered.

"Unlock the door and let me go first. Then you can jump out and protect me."

Cornelius was not sure if she was being serious, but he did not argue. He unlocked the door and pulled it down very carefully. Victoria put her arms up through the hole and pulled herself upward. It took most of her strength to pull herself up, even with Cornelius pushing on her lower torso. But she did not make a sound in her struggles as she pulled herself to her feet. She turned the doorknob slowly and pushed on the door. It opened silently, and she slipped inside. Cornelius was up and in the closet very quickly.

"Wow, that was fast," she said.

"I have done this before, remember?" Cornelius replied.

"Aye. Now what do we do?"

"Well, that is the hard part of the plan. We have to make a run for it."

"So there is no secret passageway out of here?"

"No, only this empty closet with a secret extra chamber inside it."

"Well, get inside the secret chamber. I am gonna make a bit of noise."

Cornelius did not object, but he wished for a second that he could actually read her mind. She looked around the dark closet and found him lying sideways in a small cutout in the wall. He was holding open the door to the hiding place.

Victoria kicked the door to the closet open with some force and then jumped into the closet-hiding place with Cornelius. The door slammed against the outside wall and then slammed shut. They could hear the echoes of the guard's footfalls as they ran toward the sound.

The guard on the east end of the hall arrived first. He lit the torch on the wall next to the closet just as the other guard came up. "What happened, Joe?" he asked out of breath.

"I don't know! There is a storage closet here, but they don't keep nothing in it." He pushed gently on the wall. The door opened. He shined the light in inside. "See, look, there is nothing inside."

"Then how did the door open?"

"How the heck should I know, dimwit?"

"Maybe it was a ghost."

"I don't know what it was, but there is nothing here. So we need to get back to our post. If captain catches us here lookin' at nothin', we are dead."

"I agree, but be on the lookout for a ghost. I doubt this door could open on its own."

"You are funny, Bob! I am putting out this torch. Don't be scared on your way back!" Joe said in a taunting voice.

About a minute after the footfalls stopped, Cornelius pushed open the door to the cutout and climbed down. "Why did you do that exactly?"

"Because now we know which direction to run! We go west. Bob is much slower, and he is already spooked, which should give us an extra few seconds' head start," Victoria said as she slid quietly down to the ground.

"I always wait until they change shifts and then slip by them," he said.

"Yes, but there are two of us, and I want to see my father now."

"But how are we going to get out if we alert them to our presence?"

"Easy. We convince Bob that we are ghosts. He seems to really believe there are ghosts here."

They crept slowly down the hallway in the dark. Cornelius fumbled around in his pocket until he found a small rock. "Hey, be really quiet. I am gonna throw this rock over the guard's head to the far wall. Then you make a run for it. There will be a set of stairs on your left. Go up those stairs and wait for me," he whispered as they got close enough to the guard to slip past him.

"How did you get a rock?" Victoria asked, almost forgetting to whisper.

"I always have a rock or two, in case I need a distraction," he said.

"See you in a couple of minutes." She kissed him quickly and then let go of his hand and got closer to the guard.

Just as Cornelius lifted his arm to throw the rock, he heard a voice in the darkness.

"Please, spirits, I have done nothing wrong," the voice said in a low, fearful voice.

"What?" said Victoria in astonishment.

"You are not very good at pretending to be a ghost," Bob whispered as he turned and looked at them both with a torch in his hand. "Though you could pass as one. My gosh, you look just like her!"

"Just like who?"

"Your mother. She used to sneak in this way to see the king."

"You knew my mother?" Excitement began to creep into her voice.

"Victoria, keep your voice down." Cornelius warned with his head on her shoulder. He looked back to see if Joe had heard anything.

"Don't worry about him. He is nearly deaf, and he thinks I am the idiot! And yes, I knew your mother. She was my cousin."

Victoria stood there, almost in a trance. She realized she knew his voice. She had heard it in her dreams. The recurring nightmare came back to her all at once. She remembered being carried down a dark hall. She was crying because she would never see her father again. Then she remembered Bob's voice. *Good-bye, little one. Thomas will take care of you now. But we will meet again someday.* Then she was in a different corridor. She always woke up just before they stepped into the lighted room.

"I remember your voice from a dream. You were telling me good-bye," she said in a nearly inaudible tone.

"That's right. I was on post here when Thomas came with you to escape the castle. You stayed with my wife and me until then. We live on the castle grounds so you could still visit your father. You were nearly three when you left us. My sons were very sad, but it was for the best."

"You said we would meet again and now we have," she said as she extended her hand as an introduction.

Bob took her hand and shook it firmly. Then he reached out to Cornelius, who had been standing, patiently waiting.

"Oh yes, this is my boyfriend. I mean my husband, Cornelius," Victoria said.

"Yes, the messenger boy! We have met before, though never formally. It is nice to finally speak to you. After all those times, I let you sneak in to see the king."

"Let me?" Cornelius asked in astonishment.

"Son, I have been guarding this corridor for thirty years now. No one gets past me unless I want them to. I do give you credit. We were changing shifts every time. I merely didn't point out to the idiot who replaces me. It was really his place to stop you anyhow!" Bob said with a smile.

"Now go on, you two. The king is getting worse by the day. You have four hours before you are stuck in the castle for the night. If you don't make it by then, there is always a bed at my house."

Cornelius took Victoria's hand and led her away. She turned around and followed him to the staircase. They walked silently up the stone stairs. When they reached the top, Cornelius opened the door a little and looked down the hall. There was no one about, so he and Victoria stepped out of the dingy basement and into the beautiful bright and ornate palace.

Cornelius led her to the next hall, where Justin was standing guard outside a door.

"Hi, Justin," Cornelius said.

"Well, I'll be. You guys made it. His Majesty is waiting for you. But I have to warn you, Victoria. He is very ill. His lungs don't work well."

"I know. I think I have always known, but where is the queen? What if she finds us here?"

"She won't! She is gone to the battlefields. She is beginning to fear for her sons' lives. They are all she has, you know."

"I thought she wanted the war."

"She doesn't want Kybon to kill her sons."

"But—"

"Victoria, we will discuss this later," Cornelius butted in. We don't have much time. Justin, when is post change for you?"

"Four hours is all the time you will need. He will not be awake much longer than that anyway."

"Fine, see you soon then," Cornelius and Victoria said together. She took Cornelius's hand this time as she reached for the doorknob with the other. She turned it slowly and opened the door gently. She and Cornelius walked in holding hands.

The room was dimly lit. In fact, the only light was the light given off from the dying fire. There was nothing on the walls, and there were no windows at all. There was only a lavish bed in the center of the room and a small table next to it. The king lay on it half-propped up on pillows.

"Come in, you two. I have been waiting many years to see you again, Victoria. Please do not be shy," the king said in a low, raspy voice. He didn't sound weak, just strangely breathless.

Victoria wasn't sure how to feel; she was happy to finally meet her father, but she was scared and angry and sad at the circumstances that had separated them. She also felt like she was betraying Thomas in some way. Thomas was the only father she ever knew. Many thoughts and feelings rushed around in her head. She thought for a moment that she might become sick to her stomach. Then she became livid at her own weaknesses.

Cornelius gently squeezed her hand and motioned her forward. She took a deep, steadying breath and forced her anger and fears to the back of her mind. A second breath calmed her completely. She felt a peace and spoke to her father for the first time since she was two years old.

"Hello, Father."

"Hello, Your Highness." This was Cornelius's usual greeting.

"First, I would like to say I am sorry that I missed you growing up. I hear from Justin that you two got married a few days ago."

"Yes, sir," Cornelius said. He began to feel worse about the fact that he had not been able to ask the king for permission to marry Victoria. The king was her father, and tradition called for the formality of the father's blessing.

"You had my blessing, Cornelius. Thomas made sure I knew. You even delivered messages to me about it. Do not be upset that you never asked me. Thomas raised her..."

He could not finish his sentence. Victoria felt it too. She was finally face-to-face with her father, but she did not know him. She had spent the last fourteen years considering Thomas to be her father. Cornelius was finding it hard to feel that the sick and wilted man that lay before them could be the father of such a vibrant and feisty woman.

"I do wish I could have left this castle, but I am afraid that without Kybon's herbs to keep me breathing, I would have died years ago," he said as he began to cough deeply.

"What do you mean by Kybon's herbs? Is he keeping you alive?"

"Yes, my lungs do not work the way that they should. But Kybon was trained in medicine as a boy. He keeps me alive. So if I die, one of the twins will become king. They are much stronger than I, so they could usurp his power." The king stopped talking again.

Cornelius walked to the basin on the bed stand and got the king a cup of water. The king took it and drank slowly. When he was done, Victoria took over the talking.

"So as long as you are alive, you are king and he is in control. So what of the war the twins are fighting, what does that prove? And what happens if they both die?"

"Well then, Colin becomes king since he is my half-brother. Kybon already controls him, so that is ideally what he wants."

"But even if the twins die, Kybon can't kill me so I would become queen."

"Be on your guard, daughter. You are right that he can't kill you, but he can lock you up. You can't rule the kingdom from his dungeon."

"We will not let that happen!" Cornelius said.

"I want to believe that. But it is still better than Colin's idea. If he kills her, he will become truly as evil as Kybon. But he is desperate to stop Kybon's reign. He does not want the throne. He is a good man. He wants the same things we do. He wants the peace he and I once knew."

The king began to cough again. This time was even longer. Cornelius again got the king some water. Even as he drank, Victoria knew that the conversation was over. He was too weak to continue. So she spent the better part of an hour telling him stories about her life. Cornelius took out the book he had been writing in and read some of their travels to the king. It was written up to the night of their marriage.

Then there was a light knocking on the door, but before they could answer or hide, Justin opened the door and said loudly, "Your Highness, your herbs will be down in a few minutes. I was told to make sure you are awake. The royal and mighty sorcerer Kybon will be bringing them in person." Then the door closed again.

Victoria and Cornelius knew that Justin was warning them to leave now. Victoria hugged her father, and he kissed her cheek. She promised to return as soon as she could. Two minutes later, they walked out the door and passed Justin, who winked at them happily. They went back the same way they came.

Bob was still on guard in front of the dark hallway. He stepped up two steps, clearing the way to the secret door as they walked up. He leaned in and whispered in Victoria's ear as they walked by. "See you soon, spirit!" he said, moving his eyes back and forth in mock fear. Victoria smiled as she let Cornelius lead her to the trapdoor.

Half an hour later, they were back in Aden's shop. He was hard at work, casting new weapons for them, two knives for Cornelius and a new sword for Victoria. Garvan was sitting silently in a corner facing the wall. There was no one else in the room. Cornelius sat down to finish writing their journey. Victoria pulled out her journal and began writing too.

Suddenly Kylan appeared in the room. No one heard her come in until she spoke. "Cornelius, what did you think of the conversation with the king?"

"Ahh! You scared me. When did you come in?"

"Just now. I can move silently! Answer the question, please."

"I don't know what to think. We want to keep her safe, but I know she is not willing to stay here while the rest of us are out. She is not a prisoner."

"No, she isn't!"

"Aw, I am sitting here," Victoria said in a slightly perturbed voice.

"Yes, but I know what you think already."

"Well, what do we do now?" Cornelius asked.

"Don't leave the city. Colin cannot enter the city itself," Kylan said.

"But what about Kybon capturing me?" Victoria asked.

"He will not hurt you, and contrary to your father's beliefs, you will not be there forever! There are powerful forces on your side."

Garvan walked up and sat at the table with Victoria and Cornelius. Kylan was still standing near them refusing to sit down. "Here, take this and keep it safe," Garvan said as he handed Victoria a small jar of a purple liquid.

She examined it carefully. "What is it?"

"It is a potion that will help you sleep comfortably if you are captured."

"I think sleep will be the least of my worries if I get captured."

"No. You see, you will need to stay well! Kybon will not kill you but has decided to throw you in the dungeon! This potion will keep you warm also. If you get sick and die naturally, he keeps his powers and there is no heir to the throne!" Garvan said sadly.

The realization came to the three of them at once. Victoria looked closely at the vial again. "How long will it last?"

"There is enough there for three weeks if you use it wisely. I am sorry I have no more. It takes months to make. I will have more in four months, but you will not need it by then." Garvan chuckled and went back to his corner.

That night, all seven of them gathered for dinner in the shop. Joanna cooked a meal of fresh meat and vegetables and bread. Kylan had gotten the meat from the butcher, and Rupert had gotten the rest. It was the best meal any of them had eaten in a while. After dinner, they played the game they had made up at the festival in the woods. Laughter filled the small room long into the night.

The next morning, Jeps left to go to work with his mother again. He enjoyed the work and it kept him busy. Finally, he had found a place he liked. Victoria dressed up as Mark and went out with Cornelius to explore the city. Rupert left on Thunderstorm that morning to go back to the battlefield to help Bartholomew. Though the battle was now at a standstill, the queen was trying to work out a truce in a desperate effort to keep both of her sons alive.

Two days later, Kylan came rushing up to Victoria and Cornelius as they sat outside the inn talking to Jeps and his mother. Peter was with Kylan. He looked very confused.

"I need to talk to you all!" she said nearly out of breath.

"What is it?" Victoria and Cornelius said together.

She pulled them close to her and spoke in a whisper. "Kybon's general is on his way to the battlefield. He is going to make the princes duel for the throne. But the plan is to make sure they both die! I got through to Rupert, but there is little he can do right now."

"Why not?" asked Jeps, who believed that all of his new friends were capable of anything.

"Because Colin is there. He is a sorcerer and more powerful than he is given credit for. He is currently planning a nasty spell to keep Rupert from doing anything."

"Oh no! Can you stop him?" Victoria asked.

"Yes, but while I am doing that, someone has to stop the duel."

"We will go with you, Kylan," Jeps said.

"But Colin wants to kill Victoria, Jeps. She shouldn't leave the city," Kylan said.

"But what about Bartholomew? He will fight the duel if he thinks he can end this! We have to help them!"

Cornelius didn't say anything. He knew that whatever they decided, it was Victoria's decision.

"Jeps is right. Rupert is my friend, and Bartholomew and Mathew are my brothers. What kind of a queen would I be if I let my own brothers kill each other?" Victoria said.

"Cornelius, what do you think?" Kylan asked.

"I think that I have to support my wife's decision. What kind of king would I be if I can't support my queen?"

Kylan feared that she would not be able to protect everyone. But she was not going to admit her fears to her friends. It would do no good, anyway. Their minds were made up. "Very well, the decision is made."

"Yes, we go as soon as possible," Victoria said.

Cornelius and Jeps went inside to tell Cornelius's grandfather that they were leaving. He sent them on their way with his blessing and some dried food.

"We won't need that. I can move place to place instantly. There is no time to ride there. But I can only take you one at a time," Kylan said.

"That will leave Victoria unprotected," Cornelius said.

"Not if we go in the right order," Peter said from behind them. "Jeps goes first, then me, then Victoria goes and then you. Jeps and I will be able to protect her before you get there." Peter actually meant he could protect her, but he didn't want them to know that yet.

"But how will that work?" Cornelius asked.

"Just trust me, okay?" Peter said with indignance in his voice.

Cornelius trusted Peter, though he didn't know why. So Kylan set to the task of concentrating very hard to move herself and another person through space a far distance. The whole process took less than five minutes. Kylan had actually taken them to a place on the mountain that overlooked the battlefield. No one was around to see them appear from nowhere.

Jeps and Peter were both still shorter than Victoria, but they stood one on each side of her for the minute or so it took for Kylan to return with Cornelius. They said nothing in that time. Jeps wasn't sure he completely trusted Peter, but he was just starting to learn to trust people at all. Peter had nothing to say. He knew they didn't trust him yet. But they would soon.

So they just stood there in the warm sunshine. When Kylan returned with Cornelius, she led them down the steep path to the flat ground near Bartholomew's camp. Rupert was waiting for them. He did not look well. He looked as if he was fighting the stomach flu.

"Are you okay, Rupert?" Peter asked.

"No, but Colin's spell could be worse. Garvan is helping me fight it. But never mind me. I will live. It is Bartholomew I am worried about. Mathew is much better with a sword."

"How do we stop this?" Victoria said.

"We will have to talk them out of it. But that is where it gets tricky," Rupert said, trying to hide how weak he felt.

"When is the duel set to take place?" Cornelius asked.

"Dawn!" Rupert said, dropping to one knee.

Kylan leaned over and put her hand on Rupert's shoulder to steady him. She was tired from bringing the others here, but she said a spell to herself to protect him more. He reached up for her hand, and she pulled him up. He dusted off the knee of his pants.

"So what do we do now? It will be getting dark soon. I want to talk to Bartholomew," Victoria said.

"I know. The queen has set up a bed for you in his tent. She can't talk them out of it. I think she is hoping you can," Rupert said.

"I thought she hated me?"

Rupert weakly shrugged his shoulders.

They all walked together to the camp. Cornelius kept an eye out for Colin as they walked.

Rupert walked next to Cornelius to steady himself but still tried to reassure his friend. "Don't worry too much. Colin can't kill her himself. It will have to be one of his henchmen, so they will have to actually fight her by hand. We are ready for them."

They spent much of the afternoon and evening talking to their friends at the camp. All of the boys were scared and tired, and there was a painful absence of several. The battles had taken its toll on all of them. Malachi sat quietly, looking over a paper that was well worn out.

Bartholomew was in the tent with his mother. She had been going back and forth between her sons' camps. There was a guard standing on either side of the entrance to Bartholomew's tent. Before either man could say anything, the queen came bursting out of the tent.

She was tall and thin. She had long black hair. Her eyes were exactly the same as Bartholomew's. She beckoned Victoria into the tent. But the guards stepped in front of the rest of the group. Victoria stopped and turned to one of the guards after she got a look at the faces of both of them. She pointed to Cornelius. "He comes with me."

The guard glanced at the queen. She nodded so he stepped aside and let Cornelius pass into the tent. Victoria saw Bartholomew lying on a pile of hay and blankets. He was wheezing very hard and sweating in his sleep.

Victoria rushed to his side. "Is he sick?" she asked, realizing the stupidity of the question as she asked it.

"He can barely stand up."

"Then there will be no duel at dawn," Victoria said.

"He and his brother are insisting. Mathew is as stubborn as... well... me," said the queen.

"But if he can't stand. How can he hold his sword?"

"He can't. He will die and give his brother the throne, but Kybon will see to it that they both die! I will be left with nothing."

Victoria realized the queen was only upset because she was going to lose both of her sons. It was well known that she favored Mathew over Bartholomew. Victoria wondered if the queen were hoping that Bartholomew would die in the night.

"What do you want from me?" Victoria asked.

"I want you to help me save my sons!"

"I will do what a can for Bartholomew." She would make no promises about Mathew, a boy she had never met even if he was her brother.

"You will save them both, or you will save neither!" the queen said sharply.

Victoria didn't even flinch when Kylan appeared behind the queen. Cornelius was careful not to give away what was happening.

Victoria spoke again. "I have never met Mathew. How can I save him?"

"I can't lose both of my children and my husband!"

Victoria shook her head. "I am afraid I have no power to control that." Just as she finished her statement, Kylan disappeared with Bartholomew.

Victoria grabbed Cornelius's hand and ran for the door. The queen ran after them, but she was stopped by the guards. Cornelius looked at them and realized one was his own cousin and the other was the splitting image of Bob if he were twenty years younger. Victoria nodded to both men. They both smiled broadly, each holding the queen by an arm.

Rupert hobbled up; his whole body hunched over. "It looks like he had been poisoned. I believe, Your Highness, that you had better run back the favored son!"

"I didn't poison him. I know everyone thinks I am cruel, but I love my sons. I would never willingly let him die."

"Then why is he dying now?" Rupert asked, bluffing a little.

"No! He said it only made him sick."

"Why would you want to make him sick?" Victoria asked.

"Why, to bring you here, of course!" the queen said happily.

Before Victoria could process that statement, she saw Colin running up with several men. They surrounded all of them. Kylan was nowhere in sight. One of the bigger men grabbed Victoria while a second stood in front of her with his sword drawn. Cornelius ran behind to stop him with one of his knives drawn but was thrown to the ground by another man, though he managed to wound his assailant on his way down. Rupert fell on his own as Kylan was not there to counter Colin's spell.

Suddenly Peter grabbed Cornelius's knife from the ground. But instead of running to the action, he merely yelled. "Colin, if you kill her, I will kill myself and end your powers!"

Colin put up a hand to stop the man with the sword. "What?" Colin, along with several others, yelled at once.

Peter pulled up the left sleeve of his shirt to reveal the same mark Victoria had on her arm. Colin realized at once he was looking at the keeper of his powers. Kylan reappeared and knocked down the three remaining men with the sweep of her hand.

"You wouldn't kill yourself to save her life! Proceed, Merdoc!" Colin ordered.

Merdoc smiled manically. Peter looked at Kylan and then screamed at the top of his lungs. He jammed the knife into his side, where he knew that Garvan would be able to heal the wound.

Colin fell to the ground at the same time. Kylan swung her arm again, throwing Merdoc to the ground. The sword fell from his hands. Victoria kicked the man that was holding her. Then she pulled him forward and threw him over her head to the ground!

Suddenly Rupert was standing again. The spell was broken, and his strength returned.

Kylan grabbed Peter and disappeared with him. Rupert grabbed Colin and dragged him to the guards by Bartholomew's tent. In the confusion, the two guards lost sight of the queen.

"The queen is gone, Rupert," Bob's son, Junior, said.

"That is all right. She is really not a threat to us anymore. But don't lose sight of this one."

"Can't he use magic to escape?" the other guard asked.

"Not right now! He called Peter's bluff and lost," Rupert said. Colin only let out a small whimper. He stood up dejectedly as the two young men tied him up.

Rupert walked back out to the battlefield. He explained to Malachi and the troops that Bartholomew had been poisoned but that he would be better in a few days. Their troubles were far from over—Kybon would not be happy that his plans had been thwarted. When he was done talking, he turned around to find Kylan standing behind him.

"Come on, I will take you back to Pallen," Kylan said. "We could use your help taking care of Barth and Peter."

"Wait, how are you gonna do that?" Rupert eyed her incredulously.

"Magic!"

"Oh yeah. Wait, what about Thunderstorm?"

"I think he will be fine here. I will have to come back in a few days. I don't plan to let Peter die, so I will have to come back to restrain Colin when he regains his powers."

"Aye, but let me at least tell Thunder I am leaving."

Kylan handed him a carrot she had brought back for him to give to the horse. Rupert smiled at the small gift.

CHAPTER 30

Peter's Recovery

Bartholomew was fine as soon as Garvan found the correct antidote. He was extremely tired but refused to go to sleep until someone told him what happened. Rupert quickly told him about the poison and the trap and Colin's spell. He omitted that it was the queen who had given him the poison.

"How did Peter hurting himself break Colin's spells? I thought the power keeper had to die?" Bartholomew asked.

"By the laws of magic. Because Colin did not try to stop Peter, his powers are in limbo until Peter's strength returns."

Peter lay still in the cot next to Bartholomew. Garvan and Kylan cleaned the wound and dressed it. Then they gave him sleeping herbs so that he could rest comfortably. Bartholomew slept all night and most of the next day without any sleeping herbs at all.

Garvan hovered near his charges while the others filled in Aden and Joanna on their adventure. The story was much longer than the actual events because each of them told parts of it while correcting and interjecting in on each other. Jeps spoke the loudest about Peter's bravery. He was proud of his new friend. The account was finally done being told just before midnight.

Garvan talked them all into going to sleep. "All of you need a good rest!"

The next day, they all agreed that they should lay low for the next few days. Jeps didn't even go back to work at the inn. His mother came to stay with them instead. They were afraid that Kybon would be looking for all of them now.

Kylan told the others that they needed to stay in Aden's shop because they were safe from Kybon's magic there. The high sorceress had managed a spell that protected anyone with in its walls. Kylan was the only one who left the shop besides Joanna, who had to work at the tavern. Aden left, but he took the passage within the walls wherever he went.

Kylan popped out every few hours to check on Colin. She finally decided on a way to deal with him.

"Rupert, is it all right if I tie Colin to Thunderstorm and send them off to the high sorceress?"

"You will have to ask Thunderstorm that. You know I don't decide where he goes. But if he agrees, make sure he is protected."

"Thunderstorm will be fine. Colin's powers are not fully back, and I don't see him regaining full powers before they reach Ashel. She is waiting for him."

CHAPTER 31

The Siblings Unite

It had been a full week when there came a knock at the front door of the shop. Both Peter and Bartholomew were recovered, though Peter's ribs were still sore. Kylan looked at Bartholomew.

"It's your brother at the door. He wants to talk you. Is it all right if I let him in?"

"Yes, well, is he alone?"

"No, but I will let only Prince Mathew in."

The others said nothing. They just waited. Rupert was glad for something to do. Victoria felt a pang of excitement in finally meeting her other brother. Kylan opened the door slightly, spoke to the persons outside, and then opened the door enough to let Prince Mathew slip inside.

Mathew walked in slowly. He was wearing old, tattered clothes and did not appear to have a weapon. His hair was shorter than Bartholomew's. He walked in and sat down at the table next to his brother.

"I want to call a truce! I have realized that neither of us will ever become king. We should be working together to help our father and our people," Mathew spoke with a clear voice.

"I agree," Bartholomew said, looking up at Kylan to see if he could trust his brother. She nodded affirmatively. So Bartholomew extended his hand. They shook hands.

"Where is Mom?" Bartholomew asked.

"She is back at the palace. But I fear things are not going well there. Father is getting sicker by the day. And Kybon is angry. I was listening to him talk to his general. He is going to take over the country by force. He is declaring war on us."

"You and me? Or the whole country?"

"You and me and our armies. I think we should join forces against him. Most of the guards are on Father's side. Kybon actually has a much smaller army than he thinks."

"But what about his powers?" Bartholomew asked. Rupert and Victoria listened very carefully without interrupting the brothers.

Mathew stood up and looked around the room. His eyes fell on each one of them. He lingered a second or two on Victoria. "Well, we have a sorceress here! And the heir to the throne, I presume?" he said.

"Maybe," Bartholomew said in a voice that let his brother know that he still did not fully trust him.

"Look, I know you are angry at me and at Mother, but well, we have to trust each other now. It is the only way we will defeat Kybon and take back the country that rightfully belongs to our family." Mathew then stood up and walked straight up to Victoria. "Hi, I am Mathew," he said, extending his hand.

"Victoria," she said as she shook his hand. "This is my husband, Cornelius."

"Nice to meet you both. I am sorry for the troubles that I have caused either directly or indirectly. That goes for all of you."

Everyone mumbled something about accepting his apology. Rupert didn't get a bad feeling from Mathew.

"I trust you!" Kylan said more to everyone else other than to Mathew. *If he is setting us up, he is not aware of it. He has truly come to realize that he was on the wrong side*, she thought, hoping Rupert will pick her thoughts.

"I trust him as well," Rupert responded.

The next day, Victoria insisted on seeing her father again. Cornelius and Rupert were both skeptical.

"But he is dying. I have only just gotten to know him," Victoria pleaded.

"What if Kybon catches you?" Rupert argued.

"Then he will throw me in the dungeon. My life is not in danger. I am better off there than fighting in this war."

They talked and argued for several hours, but it was finally agreed on that Rupert and Cornelius were going to go back to the battlefield with the princes and Jeps and Peter. Bartholomew promoted both of them to commanders, which was a position just below general. Mathew agreed with the decision.

Victoria went to see her father alone, while Kylan became messenger to the army leaders because she could get back and forth almost instantly. Jeps's mother and Cornelius's grandfather and Joanna began to spread the word that the princes had joined forces and were taking recruits for the army. Garvan and Aden took up the task of training the new boys and men who began to show up at the door of the inn.

Thunderstorm turned up on the way to the battlefield. Rupert had been riding Kylan's horse since she was not in need of one at the moment. Thunderstorm understood what was going on and trotted along beside Rupert and his borrowed mount.

By midday the next day, the two armies had fully merged together. Malachi and the other generals and his two new commanders were busy training and preparing the young men for a full out war.

Kylan brought Victoria to the battlefield to meet up with the others while she was on one of her trips as a messenger. Victoria was dressed in a general's uniform with her bright-green cloak where the black smock would have been. Her sword was at her side, and she was carrying one that looked just like hers.

"Bartholomew, I got your sword back. Wear it with pride," she said.

"Thank you, but shouldn't you be dressed that way? Kybon is looking for you," her brother said.

"Yes, I am aware of that, but he will not kill me. He knows he cannot. I will survive in the dungeon for a few days." She smiled at Cornelius, who looked very handsome in his new uniform. "My husband will rescue me!"

Cornelius blushed just a little bit. But he smiled at her confidence in him. Rupert was nearby too. His uniform was new as well, but he had already torn a hole in his pants. Victoria thought of the pants she had never sewed for him. It had been less than a year, but it seemed so long ago.

CHAPTER 32

Victoria's Capture

Later that day, Victoria, along with Kylan and two other women about their age, were captured in the marketplace. Since there were so few men in the city now, they were easy to find.

Just as Kybon's guards bounded forward to arrest them, Kylan leaned over and whispered in Victoria's ear, "The best place for you is in the dungeon. It is Kybon who is falling prey to his own devious plan! Drink a bit of the potion Garvan gave you. They will not find it if we are searched."

Victoria did not have time to respond. The guards seized them roughly and dragged them toward the palace. Kybon had no time to deal with them. He glanced at them from far away and had Victoria and Kylan locked in the dungeon. The other two women were sent to be part of his growing harem.

Cornelius missed Victoria very much but was reassured that she would be alive when he and Rupert went to rescue her.

Kylan simply transported herself out of the dungeon and returned to the battlefield.

"How did you get out?" Jeps asked in amazement. He had been on the errand to the marketplace with them, but Kylan warned him to let them be captured. He was simply to report back to Cornelius and Rupert what had happened. He did what he was told.

Rupert and Kylan both said "Magic" at the same time.

That night, Kylan appeared in the small dark dungeon room. Victoria was sitting in the corner with her eyes closed. She wasn't sure how much of Garvan's concoction she was to drink, so she had not taken much. It had only lasted four or five hours, but Victoria didn't know for sure how long she had been there.

"Why did it take you so long to get here?" she said without opening her eyes.

"I had to check on Rupert and your husband."

"How is Cornelius taking my capture?"

"He is already planning to rescue you."

"That is sweet."

"Yeah, well, it is going to be about two weeks before he can get here."

Then Kylan lit a small ball of fire in her hand. Victoria almost asked her how she did that but remembered that the answer was magic. In the light, she noticed that Kylan had a large pack with her.

"I brought you some supplies," Kylan said, setting down the pack with one hand.

Victoria opened it and began removing the items. There was a large, thick blanket, two candles, a pillow, and a small bottle of a ground herb, two pieces of flint, her journal, a piece of writing coal, canteen full of water, two small cups, and a spoon.

"The herb is willow-tree root. It will keep you from getting sick in the dank air in this place. Put a spoonful into that cup, and then mix it with the water from the canteen. Drink it once a day. Also Cornelius sent with me your journal and the candles so you can see. He said you will go mad in here with nothing to do."

"He is right."

"Aye, you are set. I need to go before someone hears us talking. Kybon cannot kill me either, but he can hurt me. I would prefer he not test my powers this soon." She lit one of the candles with her fire then disappeared as quickly as she had appeared.

Victoria looked at the very short candle. She wondered how long it would burn. It looked like it would last only an hour or so, but she was starting to learn that magic changed what she knew about the world.

After a minute or two, her eyes adjusted to the dim light, and she was able to examine the tiny space. The ceiling was staggered like an upside-down staircase, which explained how Kylan was able to stand at her full stature. She must have been in a room under stone steps. Judging from what she remembered of her under-castle travels, this was not a staircase she had walked up. The stairs were pointed in the wrong direction if the door was facing the wall Bob had been guarding. She stood up and leaned against the wall for a moment, and then she walked in a circle to stretch out her legs. After the better part of an hour, she had the tiny room arranged comfortably. She took out her journal and began to write to keep her mind busy.

CHAPTER 33

Kylan Returns to the Fray

When Kylan returned to the battlefield, she found her father and three of Cornelius's uncles sitting in small tent set up for the officers.

"Hello, my daughter!" Raven said happily.

"Hello, what are you doing here?"

"We came to help. You know I have the best network of spies in the kingdom. The princes are young. They will not win on their own."

"No one will win, anyway, not until Kybon dies, but, Father, no one can kill him. The council told me that if one sorcerer kills another even to protect their people, that sorcerer is cursed for the rest of their days. I am not sure I can let that happen to Rupert. The council told me not to tell him."

"Honey, calm down. Do not worry, and do not tell Rupert! He will be fine, I promise."

"But, Dad—"

"Kylan, he will be all right. Now practice guarding your mind so that you don't tell him about it as you dwell on it in your worries."

"Aye. By the way, where is he?"

"He and Cornelius are on their way to Pallen for more supplies. They took your horse along. Rupert said you would not need him," Bastien said from the corner.

"Her—my horse is a *her*, and I suppose he is right."

"They will be back later tonight, Kylan, but for now, tell me about your adventures. I have not seen you since you got your powers."

Kylan sat down and began to tell her father all the things that had happened since they left him just after the festival. As they talked, she calmed down a bit, but not enough to hide her anxiety.

Rupert could feel her tension from Pallen as he and Cornelius loaded the supplies on the horses.

"What's wrong, Rupert? You keep staring off into space!" Cornelius asked as he put the heaviest saddlebag on the Kylan's horse without Rupert's help.

"Sorry, Kylan is worried about me. I am not sure why. She is blocking any actual thoughts."

"Well, you have a tough mission. And I think she is smitten with you, so it is only natural for her to worry.

"Smitten? Yeah, maybe so, but I don't think that is why she is worried. She knows I can take care of myself."

"Can you?"

"What? Of course, I can!" Rupert felt rage as Cornelius's lack of faith in him coursed through him.

"I don't mean any disrespect, but you don't have your powers yet, so you are vulnerable. Don't get angry. I am sure that is why she is anxious. She is worried, but she can't protect you or me or the princes or Victoria. I am sure it is quite frustrating for her. Truthfully, I feel the same way!"

Rupert took a deep breath to center himself. "You are right. I can feel her calming down. I believe she is talking to Raven."

"Probably, he is there with Bastien, Benjamin, and Byron."

"Come on, let's get back to the battlefield. I am starting to get my own uneasy feeling. We are not safe much longer here."

The two of them set out for the battlefield at once. Rupert knew they were being followed, but there was nothing they could do about it but be prepared for an attack.

Kylan picked up on his thoughts. "Rupert and Cornelius are being followed as they head back here," Kylan told her father.

"Can you take me and a horse with you instantly?"

"Yes, I think so."

"Come on then."

Raven took his daughter's hand, and they quickly went to his horse. She concentrated hard. She was not sure where Rupert was. He gave her landmarks in his thoughts. She was a little off in her destination, but they appeared a little ahead of them on the trail.

Raven smiled at his daughter as he listened. "We are a bit ahead of them, but they should be visible as they come around the bend."

Sure enough, as they watched, Rupert and Cornelius came around the bend into their sight. Kylan thought Rupert looked very powerful on the back of Thunderstorm. The other two horses looked quite small in his presence.

Raven rode toward them. He waved them to a stop as they got close to him. The boys dismounted the horses and walked to Kylan and Raven.

Raven helped Kylan off the horse but did not dismount himself. "Kylan is going to take you two back to the battlefield. I will ride back with the horses," he said to the two men.

"But, Father, do you even know the way?" Kylan was worried.

"No, but Thunderstorm does. He will take me. Do not worry!

I will be back before morning."

"But there is someone following us," Rupert said.

"There are many of my spies in the area too. If I am attacked, they will be here to help me. Do not worry about me. Now, I said go back to the battlefield." Raven's tone reminded them of who was really in charge.

Kylan did not ever second-guess her father. She took them each by the hand and thought herself back to the battlefield. She nearly collapsed from exhaustion when they appeared in the officer's tent.

Rupert caught her fall. "Aye, time for you to rest," he said.

She was too tired to argue, so she just let him carry her to the tent set up for the sick and injured, though at the moment it was being used for the exhausted trainees. He laid her gently in one of the open cots. He kissed her softly and whispered to her, "Don't worry about me. We are gonna be all right. Get some rest." He almost told her that he was falling in love with her, but he decided that now was not the right time. He stumbled over the cot next to hers as he walked away. She giggled as she drifted off to sleep. Since his back was turned while he tried to catch himself as he tripped over the cot, he didn't notice Ashel appear next to Kylan.

He walked slowly back to the officers' tent. He wondered if everything was really going to be all right. How was he going to stop Kybon? It seemed that this was his destiny, but he wasn't sure how or what to do. His birthday was still two weeks away. The war was going to start any day now. He knew that all Cornelius could think about was getting Victoria out of the dungeon. Bartholomew and Mathew were trying so hard to be good leaders, but they were still very young.

Rupert began to feel helpless.

CHAPTER 34

Visits from Elders

The rest of the day went by slowly for Rupert. He tried not to dwell on the growing feeling of uselessness that was creeping into his soul. Not far off, Thunderstorm quickened his pace. Raven noticed and smiled to himself.

Kylan felt it in her rest. She opened her eyes and noticed the high sorceress watching her.

"I will talk to him," Ashel said before Kylan opened her mouth to speak.

"It is important that he does not get discouraged."

"He will be fine. Your father will be back soon, and Thomas is on his way here as well. They will take care of things. And as for the magical laws that you are worried about, don't worry. There are, as Kybon and Colin have discovered, many loopholes to the rules that govern us. I have found one or two that work to our advantage. No curse will come to Rupert when he is successful in saving us all."

Kylan smiled and went back to sleep with her mind at ease. Ashel left as silently as she came.

Raven and Thomas arrived at nearly the same time. Whoever had been following Rupert and Cornelius thought better of attacking Raven. Thomas rode up just after Raven and the two men shook hands.

"It is good to see you again," Raven said.

"I wish it was under different circumstances," Thomas said dryly.

"Yes, there is a mess of things at the moment."

"I heard Colin tried to have Victoria killed!" Thomas did not even try to hide the rage in his voice.

"Yes, but his power keeper apparently stabbed himself. He did not die, but he weakened Colin enough that the children were able to subdue him. Now he is in a makeshift jail on the edge of camp. Kylan sent him to the sorcery council. Ashel sentenced him to jail and sent him back here where he can be guarded without giving away vital information about the council's new hiding place."

"Who is controlling his magic?"

"Garvan made a potion of some kind that is keeping Colin from regaining his full powers. Ashel was here, so I am sure there are extra spells that a mediocre sorcerer like Colin cannot break."

"So the power keeper lived then?"

"Yes, he has nearly fully recovered, but he is still in the sick tent."

"Where is Victoria now?"

"She was captured by Kybon. He is holding her in one of the dungeon cells."

As they spoke, Garvan walked up to them. "Hello, Garvan," Thomas said.

"Hello, Thomas."

"I was just catching Thomas up on everything that has been happening."

"There is no time for that now. Rupert is slipping away from us," Garvan said with urgency in his voice.

"What is wrong with him?" Raven asked, but Thomas knew.

"He is beginning to feel helpless. He thinks there is little he can do for anyone here until he gets his powers," Thomas answered, realizing he had arrived just in time. He sighed and continued speaking. "You know I cannot stay long. Bale is unguarded without me there. I will talk to Rupert and send him back to Pallen."

"But what if he is captured before he gets his powers?"

"I don't think he will be." Thomas looked up at Thunderstorm. "His horse will keep him safe."

Raven turned and looked at the magnificent horse that had led him back to the camp. Thunderstorm's eyes were different than the eyes of any other horse Raven had seen in many years. The memories of his own horse and of Black Shadow came back to him. There were only thirty-two magic horses in the world. They all came from the same line, the horse of the first sorceress. She gave the horse magic to protect her child until he was old enough to protect himself.

Thomas nodded as he saw the look of realization on his old friend's face. Rupert was well protected.

"Garvan, where is Rupert?"

"He is in the officers' tent," Garvan said, pointing behind himself without looking back.

Thomas handed Garvan the reins to his horse as he walked by him to the tent. Garvan nodded and walked the horse toward the stable. Raven called over several boys to help him unburden the horses he led there. Thunderstorm stood very still as the boys gathered around him.

CHAPTER 35

Rupert's Mission

Rupert was sitting quietly in the corner of the tent with his hand over his face. He was very deep in thought. Thomas put his hand on Rupert's shoulder. He started and looked up.

"I didn't mean to scare you," Thomas said with a smile.

"Uncle Thomas! How are you? How is my mother? What are you doing here? Who is in charge of Bale?"

Thomas laughed. "Slow down, boy. I heard you were feeling sorry for yourself?"

"Well, yeah, just a little. Everyone else has something important to do. I am stuck here waiting for my powers. I feel helpless."

"Good thing your mother isn't here! She would be very upset with you for giving up. She is fine, by the way. Bale is fine. Malcolm and two of his brothers-in-law are in charge of the city. I am here to get you back on track."

"How are you gonna do that?"

"Easy, I have a mission for you."

"Really, what is it?" He tried very hard not to sound too excited.

"A hermit and his grandson live just outside of Corslan. The hermits name is Ailill. I do not know the boy's name. Ailill was a landholder in Corslan for many years, but then his oldest daughter was disgraced by having a child out of wedlock. I believe you have met that child. His name is Jeps."

"Yes, he is here fighting for us."

"Good. Well, Jeps's uncle was killed when he tried to defend his sister's honor, leaving his son orphaned. Ailill took his grandson and left the city proper. He has spent the last few years learning magic."

"Aye, but what does any of this have to do with me?"

"Rupert, stop being impatient. Patience is one of the most important traits you will need to be a good sorcerer. I am getting to the point." Thomas put his hand on Rupert's shoulder, letting him know that he was not mad at Rupert's lack of patience. "So the reason this is important—Ailill has, in his possession, a ring that belonged to your father. I am not sure how he came to have it. I am not sure he knows how he got it. But anyway, that ring belongs to you now. I have spoken with him. His grandson is gravely ill. He cannot leave the boy, so you will have to go and get the ring yourself.

"Aye, is there something we can do for his grandson?"

"I have already given him the proper herbs to get the boy healthy, but it will take a few more days."

"When am I to leave? And why do you want me to get my father's ring now?"

"I am not sure how it works. You would have to ask Ashel, but from what I understand, because your father was wearing it when he died and because of the way he was killed, it will protect anyone in his line against evil."

Rupert was not sure what to say. He looked at the book of sorcery he had not read in several weeks. A pang of guilt ran through him. He should have been reading his book instead of feeling sorry for himself. The look on his face gave away his thoughts.

"Rupert, do not be hard on yourself. A lot has been put on your shoulders. You are still very young. I am proud of all three of you for what you have accomplished. Our Lord knows I didn't give you enough information about what it was you were supposed to do!"

"Aye, Uncle Thomas, I will make a deal with you. I will not be hard on myself if you are not too hard on yourself. Neither of us asked for this."

They shook hands, which Rupert pulled into a hug. "You leave in the morning," Thomas said.

At dawn the next morning, Kylan met Rupert at the stables as he was packing supplies for his journey. "Were you planning to tell me bye, or were you just going to sneak off?" she asked.

"I didn't want to wake you. I will be back in a few days."

"Thank you for your concern. I am feeling much better."

"Um, good... I... was going to tell you good-bye. I wanted to pack first."

Kylan knew that already since he had been thinking about her for at least ten minutes. She decided to save him the trip. She was beginning to go stir-crazy in the tent, anyway. She reached up and handed Thunderstorm a carrot almost instinctively. Thunderstorm nudged her "Thank you."

Rupert jumped on his horse and leaned down to Kylan. "Bye, Kylan. I'll see you in a week." Instead of kissing her, he patted her on the head and rode away.

She stood there hating the fact that she thought him not kissing her was funny. She smiled as she watched him leave. He looked back to see if she was still there. She laughed out loud at the look on his face. She threw him the thought, *Never look back!* He thought back, *Only for you!* Then Thunderstorm galloped away.

It took him nearly three days to get to the hermitage. He had been warned to stay near Thunderstorm. He was not sure why, but he took the advice. He trusted his own feelings as well as those of his horse, who seemed to keep watch at night. He wondered if the horse slept at all in the three-day journey. At dusk on the third day, he arrived at the hermitage. Ailill was waiting for him on the front porch of the small house.

"Welcome, Rupert!" the smallish man called to him. Ailill stood up and met him at the gate. Rupert dismounted and walked in. Thunderstorm walked in on his own. Ailill thought it a bit odd that he was riding the horse without reins.

Ailill invited him into the house. There was a meal waiting for them. The grandson Thomas had mentioned was sleeping in a corner of the room.

"How is your grandson doing?" Rupert asked cordially.

"He is doin' bett'r since Thom's came here and gave me 'erbs."

"Glad to hear it," Rupert said. He had an uneasy feeling in his gut. He wondered if this man was trustworthy.

After a silent dinner, the man handed Rupert a beautiful ring. They did little discussion, and Rupert slept in the barn. He left the next morning after saying a cordial good-bye.

He settled into the three-day ride back to camp. Kylan kept him posted on the progress of the war. It seemed that Kybon had declared war, but nothing had started yet. On his second day, sometime in the afternoon, Kylan instructed him not to come back to camp but to meet Cornelius in Pallen in three days. So he went to Aden's place and waited. Cornelius arrived at noon two days later.

"Hello, how was your journey?" Cornelius asked, as he sat down next to Rupert.

"Uneventful. I had too much time to think."

Cornelius's eyes fell to the ring that was now on the third finger of Rupert's right hand. He realized he had seen it before. It had been him who had given it to Ailill to save for Rupert until the time was right.

"So why are we both here?" Rupert asked.

"I am not sure. But I would like to go see the king while we are here."

"They did not tell you why we are here?" Rupert asked.

"No, but the fighting has started, and we are not allowed to be part of the fighting! We have to live long enough to stop it. Your birthday is in six days. All I know is, Thomas told me you and I need to be here."

"Well, I guess we can try to go see Victoria in the dungeon, and I would like to meet the king before he dies."

"We can't go to see Victoria!" he said as his voice cracked.

"Sorry, man."

"It is all right. She still has a few days left of that potion to keep her healthy."

As they were talking, Aden walked in. He said hello to Cornelius but nothing else.

"Are you all right, Aden?"

"Yes, I am just.. .very busy. Metal smiths are busiest during war time!"

"Do you need help?" they said at once.

"Sure."

They spent the next two days helping Aden produce sword after sword. He had three apprentices helping as well. Rupert and Cornelius enjoyed the work, and Rupert finally felt that he was helping with the effort to end the tyranny of Kybon.

On the morning of the third day, Justin came to see them. "Sirs, if you are wanting to see the king again, you must do it soon! Kybon is no longer sending him his medicine. I fear he will be dead by tomorrow morning.

Suddenly Kylan emerged from nowhere. She was standing behind Rupert, but the other two saw her appear.

"Hi," Rupert said without turning around.

"I have gotten word that the king is dying! Thomas says she has to go today," Kylan said.

"So are we just gonna emerge in the king's room with her from the dungeon?"

"No, I am going to emerge in the king's room with Victoria. You two are going to take the secret passage!"

"Good idea. Come on, Rupert, I will show you the way," Cornelius said.

CHAPTER 36

The Final Visit to the King

Kylan emerged in the dungeon. Victoria was sleeping. The magic candle was still burning. Kylan shook her awake.

"Your father is dying. I am going to take you to see him. Rupert and Cornelius are on their way through the tunnels."

Victoria stood up and stretched as best she could with her hands flat on the ceiling. She straightened out. She put on her cloak and sword and her boots. "Okay, I am ready. Let's go."

Kylan slipped her arm through the crook of Victoria's. Victoria closed her eyes so as not to get dizzy. Five seconds later, they were standing next to the king's bed. He was barely conscious. The only sound in the room was his labored breathing.

Kylan bent over him. "Your Highness?" she said softly.

He turned and looked at her. He smiled and lifted himself to a sitting position with Kylan's help. Then she handed him a canteen of water. He sipped it slowly.

"I am dying," he said finally.

"Yes, I have brought Victoria to see you. And Cornelius and Rupert are coming too. We want to bid you best wishes in the next world. If there is a next world!"

"I believe there is. It is a paradise. But I don't know if I will be sent there. Do cowards get to go to paradise?"

"Father, you are not a coward!" Victoria said. "Kybon is evil and powerful. He would have killed you sooner if you were truly a coward."

"I only wish to live long enough to see his end."

"You will, Father. Rupert will have his powers in three days."

"You will make it until then. Kybon is not the only sorcerer who has the power to keep you alive," Kylan tried to assure him.

"I know. I can taste the medicine in the water, but promise you will let me go when he is gone. I am tired of the pain. I want to see this paradise the prophets spoke about."

Victoria reached over and took her father's hand in hers, and she took Kylan's in her other hand. "We promise, Father."

"Ah, my daughter, you look as beautiful as your mother. I miss her. I hope she is in paradise so I can tell her how beautiful you are now. She would be so proud of you."

"Can you tell her about Cornelius too?" Victoria asked through sobs.

"I will!" the king said. He began to cough loudly.

Just as he finished his coughing fit, Rupert and Cornelius entered the room. Rupert walked to the other side of the bed, while Cornelius put his arms around Victoria to console her. Suddenly they heard from behind them a sinister laugh. Rupert looked up while the other three turned around.

There by the door stood a tall, well-built man. He was dressed in fine purple silk. His sword swung loosely at his side. He spoke in a deep, icy voice. "So the four of you thought you would say good-bye to my puppet! You fell right into my trap."

"We are not scared of you!" Victoria yelled, drawing her sword and running toward him.

Kybon held up both hands. Victoria was suddenly hit with a force that knocked her to the floor. Ropes appeared around her arms.

While that was happening, Kylan was hit with the same force and thrown to the wall. But she knew it was coming and countered his attack.

He was much more powerful, but she put up a fight from the wall. He pulled his right hand from Victoria and concentrated both hands on Kylan. She closed her eyes and fought him with all of her might.

Cornelius walked to Victoria to try to help her out of her binds. She whispered to him to stay behind her. It was the only way to keep him safe.

Kybon swung around and shouted, "Leave her be, boy!"

"Or what? You will have to kill me to get to him, but if I die, you have no power!" Victoria yelled.

"Then I will kill your sorceress friend!" He spun back around to finish off Kylan. But she was now trying to stand up. He laughed maniacally. "Do not waste your strength, or maybe you should! You will die sooner."

He reared back and pulled a ball of light in his hand. He threw it toward her, but Rupert jumped in front of it with his right hand outstretched. He had turned the jewel of the ring to be in line with his palm. The ball of light flew back toward Kybon. He dodged the ball, and it crashed into the wall, shaking the entire room, maybe even the entire castle.

He stood back up and directed his attention to Rupert! "You have done it now, boy! That ring won't save you but once!"

Kybon raised a ball of light again and hurled it in Rupert's direction. Kylan lunged toward Rupert to try and divert the ball with her own ball, but she was too weak, and she fell on the ground at Rupert's feet.

Rupert held up his hands. Suddenly a ball of light appeared in each of his hands. He threw them toward the light coming at him.

The balls collided with a crashing noise. Rupert's balls of light came together and engulfed Kybon's ball, forcing it back in the evil sorcerer's direction. Kybon was hit square in the chest with the huge ball of light. He flew backward into the wall. He was on the wall for nearly ten seconds, and then he crumpled and slid to the ground.

Rupert stood in shock, wondering how he had just created those forces. Kylan and Victoria were both still trying to process what had just happened.

Cornelius stood up and walked carefully to Kybon's crumpled form on the floor. He knelt beside Kybon and placed his hand on his neck. "I think he is dead!" Cornelius said, not sure of himself. Kybon may have been tricking them somehow to get them to lower their guard.

Victoria jumped to her feet. The ropes that had magically bound her had fallen away when Kybon hit the wall.

"His spell is broken anyway, but get behind me in case he is only unconscious," Cornelius said.

Rupert leaned over. "Kylan, are you all right?"

"Yes, I am a little shaken, but I will be all right," she said as she reached her hand up to Rupert. He reached down and helped her to her feet.

"How did I do that? My birthday is still three days away."

"I don't know, but there is someone we can ask!" Kylan closed her eyes. She whispered three words in the old language. The words meant "Come, Most Powerful."

Ashel appeared in the room next to Kybon's body.

"High Sorceress!" Kylan exclaimed.

"Yes, child."

"Is he dead?" Rupert asked.

"Yes."

"But how? My birthday is still three days away."

"No, it is today! Your mother was not well when she delivered you and for several weeks after. So it was quite easy for Thomas to lie about the day you were born. It was brilliant actually. Kybon lured you here to kill you because he thought you were still mortal while Thomas sent you here, thus beating Kybon at his own game!"

"Did you know that Rupert's birthday was today?" Kylan asked.

"Yes, I was sent a message a few years ago," Ashel said.

Cornelius stood perfectly still, hoping that they didn't ask who the messenger had been. Victoria felt him stiffen his posture since his arms were around her.

"You knew, didn't you, Corn? That is why you let Rupert come with you," Victoria said.

"Yes, I..." Cornelius stammered.

"Don't worry we are not mad at you. I was for a moment when I thought that Kybon was going to kill him. I thought, 'How could you be so stupid!' But now I see that you knew he would be all right."

"Yes, I was the messenger. Thomas sent me with words, not paper. The words were 'I added three days.' I only figured it out a few days ago what he meant by that."

Rupert walked slowly across the room to look his friend straight in the eyes. Cornelius knew that Rupert would be angry that he had been lied to for so long. Rupert looked as if he was going to punch Cornelius, then he laughed loudly. "Thank you. I thought most of this was my burden alone, but we were all in this together."

Ashel put her hand on Rupert's shoulder. He turned around and looked at the high sorceress for the first time.

"Nice to meet you, High Sorceress!" Rupert exclaimed.

"I met you when you were a baby!" Ashel replied. "But now is not the time for greetings. We need to stop—"

Before she could finish speaking, the king went into a horrible coughing fit. Justin and two other uniformed guards came running into the room. He noticed Victoria hastening to her father's side out of the corner of his eye, but he was fixed on the crumpled lifeless body on the floor in the dim light. One of the other guards lit a small torch.

"Kybon is dead?" Justin said.

"Yes, he is," Ashel said. "Come on, all three of you. There is much to do, starting with ending this war and sending the soldiers home."

The three guards linked their arms. Ashel took Justin by the hand, and the four of them disappeared from the room.

Kylan pulled herself all the way to a full standing position with the help of Rupert. She squeezed his hand and whispered in his ear, "I will be right back," and she disappeared too. About a minute later, she appeared with Prince Mathew at one side and the queen on the other. She disappeared again and reappeared about thirty seconds later with Bartholomew. She let go of his hand. Rupert ran up and caught her just as she collapsed. She let him take her tightly in his arms. He looked around and saw a closet near the opposite corner from where Kybon lay. He walked slowly to it. Cornelius saw him and helped get two blankets out. Then he laid Kylan on the blankets. Rupert kissed her gently. She smiled.

The others gathered around the king's bed. Victoria and the two princes began to tell stories to each other and the king. The queen stood stern-faced at the foot of the bed.

Cornelius left the room quietly. He returned a few minutes later with Joe at his side. Joe walked in and spoke a quiet and respectful hello. Then he and Rupert and Cornelius walked over to Kybon's body. They stood over him for a minute, wondering exactly what they should do with his body.

"I guess we should brin' 'im to my place. The undertaker lives only a few houses away," Joe said. "I don't know if he should get a proper funeral."

"That is for Jeps to decide," Cornelius said quietly.

The king died sometime in the middle of the night. By the next morning, news of the deaths of Kybon and the king had traveled through the kingdom. Victoria was named queen with the support of her two younger brothers and reluctantly by their mother.

Jeps decided that Kybon should be buried in Corslan on the property that belonged to Kybon's family. Jeps, Peter, Rupert, and Cornelius carried the coffin to its final resting place. Kylan and Ashel brought Colin in chains to pay respect to his brother. Rupert's grandfather, Malic, was present to keep Colin subdued if need be.

But Colin hung his head in shame. "Good-bye, brother," was all he managed to say.

Victoria actually felt a little sorry for him even though he had tried to kill her. Her father had been right about Colin. He only wanted peace for the kingdom. Now he had lost his brother, his half-brother, and his freedom.

CHAPTER 37

The King's Funeral

The next day was the king's funeral. He was laid out on a pyre and paraded through the streets of Pallen. Everyone in the city came to pay respect to the departed king. His body was brought back to the cemetery on the palace grounds. There his body was interred next to his father's.

Victoria was among the last to leave the site. Bartholomew and Cornelius stood with her.

"I wish I had gotten to know him better," she said sadly.

"Me too!" said Bartholomew. "He was sick my whole life."

"He was sick his whole life," Cornelius said. "But he is at peace now. Thank God for that. His whole life was a struggle, just to breathe. I can't imagine what that would be like." He took Victoria by the hands and kissed her. "It is time for you to get ready for your coronation now, my queen."

She giggled while Bartholomew made a gagging noise. Ashel and Kylan appeared and took Victoria by the hand.

"He is right. It is time for all of us to get ready for a new era in history," Ashel said.

"You have to come too, Cornelius. You are both being coroneted. Are you coming too, Bartholomew?" Kylan asked.

"I will meet you all back at the castle in a few minutes. I want to stay here a bit longer. I have never been here before, and this is where my family is buried."

Kylan patted him on the shoulder. Victoria hugged him. "See you in a bit," she said as they walked back to the castle.

Bartholomew walked up looking at each carved stone in the mausoleum. He read the names carefully. His father was the last one on the stones.

Rupert walked up as he lingered at the king's tomb. "I am sorry that your family tree is carved out in tombstones."

Bartholomew laughed. "Yes, this is the first time I have read all of their names together, though I have learned the kingdom's history."

"As well you should have."

"Rupert?" Bartholomew said in a quiet voice.

"Yes, Barth?"

"I was serious before when I said I wanted to learn magic. Can you be my teacher?"

"I would like that, Bartholomew. Kylan and I will officially be put in charge of protection and magical teaching tomorrow at the coronation. Garvan will be working with us, and we start training Jeps as soon as possible."

"Good. Jeps will be a good sorcerer too and a great ally if he is a powerful as his father."

"We are making Malachi general over the Unified Army. One day, you will be the magician in charge! Garvin will retire someday soon," Rupert said with pride in his voice.

"I think I will enjoy that. I should like to see the kingdom and travel around the country."

"Yes, after they have a proper honeymoon, Cornelius will take Victoria and you and anyone else who wants to go out into each town to meet the people."

"That was Victoria's idea, wasn't it?"

Rupert only smiled, then he said, "Come on, I need to go and meet Aden to see the new swords and knives he made for tomorrow. I would like to know what you think of them."

"Aye." He turned. "Good-bye, Father." His words echoed though the mausoleum. Then he turned on his heels, and he and Rupert started off toward the castle.

Kylan appeared next to Rupert and took his hand.

"I still need to go and meet with the sorcerers council," Rupert said.

"Well, you know they are all here for the coronation. Your grandfather and I have been talking a lot about what will happen in the future. He likes trying to tell the future."

"Trying? He can't really predict what will happen?" Bartholomew asked.

"Your first lesson in magic is this. There are no guarantees on anything, especially the future. No one could have predicted that Colin was going to try to kill Victoria until the day of his attempt because before that, he had not made the decision. My grandfather is pretty close to right on most of his predictions, though. But I think he just guesses well," Rupert said with a shrug.

"Maybe!" Kylan said, smiling at Rupert.

"Don't argue with me, or I will make it rain, but only on you!" Rupert said teasingly.

Kylan laughed out loud. "I can outrun your storm!" she said, kissing him on the cheek.

"Does your grandfather think the peace will last?" Bartholomew asked, ignoring Kylan's giggles.

"I haven't asked him, but I can tell you this much. Sadly, peace doesn't last. There will always be someone wanting more power than he deserves."

"Well, I guess we will fight them when they show up then."

"Of course, we will. We have these powers for a reason," Kylan and Rupert said together.

Just then they reached the castle, where Aden and Joanna were standing in front of the main entrance. Rupert and Bartholomew left with Aden toward the blacksmith's house on the castle grounds to see the new weapons.

"Come on inside, Kylan. They are looking at the new weapons. It will be a long time before they are done. We finally have peace, and there is still no time to sleep."

Their laughter floated off the castle grounds as they walked inside the large wooden doors to the brightly lit room inside. The doors closed silently behind them.

www.ingramcontent.com/pod-product-compliance
Lightning Source LLC
Chambersburg PA
CBHW030545310726

48979CB00010B/2042/J
9781959365150